TESSERAE

SHAWNA WALLS

ISBN: 0692411380
ISBN-13: 978-0692411384

DEDICATION

For dear P.J., who always wants more of the story.

CONTENTS

ACKNOWLEDGMENTS

Many thanks once again to Cameron Harris for her brilliant editing. Thanks also to M for his undying support and encouragement, and our dear little T, whose smile reminds me every day why I write stories.

PROLOGUE

Bright picked his way along the narrow dirt path, wondering again why he'd never bothered to join the orienteering group his mother had suggested when he was younger. It certainly would have made this trek through the jungle easier.

His best friend, Third, was having an even worse time of it, and hesitated just as they were about to leave the path and duck into the dense foliage proper. He glanced over at their companion. "Are you sure about this, Petal?"

"Of course she's sure," Bright reassured him. He turned to Petal. "You *are* sure, aren't you?" When he'd met her three months ago at the bar, he initially didn't believe her—assuming she was just drunk and telling stories—but it had turned out to be true: she really did work at the mysterious military-research facility on the outskirts of the city. And, according to her, the facility was about to run a test flight for a brand-new aircraft prototype, right over the section of wilderness through which they were currently trudging. Still, he thought, she could just be playing a prank on him and Third. It wouldn't be the first time someone had made fun of their obsessive interest in secret government projects.

"Well, anything could scrub the flight, of course," Petal said, "but this time and location are what was on the message that got circulated around my department. Since I'm civilian rank, I'm technically not supposed to have access to classified data, but my boss was too busy to read the message himself, so he had me scan it first." She picked her way through the underbrush, dodging a low-hanging tree branch. "Once we crest that ridge over there, we should be able to see the flight path."

Just a short journey away, the trees parted, and a small, flower-dotted hill rose in front of them. They scaled it, and once they were at the top, they had an excellent view of the surrounding territory: the lake and city in the distance to their right, more of the dense trees and ferns ahead and to their left, and, behind them, the winking lights of the bunker and its short airstrip. The bustle of activity on the strip was readily apparent, and Bright tensed in anticipation.

"Wow," Third murmured as the craft rolled into view at the far end of the runway. As a military and transportation buff, he had been more fascinated by the story than even Bright had, and clearly, he was overwhelmed by what was about to happen. "You weren't kidding. This does look like the real thing!"

The craft, as far as Bright could see, was arrowhead-shaped, a dull gray, and relatively small—likely only large enough for a pilot—but it was definitely unlike any other aircraft he'd ever seen before. For one, it had no obvious jet engines.

"Told you!" Petal said brightly. "The craft probably won't make much noise. It has a small fermentation engine to boost its launch and hydraulic systems, but when it's at cruising speed in low orbit, it runs on some sort of magnetic drive—that's the experimental part." She glanced down at the time display on her com. "Should be launching any minute now."

Sure enough, the craft began to move, slowly at first,

then quickly gaining speed. Just at the end of the runway, it got lift and soared into the sky, the morning light throwing a pinkish cast over its hull.

"Yes!" Bright cheered as the craft soared overhead, its sleek underbelly reflecting the colors of the vegetation and observers below. He reached for Petal, to embrace her in triumph and gratitude, but before they'd even made contact, something went horribly wrong.

To his shock, a large, dark spot opened up in the skies above them, right in the middle of the flight path. It looked like a patch of starry night sky—drastically out of place in the clear, glowing dawn. The craft dodged and banked as its pilot tried to avoid the strange obstacle in its way, but it was moving too fast. In a twinkling, it slipped through into the area and then disappeared from sight. Only a few seconds later, so did the dark patch itself.

"What—?" Third turned to them, gesturing erratically. "What just happened?"

"I have no idea!" Petal stared up at the empty sky where the craft had been, just as bewildered as the other two. She glanced back at Bright, her antennae dancing furiously in the air and her wings vibrating with her surprise. "No idea at all."

SHAWNA WALLS

BEGINNINGS AND ENDINGS

The sirens were horrible. They blared and screamed and wailed, adding a sharp, painful voice to the rumbling, booming cacophony of Sasha's world falling apart around her. She clamped her hands over her ears to shut out the noise, but kept running.

"Mama!" she shrieked as she dashed through the dark apartment, trying desperately to make her five-year-old's voice heard above the din. "Mama, where are you?"

Finally she spied her mother. In a corner, under a shelf that had collapsed, a slender body was pinned under the weight of hundreds of antique paper books. Her dark hair was peppered with dust and bits of paint and sheetrock from the walls that were disintegrating around her. Her eyes, usually glittering, were dull and still.

"Mama?" Sasha called again, rushing over. "Mama! Wake up!" She shook an arm, but her mother did not move. A colossal, thundering crash drew her attention to the window near to where her mother lay. Just a few blocks down from their building, Smith Tower was beginning to fall.

She screamed.

Seattle mostly looked like an alien planet to her now. As her plane descended through the dawn sky, which was still gray and damp even this late in May, Sasha Delescu noticed a few familiar things that had survived. The Space Needle, the Wheel, the sports facilities, and some other buildings and structures that had been planned with big earthquakes in mind were still intact, but they were rare relics of the city that had lived before. A great deal of what she remembered of the skyline was gone, either destroyed by the quake or rendered unsafe and subsequently demolished.

Two decades of rebuilding had shaped the city into something new, the fallen nineteenth- and twentieth-century architecture now a late-twenty-first-century landscape of recycled glass and steel. The towering high-tension wires bringing electricity from the dams in the eastern half of the state were gone, replaced by structure-integrated panels and turbines for solar, tidal, and wind generators. The seven-lane freeways snaking through downtown and across Lake Washington had largely yielded to rails and guide-wires for high-speed mass transit. Where roads still existed, they gleamed with embedded solar panels and bright lane-marking lights. Thousands of single-family Craftsman homes—beautiful, but not originally built to withstand quakes—had been swapped out for stylish braces of small condo complexes offset by wide swaths of parks and other green spaces.

Her home city was, in its new form, a model for the rest of the world, proving what could be done to ensure that the planet would continue to be inhabitable by future humans while also making life comfortable and pleasant for the ones existing now. For all its attractive, environmentally wise, and cleverly engineered shine, however, it felt unfamiliar. This was not the city of Sasha's birth, at least as her childhood memories had painted it.

Yet even with the drastic changes, she felt a thrill of connection. The things made by humans were different, but the evergreens, the water, and the white-and-lavender mountains that framed it all remained: sentinels of the place that had existed before the first humans had crossed the land bridge to settle the continent thousands of years ago. These grand, natural landmarks anchored her in a way she'd never felt in two decades in her Grandpa Joey's flat Midwest. She had survived there, under his kind-but-detached care, but never thrived, something she greatly hoped she would do now that she was back. As the plane touched down, a wave of relief and comfort washed through her.

Sasha collected her bags and made her way through the terminal, smiling at the Native and Asian iconography and art and thrilling to see so many people here with skin tones closer to her own tawny one. Seattle certainly wasn't as multiracial as points farther south, but it was at least less overwhelmingly white than the places where she had spent most of her life. She was rarely the only brown-faced person around even in Iowa, where she grew up, but she still had always felt out of place both there and Wisconsin, where she had done her undergrad and graduate work. Here, making her way through a sea of many faces with features that had originated somewhere other than northern Europe, she felt far less conspicuous—less like her right to be in the country where both she and her mother had been born would be perpetually questioned. She was somewhat paler than her mother, being half Romanian as well as Brazilian, but many in other parts of the country still eyed her with suspicion, and rude questions about "what" she was still abounded. Seattle's position on the Pacific Rim and its Ring of Fire might well have been its doom twenty years ago, but that proximity to many of the rest of the world's peoples also made the city feel considerably more welcoming than where she had been before. With every step she took, she felt years of tension and awkwardness drain away.

As she approached the light-rail platform beyond the terminal, another, more familiar brown face lit up at seeing her.

"Sasha?" The tiny, elderly woman's voice was hesitant,

but strengthened as she drew closer. "My little *chuchu*? Is it really you? Come give your *bisavó* a hug!"

"*Óla*, Bisa!" Sasha called. She dropped her bags and rushed into outstretched arms of Carmela Hernandes, her great grandmother and effectively last living relative. "It's good to see you. I've missed you so much!"

"And I you! It's so lovely to finally see you in person again. It's been what? Ten years? Twelve?"

"Something like that," Sasha said.

Bisa shook her head sadly. "I wish we could have afforded to visit more. The vids and Stream calls just never were enough." She stroked Sasha's cheek and pulled away with a small sigh. "It always made me so sad that Joey took you away, even though I understand why he did. After we lost your mother and your Vovò Juan, I wondered if it might not be better to be in Iowa myself. But then I realized I'd just be trading earthquakes and volcanoes for floods and tornadoes, so I may as well stay put!"

"Right!" Sasha said. She picked up her bags, and they made their way to a bench to wait for the train. "Well, if it had been my choice, I would have stayed here with you, quakes or no. Iowa didn't suit me at all."

"I suppose it was better than if they had sent you to live with your father. Where did he end up again? Bulgaria?"

"He went back to Bucharest," Sasha corrected her. "I think I was two or something when he lost his job and his visa expired, and since he didn't want to marry my mom to stay here, that was that. I got a few birthday gifts from him early on, but then he found someone there and married her. They have three kids of their own now, but I don't know much more than that. Not sure I want to know, either."

"You're better off, I think." Bisa wrinkled her nose. "He was a piece of work, that one. When he and Maria started dating, Juan nearly had an aneurysm. Couldn't stand him."

"Grandpa Joey couldn't, either. We used to call him my 'sperm donor.'" Sasha giggled.

"Do you miss him?" Bisa looked up at her. "Joey, I mean. I guess he was the closest thing to a parent you had most of your life."

Sasha shrugged. "I do. I loved him, very much, and when he died, it took me a while to get over it—I had a rough school term that spring. Really, though, he always seemed distant with me. He never mistreated me or anything—he made sure I had everything I needed and was always kind—but I never felt close to him. I guess since I looked like them, I reminded him too much of Vovò Juan and my mother. It must have hurt him a lot."

"That makes sense. Probably also why he didn't want to see much of me, either. I tried not to take it personally, in any case. I just wish I could've seen you more."

"Same." Sasha smiled gently.

"It's amazing how much you've grown." Bisa gazed at her and sighed.

Sasha nudged her with a shoulder. "I still got your shortness gene, though."

Bisa laughed. "I apologize for that! But it seems like only a month ago, you were just a small thing who wanted to cuddle with the sloths when we visited my cousin in São Paulo. Such a bundle of energy you were!" The elderly woman's deeply lined face erupted into an enormous grin full of too-white, recently replaced teeth. She was always getting something upgraded these days, and was composed largely of bioprinted spare parts now. "I refuse to die," she had once said. Given that she was 112 and still sprightly, Sasha believed she might well fulfill that promise.

She returned the grin. "Well, I have grown a lot since then, I suppose, but I still love cuddling with sloths." The train pulled up to the platform with a metallic thrum. Taking her bags and Bisa's arm, Sasha boarded. "That's why I'm back here now. Well, not sloths in particular, of course, but . . ."

"Ah! Your internship. What's that place called again? Xeno . . . ?" Bisa perched on one of the sky-colored seats.

"Xenobiology Network." Sasha grabbed a handrail as the train sped away from the platform. "It's the company that launched the deep-space probes to search for extraterrestrial life."

"Oh, right. The one that found those alien critters on that planet. They called them dune somethings?" Bisa frowned in concentration.

"Dune diggers," Sasha said." Their scientific name is more complex, but that's what the team nicknamed them."

"Right! I thought they all died on the way back, though?"

Sasha shook her head. "Not all of them. One of the four samples from the planet survived the stasis process. The probe is due back home in two weeks, and I'll be involved with the study of the creature. Well, it and the creatures their first probe found on that other planet."

"Those were just bugs or something, right?"

"Arthropods."

"Arth-what? Wait. Never mind. You're the one with the zoology education. That's way over my head. I'd rather just paint pretty pictures and sell them to rich tourists." Bisa chuckled. "But in any case, I'm glad it brought you back home. I wasn't sure whether you were planning on going back to Des Moines after grad school."

Sasha shook her head. "I'm planning to stay here if I can. There's nothing for me there. Since Joey didn't get along with his family—"

"Those backward nitwits!" Bisa scoffed. "We didn't see a single one of them at the wedding. Juan felt so bad for Joey then. I threatened to send them a wedding video anyway, but Joey wouldn't let me, the spoilsport."

Sasha laughed. "Anyway, Joey didn't have many close friends or family there—just some co-workers he occasionally had over for dinner. I never had much of a social life myself, either. I was always working on school, or capoeira lessons, or volunteering at the zoo or whatever. I picked up some friends in college, but we're all scattered now, and none of them are in the Midwest anyway. We keep up on our Stream accounts, but we're all too busy to visit. So, really, there's no reason for me to go back there. Where I end up is just a matter of where work takes me—or school, if I decide to keep going and get a doctorate. My other internship opportunity would've put me in Papua New Guinea studying those new marsupial bats they found, but all in all, I'm glad I got in here. It means I get to see my Bisa again after so long!"

"Too long," Bisa emphasized, squeezing Sasha's arm enthusiastically. "I'm happy with how things turned out, and that I had a spare room for you. I hope your job doesn't take up too much of your time. We have a lot of catching up to do, and you have a whole new hometown to see!"

Sasha glanced out the window of the train as it rolled through the new city on the way to Bisa's apartment in SoDo. As they crested a hill, the evergreens parted and the roiling expanse of Puget Sound stretched out to the left, with the islands and snow-dusted Olympics beyond it. *Yes*, she thought. *I'm finally home again.*

* * *

Alex Maloney toddled into the bathroom to stand at the toilet, an enormous yawn nearly splitting his head. He'd stayed up too late again last night—playing a game this time rather than unknotting equations or toying with his actuator design project—and was reaping the consequences. His muscles felt leaden, and he could feel the beginnings of a headache rolling up his tense neck.

"Want to join me when you're done?" Gabriel called from the shower, his voice thick and teasing.

Alex blinked the sleep from his gritty eyes and glanced over his shoulder. Gabriel looked hot no matter what he was doing, but drenched in warm water, droplets glistening on his dark skin like stars in a night sky, he looked downright edible. The prospect of a nice neck rub—and perhaps some rubbing of other parts that needed attention—made Alex feel considerably more awake than before. "I believe I'll take you up on that," he said languidly and quickly finished his business before anticipation made it anatomically awkward.

Just as he was about to step into the shower, however, his arm band, sitting on the counter next to his hairbrush, sounded an annoying incoming-call alert.

"Dammit," he spat. "I should take this. Might be XenoNet." He smiled apologetically.

"I thought your internship didn't start until June?" Gabriel wiped fog from the shower door and frowned at him. "And why wouldn't they just message?"

Alex shook his head as he strode back over to look at the device. "It's actually starting Monday—the 28th—but I'm doing orientation today. I'll be getting the full tour, going through HR and security and all that, so they might need to talk to me about—oh." A cold wave of dread washed through him, and he sighed heavily. The name displayed on the screen was not the company, yet he felt compelled to answer it anyway. Tucking the device's earpiece into place, he passed a thumb over it, and tried to sound cheerful. "Hi, Mom."

"Kyla? Great." Gabriel groaned and turned away to finish rinsing off.

Alex felt a knot forming in the pit of his stomach. Much as he couldn't stand his tightly wound mother, Gabriel disliked her even more and couldn't understand why Alex had anything to do with her. To avoid the discomfort Gabriel's judgmental scowl was causing him, he ducked back into the bedroom.

"Alex!" his mother said primly. "I wasn't sure you'd answer. You haven't been in contact lately—haven't answered my messages. I was wondering if you'd died or something. Can we go to video?"

"Nope. My band's in the other room at the moment, so we're voice-only. Sorry." He rubbed his face and tried to ignore the frustrated muttering from the bathroom. "And I'm not dead—just busy prepping for my internship. You remember the one I told you about, right? With XenoNet?"

"Those people? You know I don't approve of that. We shouldn't be investigating how God made the universe, and we shouldn't think of anything other than his plan for humanity here on Earth."

"Well, that's why I haven't told you much about it." Alex bit his lip to keep from saying anything more caustic. His mother had been supportive of his aptitude for science when he was a child, but as his interests began to focus on physics, and hers on religion, a bitter distance had grown between them. Six years ago, she had generously moved the family from Boston to Seattle when he graduated high school early and won a scholarship to the University of Washington. As his college career continued, however, she'd become increasingly harsh about his study area. Now, as he neared the end of his master's program in extraterrestrial geophysics, they rarely spoke. When they did, it almost always ended in a nasty argument.

"I just don't understand why you can't do something like what your brother is doing," his mother continued. "You know he's at the top of his class in seminary? I'm so proud of him."

Alex tried to keep the annoyance out of his voice. "I know Jonathan's happy. Religion's just not my thing, though. You know that."

"It'll be your thing eventually. We all have to face judgment in the end."

"Yeah, well. I don't plan on doing that anytime soon, so for now, I think I'm going to stick with what I'm doing, OK?" He sat down wearily on the edge of the bed, finger-combing the tangles out of his haphazard mess of caramel curls.

"If you insist on angering God, I suppose I can't stop you." She paused, and her voice grew softer. "But you still have to keep in touch with me, OK?" Her tone took on the slightest edge of need. That was his weakness; it was always his weakness. He was only ten when his father left the family to take up with his dental assistant, and since then, his mother's fragility had been the thing that kept him by her side, even after she'd reinvested in the long-abandoned religion of her Irish-Catholic forebears and started badgering him about his "sinful" career.

Alex glanced up as Gabriel wandered back into the bedroom to get dressed. He bent over to dig through a bin of clean laundry, looking for a pair of boxers, and Alex's heart skipped, his thoughts quickly returning to the activities he should've been doing in the shower. They'd been together for just under a year, having hooked up after Alex assisted with the geology grad's project developing quake-smart construction materials, but things were still hot. Had Alex come to bed at a normal hour last night, he'd probably have stayed up late to play an entirely different kind of game, and his body was now reminding him that he'd made a bad choice.

"Yeah, Mom," he said absentmindedly as libido began overtaking his higher brain functions. "I'll try to contact you more often. I gotta go now, though, OK? Way too much to do right now."

"Fair enough, I—" He killed the connection before she finished, and dropped the earpiece on his nightstand.

"I still have time this morning," Alex purred, coming up behind Gabriel and slipping his arms around his waist. Gabriel's skin was warm and damp, and he smelled like lemons.

"I don't." Gabriel said flatly, peeling Alex's hands away.

Alex took a step back. "Uh. OK?"

Gabriel turned. A muscle in his jaw twitched and his warm, brown eyes were narrowed. "I've had enough. I'm tired of her getting in your way—our way—all the time."

Alex sat back down. "I don't—"

Gabriel waved a hand, cutting him off. "Save it." He fastened his jeans and pulled a shirt over his head. Then he made a noise of frustration. "Look. I care about you, and you know I enjoyed working with you on the quake-smart project—you have the most amazing brain of anyone I've ever met—but I just can't do this anymore. It feels like I'm living in some sort of time warp. Your mom may as well be Amish or something. I can't stand tiptoeing around her all the time, being afraid that something you or I might do is going to set her off on one of her sermons."

"She doesn't mind about us, though. She's not that backward." Alex huffed helplessly. Accepting her son's interest in men was one of the few concessions to modern culture she had allowed.

"No, I get that. It's everything else. I wouldn't have a problem if she was just plain Catholic. Yeah, they're still twenty years behind everyone else, but they're at least getting there. I think they're even considering a female candidate for a cardinal position now or something. But your mom's thing—this Homecoming cult she's into—is just fucked up. You have to know that." He made a face.

Alex's chest tightened. "I do know it, Gabe. Honestly." Homecoming, his mother's denomination, was a rogue Catholic sect, diverging from the Vatican not long after Pope Francis had taken the office, and dedicated to reversing the increasing secularity in both the church and outside of it. Filling a gap left by increasingly insignificant conservative Protestants, the traditionalist group was starting to gain in political power, even if its membership numbers were still small overall. Every advancement in ecumenical peace and secular egalitarianism, from U.N.'s takeover of Gaza to the hardline Wahhabists in Saudi Arabia finally giving up political power, was, to them, a sign that the world was marching toward Armageddon. Of course, they also seemed to be trying to bring that on themselves, what with helping fire up a new war with extremist factions in Pakistan thanks to their anti-Muslim campaigning. Their greatest objection, however, was to advancements in science, particularly the discovery of extraterrestrial life—the province of the company for which Alex was about to be working.

"Do you?" Gabriel raised an eyebrow. "Do you really know exactly how far gone she is?"

Tears sprang to Alex's eyes as the truth of Gabriel's words stung. "Look. I know reality isn't exactly Homecoming's strong suit—not my mom's, either. I've tried to get her to see reason, but I can't. The church is her comfort zone. She's been into it for so long that there's no getting her out of it. The best I can do is just be there—be in her life and hope that I'm setting an example for her to look to if she eventually comes back."

Gabriel ran a hand over his smooth shaved head. "Eventually is never going to come, Alex. You know that as well as I do. You need to let her go, man. She's going to eat you alive someday, and I don't think I can watch that happen."

Alex felt his limbs go numb. "So, are you saying . . ." He struggled to force the words out. "Does this mean you're telling me it's you or her?"

"No." Gabriel shook his head. "I already know you've chosen her." He stood up again and headed for the door. "I'll pack my stuff and be out this weekend."

The sound of the slamming door felt like a hammer inside Alex's skull.

XENONET

"Incoming!" Baxter shouted from across the room, only seconds before the building erupted around them.

They were supposed to be safe here in this bunker—that's what Major Andersen had said. Tucked away in a hillside fort that supposedly hadn't been used since the mid-twentieth century, Jay and his logistics team should've escaped notice from the hostiles here. Obviously, that was not the case. Rather than talking his best friend, Josie, through the plan for her next civilian-rescue run, he was instead huddling with her under a table and watching all his equipment going up in a shower of sparks and metallic dust.

"Dammit!" she cried out suddenly, and a spray of thick blood spattered his leg.

He looked over: a sharp chunk of steel had flown through the air from the last hit and was now deeply embedded in her upper arm. He crawled toward her, trying to help as best he could, but then the world exploded again.

"Fuck!" The sudden blare of a backup alert from a truck outside the lobby made Jay Lambert nearly jump from his chair at the reception desk. He did knock over his cup. The lid popped off as it hit the desk, spilling hot, peppermint-scented liquid all over his uniform. He muttered bitterly as he tended to the mess.

When he'd finished sopping up the spill, he pushed back his sleeve. The med implant still glowed a healthy green under his skin: it didn't need to be refilled, yet. Still, his jumpiness had been increasing of late, and he wondered if he might need to see Dr. Long again to adjust his dosage.

He'd left Pakistan—and subsequently the military—

two years ago. After spending some time with his family to recuperate, he ventured out again, eventually settling back in Seattle, the city of his early childhood. Life here was calm and normal, yet he'd still not truly adjusted back to the comparatively safe civilian world. His new job— heading up a five-person/six-drone security force at a small, science-oriented company as it expanded—was supposed to be quiet and undemanding. In the six months he'd been at it so far, it had proven to be exactly that, and he felt like he was finally on the road to recovery. The dreams had even stopped: he no longer saw dismembered bodies and crushed buildings all around him when he closed his eyes most nights.

Still, every now and then, his nerves betrayed him, and a sudden loud noise or the sight of blood triggered waves of panic and nausea that he couldn't easily push back down. He kept telling himself it would all go away eventually. The right combination of meds, therapy, and a calm job would get him back to recovery, and maybe someday back into the field, instead of being stuck behind a reception desk, managing a team of listless wannabe cops and mindless security drones. He had spent most of his life happily running around outside, first as a toddler in the Northwest, and then for the next 15 years in his mother's native Hawai'i after his family moved to Kaua'i. His heart longed to be back outside in the natural world, even if his nervous system was still concerned about what dangers might lurk there.

The incoming-call chime on his band sounded, and Jay was pleased with himself that the sudden noise didn't bother him in the slightest. "You'll get there, Lambert," he whispered to himself. When he glanced at the name on the display, he lit up even further with the welcome surprise.

"Jojo?" he answered, switching the device's visual feed to one of the displays at his desk. Sure enough, the face that popped up was hers. Her deep-bronze skin looked more worn, and her wiry, military-buzzed hair featured a few more silver strands than before, but it was still the same woman he had met many years ago during basic training, and one of his favorite people in the world. Hover pilot Captain Josie Montpelier had been one of his constant companions while he was in the Army, and they'd shared an especially close bond after the bombing. She had lost her arm in that attack, but Jay's quick thinking had saved her from bleeding out. He'd not seen much of her since then, however, and was delighted that she was back in touch.

"Hey, Lambert!" she said cheerily. "Glad I caught you. Wasn't sure if you had the same contact info or not, but figured I'd give it a chance. Hope I'm not interrupting anything."

"Not at all." He shook his head. "Just got into work. Does this mean you're back in the U.S., then?"

"I am! Just got in last night, actually. I'm staying with my dad down at his ranch in Enumclaw for the moment, but my time in Pakistan is officially over."

"Well, thank goodness for that. I'm surprised you went back after the surgery, to be honest."

She shrugged nonchalantly. "You know me. It'd take much more than having to get an arm replaced to keep me out of getting myself in trouble. Though they did insist on parking me way the hell away from the front. I ended up playing taxi pilot for brass more than anything else. Finally got sick of it and decided to come home for a while. I'm still technically on active duty, but they're switching me into training pilots at JBLM."

"So you're here for a while, then?" he asked hopefully.

"Yep! And I plan to annoy your scrawny ass every chance I get." She chuckled slyly. "What are you up to, anyway? Just got to work? Where?"

"I'm heading up the little security force for XenoNet— the company that did those alien-life probes. One of the probes is coming back to Earth next week, with a passenger. The whole place is complete chaos these days as they shift into research mode. I'm working on getting my team together for the landing at Paine Field, though I'm planning on staying behind—just hanging out in my office pushing data and coordinating resources, all that."

"All the stuff you're best at, in other words." She grinned broadly. "Sounds like a relaxing gig. You doing OK with the . . . issues you were having?"

He nodded. "I am, yeah. On some good meds, have a good doc helping me out. Not even having many of the nightmares anymore."

"That's damn good to hear. Y'know, I was way worried about you when you had to leave. Wish I'd been able to spend more time with you before you shipped back home, but I was stuck in Ankara at the reconstruction center while they built my arm."

"I know. Wish I could've seen you then, too, but after Bachman saw that breakdown I had, they just bundled me up and sent me off to go hang with my parents at the villa in Lihue."

"Your mom's family's place?" Josie asked. "I loved it there when we visited ages ago. Wish I could go back someday and drink my way through their wine cellar."

Jay chuckled. "I'm sure they'd love to see you again. You made my dad laugh, which is pretty rare—he usually only laughs at tacky Belgian comedy vids. Anyway, I spent a year there resting up, eating his cooking, playing with my cousins' toddlers, gaining back a few kilos, all that. Then I came back home and went job hunting. Just couldn't be away from the rain that long, I guess. This job has been good for me so far. Lots of interesting stuff going on most days, but next to no stress."

He sat down at his desk and brought up his video feeds. The company was starting its morning buzz of activity: people milling about, fueling themselves with various hot beverages as they headed to work stations. Drones zoomed around everywhere, getting security footage, making deliveries, and transporting equipment.

"Well, I'm seriously happy we're both going to be local again," Josie continued. "As soon as I get my shit together, I'm taking you out and getting you properly liquored up. Gonna be like it was right after you passed basic training!"

He groaned and waved her off. "Not sure I could take those hangovers again, to be honest. I'm pushing 30 now, you know."

"Ah, you'll be fine. Age didn't slow me down!" She shrugged. "I'm guessing you don't get out much on your own. It'd do you good. Maybe you can meet someone, yeah? Oh! Unless you have already. I didn't even think to ask. You paired up these days?"

He shook his head. "Nope. Went on a couple of dates with a guy I met at the gym in my building, but that didn't go anywhere. Otherwise, I've been more or less antisocial. Didn't want to burden anyone with the whole post-war, head-screwy stuff. What about you?"

"Had a torrid, six-month fling with my physical therapist's assistant while I was working in the new arm. She was . . . damn, she was smoking hot—but also way too domestic for my tastes. She wanted us to get an apartment and a dog and, well . . . Yeah. Not me." She shivered in revulsion. "You, my dear friend, probably at least need to get laid, though."

He flushed. It had indeed been a while. And then, as if to punctuate his sudden remembrance that he had such needs, a pale, soft-featured young man strode into the lobby and approached his desk.

A sudden rush of delight ran through Jay as he recognized the face—one so cute that it had been burned into his memory from the moment he first saw it a week ago.

"Gotta go, Jojo. Work's calling. I'll message you later, though, yeah?"

"You'd better. Over and out!" She threw a lazy salute, and the screen switched back to its default feed of the front entrance.

Jay got up and strode to the counter where the young man waited. "Hello! Alex, right? Mallory, is it?" He stuck out a hand. "Welcome!"

"Thanks. And it's Maloney." The young man flashed a weak smile. "I'm sorry . . . I don't remember your name." He shook the hand.

"Oh, I didn't expect you to. We only met briefly when I checked you in for your interview last week." He let go of Alex's hand. "Jay Lambert. Some people around here call me Captain Lambert, but you don't need to. That's my old military rank, and I'd sooner forget the army. Figured a domestic security gig would be a lot less deadly than Pakistan . . ." He flushed and trailed off. He was exceptionally competent with military logistics, and until the bombing incident, brave as well, but a cute guy could always reduce him to pointless babble. It was a weakness his army buddies always teased him about—at least until he knocked them on their asses.

"I see," Alex said politely, seemingly unfazed by the jittery rambling. "Jay it is, then."

For the first time, Jay noticed the young man's blue eyes were red-rimmed and swollen. Slightly startled, he stepped back, figuring there was something else going on for the new intern, and that this awkward friendliness was probably an intrusion. He cleared his throat. "Anyway. So, there's just one more person coming in for orientation this morning. Feel free to have a seat anywhere. This won't take long."

"Thanks." Alex plopped down in a far corner of the room and began playing with his band, oblivious to the world. Then, suddenly, he perked up and stared at the door.

A short, lithe young woman with huge, dark eyes and a shoulder-length cascade of loose, black curls pushed open the door and strode in. "Am I in the right place?" she asked Jay. "I'm Sasha Delescu. I'm supposed to be here for HR intake and orientation."

"Hi!" Alex chirped, standing up and approaching her. "I'm Alex. Also here for orientation. Are you going to be in the physics department? Because it would be awesome to work with you."

Sasha raised an eyebrow, but she shook Alex's offered hand. "Bio, I'm afraid. I'll be working with the specimens."

"Well, if you ever have any interest in the other side of things, you should come over to my wing." Alex smiled significantly, but backed off after Sasha snorted a laugh. "Or not. As you like." He flashed a friendly, non-confrontational grin and seemed relieved to get one in return.

Jay rolled his eyes. *Of course*, he thought with a rush of disappointment. He'd never be so lucky that such a cute guy would be inclined the right way. Though he still could be, Jay reconsidered. After all, it wasn't like he himself didn't think the new arrival was attractive, if not his type. He hadn't dated many women over the years, but it wasn't out of the question. Perhaps Alex might be the same way from the other direction . . . Shaking his head to clear the pointless speculation, he went into professional mode. Clearing his throat, he handed over a pair of prox bands to the new recruits.

"Here are your temporary IDs—they'll get you in the buildings until your personal bands are registered on the internal Stream—and if you two will just follow me into the conference room, we'll start the process. Welcome to XenoNet!"

* * *

Alex had never been into actors or pop stars the same as the kids with whom he went to school, but at the moment, he entirely understood the kind of all-consuming excitement they might've experienced when meeting one of their idols. That his idol was a tiny, soft-spoken woman whose Tibetan-ancestry features showed evidence of her north-of-70 age didn't dampen the feeling in the slightest. He fidgeted outside the door to her office, staring obsessively at the electronic nameplate on the wall: "Jan Leung, CEO."

As a boy, he'd heard about Leung's breakthrough in deep-space propulsion technology and he'd since been glued to every report about her project. It had even driven his desire for a proper physics career in the first place. He'd been plenty into science before, of course. When he was growing up in Boston, he built model rockets and reverse-engineered the nav systems on his hover toys. Learning about the great Seattle quake when he was in kindergarten inspired him to get into geophysics in particular, and to work on Gabriel's development project for the quake-smart construction nanotech that now lived in nearly every new building in a seismic zone.

It was always Leung's work that had fascinated him the most, however Not long after retiring from her job heading Boeing's space program, she and a small team of engineers finally created a working slipspace propulsion system. Funded by grants from the government and a tech-investment company, she started XenoNet and built and launched the first probes, aiming them for the planets that astronomers had said were most likely to host extraterrestrial life. When Alex was just getting into middle school, the probes had reached their destinations. A year later, one had returned close enough to report that it had cargo: half a dozen small arthropods and a whole host of flora, minerals, and other samples. Two years after that, another probe reported that it had even more interesting cargo: a small mammal. That probe was now about to return to Earth with its precious passenger.

His mother's religion, among a few others, reacted badly to the news that humans were not alone in the universe. He was clever and observant enough by then to understand why: their faith was built on the idea that God had created all life, and that only the life on Earth—that described by the Bible—existed. In addition to their other objections to humans "playing God"—abortion, euthanasia, contraceptives, gender-related body modification, artificial reproduction—they objected to the search for extraterrestrial life. If found, the logic went, it would seriously damage their faith's claims about the origin of life and therefore about sin and salvation—its stock in trade. Most other faiths, of course, took the news in stride. They reinterpreted their scriptures and teachings as they had done with every other scientific advancement, and incorporated these other planets into their concepts of what their supreme forces or beings had created. But the scripture-literalist sects, including his mother's, continued to insist that the whole thing was either a hoax by evil scientists or an illusion created by Lucifer himself.

Perhaps it was his mother's objection—which always felt like a rejection of Alex himself—that drove him on, however, and fueled his undying interest in XenoNet and its work. Nearly every day since the probes launched had been devoted to trying to live his eventual dream of working for this company and this woman. That he was now not only employed there—OK, interning—but summoned to the CEO's office at the end if his first week was almost unreal.

The door swung in. "Alex! Thank you for coming."

"Of course!" He felt like he should genuflect or bow or something, but that seemed excessive, given that she was in jeans and a faded t-shirt and, to his surprise and amusement, also barefoot. Instead, he stuck out a hand, which she shook firmly. "It's such an honor to meet you, Ms. Leung."

"Jan, please!" She grinned. "Come have a seat."

He followed her inside. Her office was, frankly, a mess, but entertainingly so. The shelf along one wall was laden mostly with physical renderings of various space-going vehicles, plus a smattering of awards—including her Nobel, which had a thin layer of dust. The shelf also bore a few old paper books—likely relics from Leung's childhood, given the Mandarin characters on their spines. On her desk were the remains of a bagel and an enormous cup of coffee, plus a few colorful figures and toys. The vid window behind the desk was currently clear, displaying a lovely view of Lake Washington.

"How was your first week? Settling in well, I hope?" She plopped down in her overstuffed chair and nodded at the bright-red seat opposite, upon which Alex nervously perched.

"Great! I'm having plenty of fun with Dr. Kumi and her team, getting ready for the probe landing."

"That's good to hear!" she said, picking up a wooden puzzle cube and toying with it. "When I heard about your work with the quake-smart project, I was hoping I could get you on here to help us go through the geological samples and data the probe is bringing back. I actually tailored the internship in the hope of attracting you to it."

He gaped. "You've . . . heard of me?"

"Of course. Oh, I know Gabriel Jackson's name was all over the publication, but you did most of the heavy lifting."

Alex flushed. He had, in rare moments of ego, thought the same, but had never given voice to the idea. He was usually too busy admiring Gabriel to acknowledge that his boyfriend wasn't quite his intellectual equal—not that many people were. Now that they had split, however, he allowed the thought. That his idol had brought it up didn't hurt. "Well," he demurred, "I was just one person on the team."

"Of course." She nodded. "But even so, I admire your work, so I'm glad the internship appealed to you. We had a few other candidates who applied, but none of them came close to your qualifications."

"Wow! Thank you." He suppressed the impulse to squeal.

"I've done most of my own work in propulsion, of

course, but I had a big fascination with geophysics when I was younger. Reading about the landscapes and composition of other planets is what started me thinking about finding ways to physically survey them. The interest in extraterrestrial life came later—my second ex was into biophysics—but it did help me get more funding to start this company. I'm now about equally interested in both the creatures and the other things we're finding with the probes."

Alex grinned. He of course already knew everything she was talking about. He had done an eighth-grade book report on her biography and regularly monitored and edited Stream encyclopedia entries for her, to be sure they were accurate. He didn't say so, however. He worried that she might find him creepy and decide not to let him intern for her company after all. "I'm glad my work was able to interest you. I'm looking forward to helping out."

"I'm pleased to hear that. Of course, most of the daily work you'll be doing involves analyzing what the probes bring back, but really, that's just an excuse to get you here, so I can pick your brain. And also," she leaned over her desk, dropping her voice to a whisper, "I wanted to make sure you were working for me and not for Belenko."

He frowned. "Kristov Belenko? Dark Matter Technologies? I admit I hadn't even considered working there."

"Good!" She smiled. "And I admit I hope you never do."

His mind scrambled. Over the years, he'd been focused enough on Leung and XenoNet to pay little attention to other companies in the same general field. He knew at least a few things about Dark Matter and its larger-than-life CEO, who had started up his moon- and Mars-tourism businesses years ago, but not enough to understand why she'd be so opposed to Alex working there. "I'm afraid you've lost me. I mean, yeah, Belenko seems like a jerk—trying to mine Mars and going on safari hunts and all that—but otherwise, I'm not sure why I specifically shouldn't get involved with him."

She sighed and tipped back in her chair. "OK, then. Let me tell you a little story—one that isn't known to the general public, so please respect that."

"All right. Lips sealed."

"Many years ago, when I was still in Boeing's space division, there were a lot of players in the space-vehicle game. Elon Musk, Richard Branson, et cetera, all spent a lot of money trying to find ways to replace the space shuttle program after it was decommissioned, with varying levels of success. One other person, however, was just coasting along, waiting to see what else happened, to find a way to slide in once the standards had been set by others. Belenko was originally a member of Vladimir Putin's cabinet, working with their space program, when the conflicts between Ukraine and Russia began. As Belenko was Ukrainian, Putin considered him a potential spy, and had him fired and deported back to Kiev. All of Belenko's work was left behind. He didn't get to keep any of it, since it belonged to the government, and couldn't even apply his own findings to any new work for international patent reasons. So he left the profession—and Ukraine—entirely and took a job with a mining company in Belarus. That's where he struck gold. Well, titanium, to be precise. He made his way up the career ladder with the company as it grew from its new resource claim, and eventually took over as CEO. When the vein started running dry, he cashed out and moved to the U.S. As soon as he got here, however, he changed his name, had some cosmetic surgery to change his face, and falsified his CV and passport so he could get back to work in aerospace. That's where I met him."

"He changed his name?"

"Yep. His real name isn't Belenko. I didn't know that at the time, though. I just saw a good CV and a good interviewee, and hired him on the spot. I didn't run as thorough a background check as I should have, because I was too excited by his skills." She paused, and rubbed her eyes. "I've made a lot of mistakes over the years, but that was the biggest one. Because not three years into him working for me, he passed off some of my research as his own, and landed a contract with an independent space-vehicle company in Nevada. Four years later, he bought controlling interest in its shares, fired the founder, and took over."

"Wait. That part is starting to sound familiar. That's where Dark Matter started, right?"

"Right. Unfortunately, he left Boeing before we hit it big on some of the propulsion tech, so all he was able to do was build near-Earth vehicles. He used them to start up his tourism business, and made the rest of his considerable fortune that way."

"That's all Dark Matter does, though, right? I don't understand why he would be a concern for you."

"Ah, but it's not all, and that's the problem. You see, Belenko never lost his interest in deep-space vehicles, and when I started XenoNet and built our probes, he was furious. He actually thought that I had stolen some of his own research—instead of the other way around—and wanted to sue me for a portion of whatever profits we generated with the project."

"But he didn't sue you, did he?"

"Nope." She shook her head and smiled grimly. "But only because I threatened him with something he couldn't fight against."

"Which was?"

"His real name. When we were working together, I took him out for drinks one night not long after his second trophy wife left him. He got hammered and ended up confessing his whole story to me. If word ever got out about who he really is, he would be in a lot of trouble. Problem is, that's my only leverage on him. He hates me and everything I've done—he thinks all of this should be his—and he's always trying to find ways to put me out of business or leapfrog over me and do something better. Hell, he even threatened to out me once. I jumped the gun on that by outing myself. Apparently he was still living in the twentieth century and thought it would be shocking or something. It might've been a problem for me if my parents had still been alive—they did consider it a dishonor at the time—but they were long dead, so I didn't care."

Alex raised an eyebrow. When he was still in middle school, Leung issued a short media statement noting that she had been assigned male at birth and had transitioned soon after emigrating to the U.S. "Oh! I had wondered what inspired that. It seemed sudden at the time."

She grinned. "Now you know. Anyway . . . Belenko has a bad enough reputation that he has a hard time getting the best people to work for him, and has been known to be sneaky about luring people in. I don't know for sure whether you're on his radar, but even if not, it wouldn't be long before you were. Your particular interest in geophysics is something he would definitely want on board when and if he ever gets a long-range probe going. He wants to mine every place we can send a vehicle to, and someone with your knowledge of extraterrestrial geology would be invaluable to him."

Suddenly, it all made sense. Alex had been mentally cataloguing the physical makeup of every known planet and moon since he was a child. He probably knew as much or more about it than people who studied the subject for a living. Someone who saw other planets only as fresh repositories of natural resources would definitely want his knowledge. "Well, you don't have to worry, Jan. I wouldn't help him hack up other planets no matter how much he paid me. I'm all yours."

"I am so glad to hear that." She stood up. "I'm sure you're wanting to head home now—you've had a busy week!—but I'd like it if we could have regular meetings to catch up. Send me a scheduling request when you can."

"Of course. Thank you." He rose and shook her hand.

As he left her office, he seriously considered not ever washing that hand again.

WELCOME TO EARTH

"Alex?" His mother's voice was already harsh. "What are you watching?"

Immediately, he tried to turn off the vid feed, but it was too late: she'd seen it. "It's nothing, Mom," he lied anyway.

She snatched the device from his small hands and restarted the feed.

"It's up!" The reporter on the scene at the launch pad in Seattle cried as the fiery tail of the craft disappeared into the sky. "Xeno Two, the first returnable deep-space vehicle in human history, has launched. The crowd here is ecstatic, and I admit: I am, too." She wiped away a tear that had trickled down her cheek.

His mother stopped the video again. A look of tired disgust crossed her face. "Alex, we've talked about this. I don't mind you playing around with some science, but this space stuff . . . it has to stop. It is not for us humans to understand the heavens. That is God's territory, not ours."

He began to cry.

As he scanned the data displays showing the probe's gentle progress back to Earth, Alex practically vibrated with nervous energy. The person on the other end of the connection on the vid window to his left noticed.

"I don't think I even need to be there!" Jay teased. "You're making me tired just watching you!" The security chief was remotely watching the proceedings from his office and had been idly chatting with the team as they set up. Since starting his job, Alex had formed a fast friendship with the ex-soldier, who contrary to Alex's admittedly uninformed concept of military men, was witty and had a great sense of humor. He spent the majority of his time getting to know his boss, Dr. Prita Kumi, and the other people in his department, but he did enjoy dawdling in the lobby in the mornings and afternoons, chitchatting and catching up with Jay. It was a refreshing change of pace from the jargon-laden conversations with his team, and a welcome bit of social interaction when he otherwise had little time and energy these days to keep up with his friends from school, most of whom were off on their own internships now. Besides, many of his old crowd were also friends with Gabriel, who seemed to have taken custody of them after the breakup. He'd never imagined he'd make friends with a war veteran, but life was strange that way, he figured.

"Yeah, well." Alex shrugged and flashed a grin at the camera. "You're missing out! It's like the air is vibrating here. I'm completely sparked." He glanced over at another monitor; the probe was only minutes away. "And here we go!"

"You ready for this?" Dr. Kumi nudged him, her eyes twinkling in her own excitement. Behind her, Leung fidgeted, scanning every vid window in the room for the tiniest unexpected blip. Alex tried not to be unsettled by her presence.

"I think I've been ready for ten years," he admitted.

Nearby, another young face anxiously scanned the skies above the control center's dome. He hadn't had much chance to talk to Sasha since they'd met in the security office, but he'd seen a lot of her. Every time, he couldn't help being distracted. She was definitely attractive, reminding him of a soccer star one of his exes used to be into, but that was only a small part of the attraction. More important was that she was also undoubtedly his equal—and maybe beyond—in her own field. When the landing team had its prep meetings, she'd speak up confidently, contributing just as much to the conversations about the alien creature as her department boss, Dr. Takeshi Hideo, did. Alex could only dream of being so articulate, still sputtering when it was his turn to speak up. Not that being around her helped him stay focused, however. As she chatted animatedly with Dr. Hideo, Sasha pushed a lock of hair behind her ear, and her tongue flashed out to moisten her soft, full lips . . .

"Alex?" Kumi nudged him.

"What?" He blinked, turning toward her.

She glanced over in the direction of his gaze and grinned knowingly. "Want to head to your station?"

"On it!" He threw a cocky salute and trotted over to the controls, the non-lizard areas of his brain kicking back in. Much as parts south might want to interact with a prime specimen of Earth's dominant life-form, the well-being of the creature now arriving from the planet they'd nicknamed Aurora was dependent in part on him doing his job.

"Xeno Two entering atmosphere," the AI driving the ship announced. "Ready for transition to manual pilot operations."

"That's our cue!" Dr. Kumi called, and her fingers began furiously dancing over the screen in front of her. "Deploying heat shields."

"Engaging wing and tail guides," Simon, the vector specialist, checked in from his station.

"Internal systems steady," said Dr. Kumi. "Ready glide drone."

"Glide drone ready," Alex said, his voice unsteady. Honestly, guiding the craft, the surface-to-air drone plane on which the probe would piggyback to get back to ground, wasn't much more complicated than playing a game. It was just that the fate of science rested on him doing the job right. "Docking ports opened."

The satellite image showing the docking process was slightly delayed, so every move the team made had to account for what they saw being a fraction of a second slower than what they did. Jumping the gun could cause the probe to crash into the drone instead of docking. Alex felt like he could barely breathe for fear of his excitement making him act rashly.

"Docking locks extended. Speed and vector synchronized. Hand reaching for glove," Simon said.

"Magnetic field engaged!" Alex squirmed in glee. "Docking complete in five... four... three... two... one. Locked!"

"Xeno Two AI disengaged. We're flying home, folks!" Dr. Kumi let out a cheer. Seeing Alex's nervousness, she tapped his arm gently. "Shall I finish the landing?"

"Be my guest!" Alex scooted over and let her have the drone's controls. Keeping the thing steady in the troposphere wasn't terribly complicated. Actually piloting it was somewhat beyond him, though he did long to get a pilot's license one day and zip around the region in a nicely tricked-out hover.

Wiping his sweaty palms on his jeans, he turned, glancing over his shoulder at the assembly behind them. To his great delight, Sasha was staring right at him and favoring him with an enormous, proud grin. He grinned back, envisioning her someday sitting beside him in his swanky aircraft as they buzzed over the city.

* * *

Sasha fidgeted and tried to see over the shoulders of the people in front of her, once again cursing the genes that had made her shorter than most.

"Vitals steady," the AI announced flatly. "Specimen has

adjusted to Earth-standard gravity and atmospheric conditions and may be removed from the transport pod."

Hideo turned to her, smiling. "Want to do the honors?"

Her heart thumped wildly. She was excited just to see the creature. The idea that she'd be allowed to transfer it from its tiny stasis chamber on the probe's science deck into its new enclosure made her head spin. "Absolutely!"

Hideo stepped aside, and she entered the small room and approached the chamber gingerly.

Looking something like a squirrel-sized pangolin with a dash of chameleon DNA, the blue-scaled mammal fixed a luminous, golden eye on her. He—the creatures had been sexed on the journey—tilted his head and issued a soft clicking sound from his throat. Tentatively, he took a step forward.

"Hi," Sasha whispered, trying to radiate as much calm as she could muster under the circumstances. It seemed to be working, however, as the creature wasn't displaying any of his species' known fear behavior. Instead, he almost seemed—she tried not to anthropomorphize him, but couldn't help it—happy to see her, as if he was delighted to meet the first biological creature he had seen since a faceless robot had carried him into space.

She opened the seal on the chamber and carefully reached in a gloved hand. For a second, the creature shrank back, hugging close to a large rock taken from his home planet as part of the environment created for him. But then he wandered over, flicking his long, purple tongue in the air and sniffing at her. In a flash, he reached for her. His dexterous forepaws wrapped around her fingers, and he hopped into her palm.

Even through the glove, the intense warmth of the creature's touch was evident. His region of his planet was several degrees warmer than most Earth locales, and his body temperature was an amazing 50 degrees. It felt, she thought wildly, like wrapping her hand around a just-cool-enough-to-eat burrito. As she drew him from the enclosure, she also felt something else entirely: a sharp, electrifying rush that caused her to sprout goose bumps and brought a wave of tears to her eyes. She'd never before felt any stirrings of parental desire, and even all the wonderful creatures she'd loved and studied didn't necessarily inspire any feeling of longing, but this time was completely different. In the space of a second, all she could think of was being as close to the creature as possible and protecting him with every ounce of fortitude she had.

That's impossible, she thought. Still, it was undeniable: whatever pheromone or other mechanism the creature had just used, he had used it to bond with her, the way a newborn bonds with its parents. Though he might be countless trillions of kilometers from the planet of his birth, while nestled into Sasha's hand, the creature apparently felt at home. Reaching out with her index finger, she stroked one of the tiny feet pressed against her palm and whispered, "Welcome to Earth!"

The sun was dipping below the horizon and most of the bio department's staff had gone home to sleep off the day's excitement, but Sasha was still wired. She couldn't yet bring herself to leave the lab, lest she miss something wonderful that the charming little creature did, so she had volunteered to keep watch until the late shift came in.

"How's he doing?" A warm, low voice broke her reverie. She turned to see the company's security chief standing in the doorway to the lab, backpack slung over his shoulder.

"Oh! Hi, Captain Lambert." She smiled warmly and waved her cold cup of coffee at him. "Please come in."

"Jay, please." He returned the smile and strolled over to where she stood in front of the creature's enclosure.

"Jay. Got it." She nodded. "Littlefoot's doing great," she answered. "He seems to be adjusting to life here on Earth just fine."

Jay frowned. "Littlefoot?"

"Oh!" She flushed. "That's just . . . it's a nickname I've given him—because he has such tiny feet."

Jay chuckled softly and moved closer, standing behind her to watch the energetic creature. "So I see. Have you discovered anything new about him yet?"

"Well, Hideo and the other full-timers have done most of the work." She shrugged. "I've just been hanging back and observing: feeding him, cleaning his enclosure, that sort of thing. They've found quite a few interesting things about him already—stuff that the AIs wouldn't have been programmed to look for." She turned back to the creature, who was rubbing up against the Plexiglas of his enclosure, and chirping merrily. "Behavior, for instance. He recognizes different humans and knows when there's a new one. You, for instance. He hasn't seen you yet, so he's excited, and he wants to meet you."

"Really?" Jay flashed a surprised smile.

"Yep! You can introduce yourself if you like. Just run your hands through the ion sanitizer over there and put on some gloves, and then you can reach in. Can't take him out yet—we're still making sure he's not allergic to anything here—but you can give him a pat if you want."

"OK." Jay cleaned his hands, and she stepped back so he could get closer to the enclosure. She waved her palm in front of the security pad, and the seal on the enclosure hissed open. Jay hesitated for a moment, glancing back at her. "He doesn't bite, does he?"

She shook her head. "Nope. He has teeth, but his defense mechanism is his tail. See the little spines down the side of it? Those pop out when he's agitated. He's never shown any hostility to humans, though. The most he might do is grab your fingers and try to taste them."

Jay carefully reached in, moving slowly as not to startle the creature. Littlefoot did exactly as she'd said: first getting a taste of Jay's glove and then grabbing hold of his thumb and nuzzling against it.

"He's marking you," she said. "He has scent glands in his chin. As far as we can tell, it's possessive marking, not identification. He recognizes us by sight and sound and something else we haven't pinned down yet. Hideo said he apparently knew when I was standing out in the hall— when he had no way of seeing, hearing, or smelling me. Might've been infrared, but he doesn't seem to have the visual structure for that, as far as we know. He does a different greeting dance for each of us, so it was definitely me he was reacting to and not just random behavior."

"Is that unusual?" Jay asked as the creature kept rubbing over his hand.

"Not entirely. Most Earth creatures communicate with the basic senses—sight, sound, and of course smell in many cases—but a few use other methods, like feeling and sending vibrations through their environment. That sort of thing is found primarily among aquatic creatures, though some land animals—bats, for instance—also do that. It's definitely rare to see that happen between species, though."

"That's seriously cool," he said reverently.

"It is!" Sasha beamed at him. She hadn't expected the security chief to show so much interest in the details of the company's work, but it pleased her all the same. A voice in the back of her head prodded her to ask more about that—and about him in general—but she tried to ignore it. She had noticed on her first day that he was attractive, but she loved this job way too much to risk messing it up by flirting with a colleague. Still, there was no harm in being friends, she supposed.

Finally, Jay stepped back, giving Littlefoot's head one last pat, and she resealed the enclosure. "That was amazing." He smiled big. "Think he likes me?"

"Absolutely," Sasha said confidently. Her baser side got the better of her, and she blurted, "What's not to like?"

Jay looked at her strangely, then chuckled. "Thanks?"

Time to change the subject. "Anyway, I should

probably go home at some point. Tate's on overnight monitoring duty, and she should be here shortly."

"Lindsey Tate? Yeah. I checked her in at the front desk a while ago. She was chatting with Leung when I packed up to leave." He nodded at Littlefoot's enclosure. "I'm guessing he's going to miss you when you're gone, though."

"Oh?" She turned back. The creature chirruped happily as he met her gaze and did his squirmy dance of excitement. She hadn't wanted to tell anyone exactly how bonded she felt with him, lest they think she was being unprofessional and take him away from her, but truly, if someone with presumably no animal-behavior training could sense it, maybe there was something to it after all. "Yeah," she said with an absentminded smile. "I guess that's probably true."

* * *

As he made his way back down through the lobby to the parking garage, Jay ran into him again: the painfully cute intern. Jay had tried to be professional every time they'd met since Alex started, but his resolve was beginning to crack. It was impossible to avoid him, after all: he crossed in front of Jay's security desk every morning and evening as he checked in and out. He'd been friendly, too, waving and even stopping to chat a time or two when he had a few moments. Every time, Jay felt like he had to suppress an impulse to proposition him right there in the lobby.

"Damn!" Alex suddenly spat as he looked down at his band.

Jay froze at the outburst. "Something wrong?"

"Oh! Sorry, Jay. I just noticed the time, is all. I got hung up with something on my way out, and I missed the last shuttle to the train station. Naturally, it's pouring out."

"Ah, I see. Well, if you like, I can give you a ride there.

I usually take my Ducati in; there's an extra helmet in the saddlebag." He nodded toward the parking garage.

Alex tried to wave him off. "Oh, I don't want to impose—"

"No imposition at all. Hey, it's my job as security chief to make sure you folks are taken care of, yeah?" He smiled hopefully.

Alex still looked unconvinced. "Are you sure?"

"Absolutely."

The ride to the station was only twelve blocks, but to Jay, it felt like hours of bliss. Alex's arms wrapped around his waist felt like they belonged there, and the cheery chatter over the headsets in the helmets made him smile. Alex sounded surprised that Jay understood some of what he was working on, and also pressed him for more info on Leung when he found out they were friendly.

When they arrived, Alex stowed the helmet and ran a hand through his smushed-down curls to fluff them up again. "Thanks so much for doing this. I totally owe you. Let me bring you coffee on Monday, yeah?"

"You don't need to do that, but if you want to, sure. Only not coffee, if you don't mind."

"No coffee?" Alex raised an eyebrow.

Jay shook his head. "I don't do caffeine. So some sort of herbal thing or cider, maybe?"

Alex looked confused. "No caffeine. Oh. OK." He scanned Jay's face, seeming to try to figure something out.

"What?"

"I'm—this is rude. I apologize—but I'm just curious. Why the no caffeine? Is it a religious thing?"

Jay laughed and shook his head. "No. I'm not a devout anything."

"Me neither. My mom . . . well, that's a long story. If it's not religion though—wait." Alex looked him over again. His eyes lit on the small, illuminated bulge under Jay's forearm, then noted the tattoo close to it. "You said you were ex-Army . . . Pakistan."

A prickly feeling crept up Jay's neck.

Alex smiled. "One of my profs had one of those." He nodded at the med implant. "He'd been in the Siege of Damascus back in '27. Lost his whole family."

Jay looked away and bit his lip.

"Sorry," Alex said quickly. "None of my business."

He shook his head. "No. It's OK." Oddly enough, he meant the words as more than just courtesy. Something about Alex made him feel comfortable. He could almost see himself telling Alex the whole story someday if he wanted to know.

The train hummed into the station, and Alex turned. "That's me," he said. "Thanks again for the ride. Lemon OK?"

Jay frowned. "Lemon?"

"Beverage. Monday."

"Lemon sounds marvelous." Jay smiled big and waved as Alex dashed off. Then he sighed. It had been years since he'd had a crush this pointless. He felt like an adolescent again. It wasn't a bad feeling, at least. The only problem was the shit he was going to get from Josie if she found out.

* * *

Alex chewed his lip and fondled the strap on his bag as the train sped north. Looking around at the rest of the passengers, it seemed none of them cared about the amazing scientific achievement that had just happened today. They played games or read on their various bands and other devices. They watched the programs on the train's vid windows. Or like him, they mostly gazed out cleared windows at the setting sun. The train was fairly full—his was one of only two seats that didn't have both occupants—but Alex still felt alone and wished there were someone else here with whom he could share the excitement of the day. The ride to the station with the nice security chief had been pleasant, but it wasn't what he was hoping for—though he wasn't entirely sure what that was.

The rest of his team, after a quick round of champagne at the landing site, had all gone back to their offices to finish up work, out with friends or co-workers, or home to their families. He'd gotten a few messages of congratulations from some of his college friends, but no one had offered to take him out for a celebratory meal or drink, and he didn't know anyone on the team well enough to feel comfortable tagging along on their outings. He had thought for a moment about asking Sasha if she wanted to go out, but knew she'd likely want to stay late at work, getting to know the new occupant of the bio wing. He'd also considered asking if Jay wanted to go get a drink or something, but somehow that felt even weirder. Technically, he could have stayed and helped the engineering crew dismantle and repair some of the equipment retrieved from the probe, but that sort of hands-on work wasn't his specialty; he figured he'd just be in the way. So, after saying goodbye to his team and getting another round of thanks and admiration from Dr. Kumi, he headed back to his empty apartment. Truthfully, Alex didn't want to be there, with all its reminders of how alone he really was right now, but he also had nowhere else to go, unless he gave up avoiding hookup bars and tried to drown his sorrows in cheap booze and meaningless sex.

As tiny as the place was, Gabriel's absence made it seem cavernous. The table by the door still had a void where his band charger used to sit. The shoe rack had four fewer pairs than it should have. The fridge no longer had the almond milk and sesame paste he loved. And the bed, well, that was just wrong—and cold. Alex even found himself missing the tiny curls that collected in the sink every time Gabriel decided his hair had gotten too long and took a razor to his head. When Alex closed the door, even his breathing seemed to echo in the space.

Rubbing a few stinging tears from his eyes, he poured a

bowl of cereal and sat down in the living room, idly scanning through the day's news and chatter on the room's vid window. To his astonishment, his own face came up on one report of the landing, though he hadn't been named. He couldn't help a satisfied chuckle. "I must be famous now," he congratulated himself. "If Mom could only see me . . ." He sighed heavily and shoveled another spoon full of crunchy squares in his mouth. His mother would undoubtedly be avoiding any science-related news, especially news about the arrival on Earth of another species that was decidedly not on Noah's Ark.

An alert popped up in the corner of the window. New message: Jonathan Maloney. Alex nearly choked on his cereal and brought the message up. It was text-only, though the face attached to the account was a recent picture. His brother looked older now, and he'd put a few more kilos on his already well-padded frame, but still had the same round, freckled cheeks. He also wore the stiff collar of a seminary student.

"Just saw you on a news report about the probe landing," the message read. "Congratulations. I know this is important to you. I'll keep you in my prayers tonight. God be with you."

Alex set aside the bowl; his stomach was no longer capable of processing food. He could see eventually living entirely without his mother, if he couldn't ever get her to see reason, but his baby brother was a different story. From the moment he'd been born, Alex had doted on him, helping with his care and feeding and playing with "Jon-Jon" every chance he got. He read to him, sang to him, helped him build things with his blocks, and held him when he cried. He had been especially protective after their father left, when Jonathan, with a six-year-old's logic, believed he'd done something wrong to make their parents split up. Yet their bond had broken as Jonathan drifted onto their mother's path when it began to deviate from the more-or-less secular one it had been before. Alex wondered sometimes if it was his fault—if being so heavily into finishing school early and embarking on his career had pushed Jonathan to seek stability in something else, instead of his absent brother. It was too late for regrets now, though. Their lives were different, now—too different.

Yet Jonathan had sent the message. Alex's hand hovered over the controller as he wondered whether he should reply. Eventually, fear won out. He wanted to have a relationship with his brother again so badly it felt as if every cell in his body was crying. He also knew that the kind of relationship he wanted wasn't possible. The pride he felt at what he'd accomplished today was something Jonathan wouldn't ever truly understand, much less support, the words on the message notwithstanding. Closing the message alert, he dropped his hand back into his lap and curled up into a tighter ball on the sofa. He stared at the screen, hoping the comedy vid now playing would somehow suck him in, away from the real world and the real pain that was never far away.

FAMILY

"Lambert, is it?" the tall, imposing woman in front of him barked. He recognized her—she had been leading another company that was going through basic training at the same time he was—but they hadn't properly met.

He tried to stand as rigid and still as possible. *"Yes, ma'am!"*

"Can you explain to me why your uniform is not in regulation condition?"

Jay blanched and glanced down. He thought he had put everything back on correctly after his quick fling with Tito behind the barracks, but clearly, he had not: his shirt gaped where one of the buttons had not been fastened. He quickly fumbled with it, hands shaking. *"Ma'am, it was just an oversight!"*

"An oversight? Have you been walking around all day wearing an oversight? I ought to report you to your CO."

"Ma'am, please, I—"

"Or maybe you didn't spend all day like this. Maybe you just got dressed. Maybe you were doing something you shouldn't. Maybe with Private Morales?"

His stomach turned. Had she seen? His mind raced to come up with an excuse, but the words just wouldn't form.

Suddenly, she punched his arm.

"Ow! What—?" He tried to avoid rubbing the spot where her

47

solid fist had landed.

"What, MA'AM?"

"Ma'am . . ."

She erupted in a gale of deep laughs. "At ease, Lambert."

"Ma'am? I don't—"

She dropped her voice to a teasing purr and leaned in. "I know very well what you were doing with Private Morales, you naughty little boy."

"Uh?"

"Relax. I'm not going to report you. Just suggest that you find a better location to get it on. Shantal and I—" she nodded over her shoulder to a pretty, petite young woman standing nearby "—we usually use the mechanic shop after dark. No one around, and the soundproofing is decent."

Finally, he understood. For all that the military had allowed folks like them in for decades, the older top brass still didn't overlook same-sex dalliances the way they did those engaged in by straight soldiers. "Noted!" he nodded and smiled at his new ally

"Noted what?" She raised an eyebrow.

"Noted, ma'am?"

"Good job! Now back to your barracks, or I really will report you." She winked and turned to go.

"Ma'am?" he called after her.

She turned back. "Eh?"

"I'm sorry, ma'am. I didn't catch your name."

She pointed at the patch on her chest. "Montpelier. Josie. When you're not saluting, you can call me Jojo."

"Jojo, then. I'm Lambert—well, you know that. Julien."

"Julien? What the fuck kind of name is that? Y'know, fuck it. I'm calling you Jay. That work for you?"

He once again found himself cursing his Belgian father's idea of a name for his son, though at least he didn't often have to contend with haoles trying to pronounce the Hawai'ian middle name his mother had given him. But Jay? He could live with that. "Jay it is. Ma'am."

The pub was exactly as he had remembered it from his days haunting the place shortly after basic training. Same dark, polished wood, though nicked with a few more scars. Same bioprinted-leather seats. Same peppy, Britpop-revival music on the player. And, to his delight, the same sassy bartender, with whom he'd drunkenly flirted a time or two.

"Lambert? Jay? Fucking hell, mate! Where have you been? It's been years! You still drinking the same stuff?"

"Hey, Colin!" Jay reached out to shake his hand. "Yeah. Whatever IPA you have around is cool." He perched on a stool and began fiddling with the coaster Colin put in front of him. "I've been here and there. Did a couple tours in Pakistan. Got kinda blown up, had to spend some time healing."

"Ouch. My cousin Reggie had the same issue. Someone reprogrammed the guidance system for one of his drones and sent it to bomb his camp. Poor bloke lost a hand."

"I think I heard about that. We were the ones who had our bunker in the south get attacked."

"Ooh. Not fun. What're you doing now? Did you leave the service?" He set a full, dark pint glass on the bar.

Jay nodded. "Retired from duty and doing a security gig now."

"Playing with a bunch of science nerds, more like." A familiar voice behind him rang out.

"Jojo!" Jay cried and zipped over to her.

Josie swept him up in strong arms and planted a sloppy kiss on his cheek. "Hey, Cap'n!" she purred into his ear. "Dang, have I missed you."

"Same." He pulled back, grinning, taking in her tall frame and angular jaw and reveling in their familiarity.

"Colin! How the fuck are you?" Josie grabbed the barkeep's hand.

"I'm well, Montpelier!" He smiled and, as soon as she released his hand, began drawing her a pint.

"How's that gorgeous sister of yours these days?" Josie leaned on the bar and grinned rakishly.

Colin raised an eyebrow. "Tina's married now. I think you breaking her heart made her want to settle down, so she's now living in wedded bliss with a gal named Katya. She's a physician's assistant or something."

"I'll be damned!" Josie hooted. "All this time I've been feeling bad about our breakup, and she went off and did that! Maybe I should break hearts more often."

Jay nudged her with a shoulder. "I think you've broken enough, Jojo."

"Eh, you're probably right." She took the pint Colin handed her. "Keep these coming. Put it all on my account." She slid her finger down the print reader nearby to confirm the transaction. "Lambert and I have way too much catching up to do."

"Sure thing. And I'll tell Tina you said congratulations."

Josie wandered off to a booth in the corner, Jay on her heels. Once they'd settled in, she kicked him gently under the table. "So! I saw the news about that probe thing. I guess that new gig of yours is hot."

He nodded. "It is, yeah. I'm fascinated by the whole thing. Even though I wasn't on site for the landing, I watched it all from my office. I've been keeping up with the project as much as my non-expert brain can. I understand some of it, but not a lot."

"Your dad's some sort of scientist, right?" She pulled back a hearty draught of her beer.

"Yeah. He did his undergrad work in engineering, but ended up going to law school and then working in Boeing's legal department for a couple decades before he retired. Mom was an epidemiologist; she still gets occasional calls from the CDC. Oh, and my sister Lucia's currently in Antarctica tracking receding ice or something. She messages me every few months to send me video of a blizzard."

"Right. So the science thing is kinda in your blood. Guess it makes sense you'd be working for that Xeno company, then."

"Yeah. I could've worked for a hundred tech companies around here, but this one seemed like the best fit. My dad worked with Jan Leung when she was trying to get some of her propulsion systems stuff patented. Might be why she hired me on—she recognized the name, at least."

"And you're enjoying the work? Seems like it'd be decent fun, at least."

"It is, yeah. Honestly, wrangling scientists and a handful of drones is basically nothing. About the only excitement we get is when the bio-recognition panels break down and I have to check people in manually. We did have one incident when a dude from R&D found out his wife had been cheating on him and he lost it. Trashed his office, punched a co-worker—lots of fun, that. He was canned immediately, of course."

"Wild times! Sure you'd rather not be back in an actual war zone?"

He shuddered. "Very. I think I've had my fill of life-threatening situations."

She nodded in understanding. "Me, too, actually."

"I never thought I'd hear you say that, Jojo! Always admired your ability to get through any traumatic situation more or less intact. Me, I'm just not as tough as you are. I probably wouldn't have even enlisted had I known I might be deployed. When I was a kid, I think I just romanticized the idea of the military what with the bases and war memorials and such in Hawai'i. I didn't honestly think about the reality, and then the stupid war broke out. I'm sure you were a lot more OK with that."

"Oh, I'm not as tough as you might think." She shrugged. "I guess I just got immune to being affected by violent chaos as a kid."

"Well, growing up in the middle of the St. Louis riots will do that to a person, I imagine."

"Yep. Saw something like half a dozen dead bodies before I'd even finished grade school. I always kind of liked being in combat after that because at least if I was handling a weapon or piloting an attack hover, I had some control over the situation." She ran a hand over her head. "Still, even I couldn't have put up with Pakistan for much longer than I did. Glad I got the chance to get out of there when I could."

"I'm glad, too. Selfishly, I should admit." He flashed a grin. "I'm so glad to have you back, Jojo."

"And I'm glad to be back." She kicked him again, then waved her now-empty glass at Colin. "Next!"

* * *

"You survived your first week with the new alien critter!" Bisa gave Sasha a warm hug as she came through the door.

"So it seems!" Sasha returned the hug and set about to taking off her shoes and dumping her backpack in its usual spot.

"Anything you're allowed talk to me about yet? Bearing in mind that I probably wouldn't understand the slightest bit of anything technical, so I couldn't tell anyone else about it anyway."

Sasha laughed and wandered into the kitchen to make herself a cup of tea. Bisa scurried after her. "I can't tell you anything yet about Littlefoot—the new xeno—but I can tell you that I've learned a lot about the arthropods so far. They're not exactly my area of specialty, since I'm more interested in rare mammals and marsupials, but it's fascinating to work with them."

"Bugs. Ech." Bisa wrinkled her nose. She opened the fridge, pulled out a plate of sliced melon, and set about to nibbling on it as they talked.

"Well, these aren't bugs," Sasha corrected her. "That's the name for a certain kind of insect that—OK. Technical. Sorry."

"Right! I thought you had some experience with those kinds of critters, though. Didn't you do something in college with them?"

Sasha nodded. "Sort of. I spent a month in Venezuela a couple of summers ago helping to catalog the endangered Lepidoptera—butterflies—there. Honestly, I only went because I wanted to see some of the other creatures out in the jungles, but yeah. I did learn a lot about those, at least."

"Ah! Venezuela." Bisa sighed happily. "One of my girlhood friends was from there. Her father left when Chavez died, and they ended up in Sao Paulo. She was a wild little thing. I adored her. What was her name . . ." She hummed briefly. "Oh! Of course: Maria. I should've known. Juan met her a few times when she visited us in the States, and I think he picked up on the name when your mother was born."

"My mom was named after your friend?" The bevbot hissed as it finished brewing her tea, and she sat down at the kitchen table to sip at it.

"Not exactly. I think he just liked the name." Bisa sat down opposite her and shoved the plate of melon in her direction. "Eat, child!"

Sasha took a chunk of melon and nibbled on it as her tea cooled to a drinkable temperature. She still had vids and pictures of her mother, but her own memories had faded over the years. The strongest was the moment she had found her after the quake. It had always bothered her that she knew so little about her and about her *vovò*. Being a brown-faced child raised by an old white man in Iowa, she'd always felt disconnected from that side of her culture, but he never wanted to talk about her Brazilian relatives.

Bisa seemed to be reading her mind. "You miss her, don't you?"

Sasha nodded. "And Juan. Though I honestly barely remember either of them. They're more like ideas to me than real people. The only thing Joey ever told me was how they ended up with my mom."

"Well, that's a good story, at least!"

Sasha grinned. "It is, yeah. I didn't even know that until

I was nine, though. I guess Joey didn't think I was old enough to understand."

Bisa snorted. "What's to understand? Juan met a Brazilian flight attendant when he was on spring break in Vegas. They got married in a little chapel off the Strip and divorced the next day. Eight months later, she shows up at his dorm room asking if he wants first dibs on the baby before she talks to an adoption agency."

Sasha's eyes grew wide. "I didn't know about the marriage! Oh, man. That makes the whole thing better. But he was already dating Joey when she came around again, right?"

"Yes. I know Joey was kind of irritated by it—he'd been under the impression that your *vovô* was entirely gay, so that was more than a bit of a shock—but to his credit, he handled the whole thing well after the initial freak-out. Juan once told me that he thought Joey had been about to propose to him anyway before the baby came into the picture. He was definitely the settling-down kind, so he probably thought having a ready-made family like that would be fun."

"Wow. I admit I can't imagine him being like that."

"I'm sure. You never got to see that side of him—before he let the grief take over and change him."

"Not really, no. He had his moments, but he was always subdued."

Bisa's age was suddenly apparent on her face, and she sighed heavily. "Well, I was too, at first. I understand that he lost a husband and a daughter—that certainly would've been hard—but I lost a child and grandchild, too. I was absolutely bereft for a long time. I had hoped that we might be closer—that we could've bonded over our losses, and maybe tried to salvage a family with you—but he never wanted that. He just wanted to forget everything."

"I'm so sorry." Sasha said. "I never understood that, I guess."

Bisa shook her head and smiled sadly. "How could

you? You were just a little girl. We tried to keep our disputes away from you so it wouldn't hurt you any more than you already had been. Anyway, it's all past and gone now. We should talk of better things."

Sasha nodded in understanding. "Sure. I'd like to know more about my family history someday, though."

"Of course! Any time." Suddenly, she paused and unsuccessfully tried to stifle a huge yawn. "For now, though, I am way past my usual bedtime. I like to get up early—dawn's the best light in my studio, so I do most of my work then."

Sasha nodded again. "Don't let me keep you up. Maybe we can go out to lunch or something this weekend."

"Sounds lovely! G'night, Meniña." Dropping a kiss atop Sasha's head, Bisa headed down the hall to her room.

Sasha was far more of a night owl than the elderly woman, so sleep wasn't on her agenda at all yet. She remained at the kitchen table and fidgeted for a while, finishing her tea and the plate of melon. She opened her band and tried to read, play a game, or make a few more notes about Littlefoot, but she still couldn't calm down. The week had simply been far too exciting, and she was far too buzzed to relax.

After yet another failed attempt at zoning out over news, she glanced at the time: still only 10, which was plenty early enough to go out and see if she could burn off energy by dancing . . . or doing other physical activities. After taking a moment to freshen up and change into something more attractive, she quietly left the apartment.

Sasha's hair got caught under his hand, and she yelped.

"Oh! Sorry." He squirmed away.

"No, that's fine!" she laughed breathlessly. "Keep going!"

In the bliss of the moment, such things weren't a big deal. Nor was his name, how old he was, whether he had any other partners, or anything else. After the day's intensity, she needed something physical to help her calm down. And this hot, if lacking in conversational skills, young student she'd found at a bar near the university was providing exactly that.

Still, the romp, while fun, wasn't quite clearing her mind as much as she'd have liked. Something about the way he moved, or his dark hair and eyes, or perhaps his voice kept reminding her of Jay and the ridiculous crush she seemed to be developing on him. Though maybe that was why she'd chosen this particular guy. Pursuing the one she actually wanted would be stupid and counterproductive, and anyway, the way she was feeling about him was probably just hormones. If she could burn off the need with this meaningless, if not exactly expert, roll on a small bed in a messy apartment, maybe she'd be able to face Jay in the mornings and not make an ass of herself as she almost did when he visited the lab.

So, she tried to focus on the moment, accidental hair-pulling notwithstanding, and it worked—sort of. At least well enough that the release calmed her down to where she thought she'd be able to get some sleep and function for the rest of the weekend.

"That was fun, thanks." She glanced over her shoulder as she buttoned her jeans.

The kid looked crestfallen. "You sure you don't want to stay the night? I can make you pancakes in the morning."

"Nah. I need to, uh, get to work early tomorrow. Boss will kill me, all that. But I'll see you around, hey?"

"Sure thing. Can I look you up on the Stream?" He flashed a hopeful smile.

"Oh. Yeah." Sasha slipped her top over her head and fluffed her hair.

"What's your last name?"

"Donovan. Shannon Donovan." She smiled tightly.

"Got it. Thanks, Shannon." He leaned over for an awkward kiss.

As she left his apartment, she sighed heavily. He didn't,

now that she thought about it, remind her all that much of Jay. Alex, on the other hand . . .

* * *

Jay jerked as he started awake, out of another nightmare about Pakistan. It took him a moment to get his bearings and realize that he was not, in fact, trying to save his best friend from a catastrophic injury in a war zone, but at home in bed in his high-rise apartment in Queen Anne. Said friend had indeed been saved—he'd even seen plenty of her so far this summer since she came back. She'd been busy still working with the Army, but at least every other weekend, they'd gone out to down a few beers and reminisce—though discussions about the bombing never came up.

As the fog of sleep finally left his brain, Jay realized that the booming that had echoed in his mind wasn't just a dream: some sharp noise had inspired this particular flashback. He glanced around, but nothing was rattling. Not a quake. Then he heard something else: a high-pitched whine followed by a colossal wet slap, as if an enormous whale had just breached and crashed back into the surf. He scrambling out of bed and dashed to the window. Waving his hand past the sensor to clear the privacy fog, he stared out at the expanse of Elliott Bay visible between the buildings. It was a clear, August day, and the sky was just beginning to brighten in the early dawn; it was light enough to see the surface of the water. Sure enough, in the middle of the bay just beyond Pier 55 was a frothy oblong of disturbed water, more than 10 meters across by his reckoning.

As his brain finished booting up, he realized what the first sound must have been: a sonic boom. Clearly, some sort of large, high-speed aircraft had just streaked through the skies over the city and then crash-landed in the surf. But what? He pushed his memory, trying to think of what craft would be that size and shape. Most commercial jets would've been longer. Most short-range hovers, while they had a wide wingspan, would be considerably narrower at the tail. But nothing except military craft could move that fast.

He hesitated for a quick moment, but then grabbed his band, flipped it into flat-screen mode, and hurriedly typed out a message: *Call back. Urgent. Military thing?*

Josie's voice was thick with sleep when she responded with an audio call. "Lambert? What the hell?" Her video feed remained off.

"Hey, Jojo. Sorry if I woke you." He tried to sound deferent, knowing that if he had indeed disturbed her, she'd probably tear his head off. "Did you happen to hear that sonic boom?" She lived an hour south, but the boom had been big enough that she'd surely heard something.

"Is that what that was? I thought we were having a thunderstorm. Ignored it." She yawned noisily.

"Not thunder. An aircraft of some sort. It just crash-landed into Elliott Bay. Do you know of anything supersonic in the area?"

"At this time? No. Here, gimme a sec." She went quiet. He figured she was looking up information on the military Stream to which she, as an active-duty soldier if not a deployed one, had access. "Nothing. But . . . Dude! There's some serious chatter on—oh, hell. I'm being scrambled. Guess I'm headed up to the bay!"

"Meet you there?" he asked hopefully. "Just to watch from a safe distance," he quickly added. Though he feared any potential chaos, this at least seemed like it might be a semi-controlled situation in which he could test out his resistance to trauma reactions while not being directly involved.

"You're a civilian now, Lambert," she said.

He made a frustrated noise.

"Job that boring, is it?" She chuckled softly. "A'ight. Get your ass down there before I do."

THE CRASH

"You mean like E.T.?" Jonathan's luminous blue eyes already seemed to take over half of his cherubic face. The news, as Alex explained it to him, that humans had finally found evidence of life on other planets had made those big eyes seem downright enormous.

Alex laughed. "Not really, Jon-Jon." To be honest, the fact that he'd even shown the old movie to his baby brother would probably have gotten him in serious trouble if their mother ever found out. "These are just spiders and scorpions—or at least stuff like that. They're not like people. They're not even like dogs or cats."

Jonathan's face fell. "Oh. That's too bad. I was hoping we could have an alien friend. Or have one over for dinner or something."

Alex felt a sharp pang in his chest. Since their mother had started going to that new church, she had forbidden them to see most of their old friends. He was getting past it—burying himself in his studies and experiments—but little Jon-Jon wasn't taking the newfound isolation well at all. "Yeah, that would be fun. No friendly aliens this time, though. There might be some out there, but we don't know about any of them yet."

"But maybe we will someday, right?" Jonathan looked hopeful.

"Sure! Someday." Alex threw an arm around the small shoulders and squeezed. At this point, an alien would probably be their only chance at making any new friends at all.

* * *

Alex paced uncomfortably on the dock. Being functional at this hour on a Sunday morning wasn't his usual habit since he spent most Saturday nights up until the wee hours hacking at computer-generated zombies and goblins in his living room. Still, the combination of the massive jug of coffee he'd downed and the excitement of the event in question was making him ridiculously twitchy.

"Alex, would you stand still for a minute?" his boss chided him, though her eyes twinkled with amusement. "You're making *me* nervous!"

"Sorry, Dr. Kumi!" He grinned and trotted over to her, trying not to stray too much. "I'm just a little gobsmacked, is all. I thought I'd be crunching numbers and writing reports the entire summer, not getting into a submarine to go investigate a UFO."

"Yeah, well. It's unexpected for me, too," she acknowledged. "I'm glad Leung is letting you and the bio-department intern—Sasha, is it?—come along on this ride. Definitely something to write a good report about, don't you think?"

"Oh, hell, yes." Alex beamed. He glanced over to where Sasha was nervously chatting with her own supervisor. She looked considerably calmer: standing still, her hands clasped behind her back. Her expression, however, betrayed something else: she was utterly petrified. His impulse was to head over there and perhaps reassure her, but then his band chimed an audio-call alert.

"Who the hell—?" He felt queasy when he saw the name on the display. After excusing himself, he strolled over to the edge of the dock. "Jonathan? I'm kind of busy. Do you need me right now, or can you message me?"

"Oh! Sorry. I won't take much of your time. My flight just landed—I was in Boston visiting Aunt Jenna—and I just saw the news about the military plane going down in the bay. I figured if anyone knew something about that, you would."

Alex hesitated. He knew that he couldn't tell his brother the real story of what the initial military investigation had found: The craft was of alien origin. Homeland and the military had secured the site, but as XenoNet was the only nearby facility even remotely capable of dealing with alien craft and life-forms the government put the company in charge of further investigation and salvage. "Oh, yeah," he tried to sound casual. "Military thing. The, uh . . ." He glanced around and caught sight of Jay, suiting himself up in protective gear at the nearby transport hover. "One of the guys I work with—our security chief—he's ex-military. Told me all about it. It was some green pilot doing test runs with something supersonic out of JBLM. Pushed the wrong control, and *boom*. They've set up an exclusion zone for about half a mile around the crash site while they're salvaging it. It's a madhouse down at the waterfront—trying to keep private drones away and such."

"That must've been the activity I was seeing from the air—couldn't see details though, of course." He laughed lightly. "Never a dull moment in this city, hey? Trust you to make us move to where all the action is, big bro."

"Yeah, well. Boston just didn't have what I needed, that's true." His voice tightened. Jay had finished kitting up and strolled over to talk to Sasha. Her fearful expression had vanished in the presence of the handsome guard; instead, she was gazing up at him in rapt attention, her pupils wide and her smile open and flirty. "Aw, man," Alex muttered to himself. Much as he liked Jay and also found him attractive, he felt a flash of jealousy at Sasha's obvious interest in him. Being short and decidedly non-athletic, he was used to being passed over for guys who were more buff, but he'd been hoping the clever biologist would be less shallow. He sighed. "I so need to start working out."

"What was that?" Jonathan sounded confused.

"Nothing, Jon."

"Anyway, the crash thing wasn't my only reason for getting in touch." His brother's voice hitched. "I was— well, I don't know if you'd be interested—"

"Interested in what?"

"I'm graduating from seminary next week. I'm going to be ordained. I'd like it if you could come. I know it's not your thing, but . . ."

Alex stiffened. Much as his heart wanted to be supportive of his baby brother's ambitions, the idea of being anywhere near that many Homecoming adherents— and of course his mother—gave him chills. "I'm not sure," he equivocated. "I'll have to look at my work schedule. We have a big project coming up and I might need to pull some overtime. I'll, uh, talk to my boss and get back to you, OK?"

"Sure thing. Don't want to get in the way of your internship. I'm sure you're enjoying the work. I know Mom doesn't like it, and well, I admit it makes me uncomfortable, too, but I know it makes you happy."

Alex flushed with an uncomfortable combination of love and guilt. Jonathan was, in general, far kinder and more open-minded than their mother, but he was still pious, and after three years subsumed in dogma that would've been more at home during the Crusades than the latter half of the twenty-first century, being so kind about this was unexpected. He began to wonder if the message from a few weeks back wasn't a fluke after all.

"Thanks," he said. "I'll be in touch about the ceremony." He was nearly certain that he wouldn't be able to stomach the event, but it was still possible he'd change his mind. "And congrats."

"Thank you. I hope you can make it. In the meantime, you might want to keep away from the waterfront. Never know when a plane might fall on top of you!" Jonathan chuckled.

Alex squirmed. The sub had come up to the dock, and

Kumi was now beckoning him over. "Yep. Wouldn't think of going down there now."

* * *

So far, Sasha had kept a lid on her fear, but as the sub carrying them dipped below the surface of the bay, a flutter ran through her belly, and her heartbeat sped up. She shuddered.

Jay noticed. "You OK?" He was in full combat gear and was effectively their only real defense. The sub was a small model—usually used to transport small maintenance crews to the tidal generators at the bottom of the bay—and didn't have room for more than six people. Aside from Jay, there was only the sub's pilot, her, Alex, and their supervisors. Alex had joked that the reason the two interns were sent along on the mission was they were considerably more expendable than regular staff. Sasha hadn't found that funny in the least. He was currently up front, chatting with the researchers, and looked downright giddy to be going down to investigate the wreck. She felt the same—mostly.

She shook her head, trying to clear the worry. "I'm fine, Jay."

"You sure?" He raised an eyebrow.

She flashed a nervous smile. "Just . . . I'm used to the creatures I deal with being small and not exactly threatening. Dunno what we're going to find down there."

"Well, that's what I'm here for." He patted her shoulder reassuringly. The touch was unexpected—and sent a tiny thrill through her. Under the circumstances, that wasn't a feeling she could pay attention to. Given the danger of the situation, Jay could've looked like a diseased warthog, so long as he knew how to use the array of weaponry he carried.

The mission they were on wasn't exactly what she had expected to be doing when she took the internship. She'd been greatly enjoying her work with Littlefoot, with whom she'd become thoroughly bonded, and was perfectly content with just that. Investigating a ship obviously made by an intelligent species hadn't even been on her radar.

But six hours ago, the thing had shot through the pre dawn sky and crashed into the bay, coming to rest on an underwater shelf some 15 meters down. The craft's sudden appearance was utterly baffling. It hadn't been seen on any satellite or radar scans until it was already only a few meters above the surface of the water, nor did anyone on the ground see it. Only a news camera drone, sent to get footage of a nearby tram-pedestrian accident, got a brief shot of the craft before it was swallowed up. It was as if it had literally just appeared out of thin air. Exciting, yes, but also not what she thought she'd wake up to this morning. Even without knowing the details, which Sasha couldn't divulge, her Bisa was even more alarmed, practically begging her to stay home and stay out of the way of whatever chaos was going on. However, Sasha's innate curiosity overrode any fear—until now.

"You guys should come see this!" Alex called back to them. "It's amazing!"

Jay looked down at her. "Shall we?"

She returned his kind smile. "Yeah." She nodded at the twitchy young man ahead of them, whose grin was currently threatening to take over his face. She heaved a steadying breath and started toward him. "What are you seeing out there, Alex?"

Without warning, the sub sharply lurched forward, and she lost her balance, going down hard on one knee.

"Ow! What the hell?" she barked.

Jay, already on alert, helped her to her feet, and they rushed to the front of the sub.

"I don't understand!" The pilot's voice was full of sudden panic. "It's like we're suddenly accelerating, but I haven't touched the throttle." He poked at a keypad, bringing up a diagnostic display in the front window and quickly scanning the data.

"What's wrong?" Hideo frowned him. "What's happened?"

Alex saw the key readout first. "We're being pulled . . ." He looked beyond the display to the dull-gray hulk looming in the murky water ahead of them. "It's the craft!" he cried. "It must use some sort of magnetic drive!"

Kumi shook her head. "That's impossible. The scans the military took from the air would've shown a magnetic field, and the drone subs they sent in before would've noted it, too, since they would've been pulled in as well."

"Not necessarily," Alex countered. "The systems may have just been offline from the crash, and they somehow fired up again after a reset period."

"Give me a minute," the pilot muttered, hands flying over the controls. "I'll get this thing maneuvered properly." Despite his best efforts, however, the sub continued to hurtle toward the craft, picking up speed.

"It's no use!" Jay called, his voice sharp with panic. "We're going to impact! Brace yourselves!" He grabbed the two closest to him, Sasha and Alex, dragged them out of the front cabin and pulled them down into a crash position. In just a couple of seconds, the sub slammed up against the hull of the downed ship.

When they finally stilled, Sasha looked up and was horrified at the extent of the damage. The sub's front hull had collapsed, and the three who had been in the forward compartment were bloodied and still. Jay crawled over to check on them and glanced back, his expression confirming what the positions of their broken bodies already seemed to suggest. Water seeped in from cracks in the windows and fuselage, the electrical systems sparked and flickered, and the sounds of stressing metal horribly echoed all around them.

"What's happening?" she shouted above the din, and struggled to her feet.

Alex stood up, too, looking around. Then he paled.

"Holy shit."

She grabbed his shoulder. "What?"

"We're screwed," Alex spat. He began pacing the cabin, pulling open storage cupboards until he found what he was looking for, and then stalked over to the sub's two-stage escape hatch.

"Maloney, what are you doing?" Jay shouted. His face had gone pale, and he trembled in a way that seemed incongruous with his physical strength. "We should call the crew on the surface and wait for rescue."

"There's no time for that." Alex shoved a couple of packages at them. "This sub is dead, and we will be, too if we don't get out as soon as we can."

"But we're down too far," Sasha protested, her mind racing as she remembered bits of diving lessons from a spring-break trip to Cozumel. "We can cope with the water pressure at this depth, but we'll drown before we can get to the surface, even with floatation vests. We could use rebreathers, but—"

Jay finished her thought. "If that ship's magnetic, our equipment will be sucked in, just like the sub. The water down this far is too cold for us to be in without proper wetsuits. We'll freeze before rescue can come peel us loose."

Alex voice was tight with frustration. "Yes, our equipment will be attracted to the craft, but *we* won't be. We just need the rebreathers long enough to get free of the sub. This—" he waved a wrapped package of bright-yellow nanoplast and a bundle of netting"—is what will get us out, and if we work fast, we won't freeze. Now would you please help me get this hatch open?"

Sasha was utterly terrified, but something about Alex's certainty of his plan—and the way he looked at both of them—calmed her. Putting her life in the hands of the young genius, she and Jay helped open the hatch, stripped down to avoid getting tangled up in sodden clothing, and followed Alex through.

The shock of the cold water was enough to take her breath away, but before she had time to think about that, she and the others were careening toward the craft, pulled there by the metal bindings from their oxygen generators. They came to rest on the side of it with an uncomfortable thunk.

Following Alex's lead, Sasha and Jay wriggled free of their equipment, keeping only the non-metal masks and tubing that were still connected to the tanks now stuck to the craft's hull. As they continued to breathe and fight off impending hypothermia, Alex went to work, tearing a small hole in the package. Getting a big lungful of air, he removed his mask and swam over to the exterior ports on the collapsing sub. Wrapping the package around the end of one port, he wrenched it fully open, and the sub's cabin air began pumping out into the package.

Sasha was the first one to understand. Gesturing to Jay to help, the trio swam back and forth between their oxygen generators and the port, shaping the life raft into a useful form, surrounding it with the netting and sealing its open edges around them as it inflated. With some wrangling and wrestling with straps to close it up, they were soon surrounded by an air-filled, if soggy, underwater balloon. Sasha, the smallest, finally swam up inside, and they tied up the end and let go of the port. In just a few minutes, they floated to the surface, while beneath them, the sub's structure finally failed.

They huddled closely together on the hover as it sped away toward the nearest hospital. Though wrapped in emergency blankets and being tended to by medics, Sasha was still shivering and queasy. It was a narrow escape, and one she definitely wouldn't have been able to make on her own. Jay seemed to feel the same. His soldier's bravado was utterly gone, and he couldn't stop staring at Alex, an awestruck expression on his chiseled face.

"You saved our lives, Alex," he said quietly, jaw still

quivering with the cold. "Thank you."

Alex's pale cheeks went pink. "You're welcome. But I couldn't have done that alone, either." He glanced quickly over at Sasha, smiling shyly at her. "We all did that."

"We did, yeah." Sasha nodded at him. "Guess we make a pretty good team, hey?"

Jay looked back and forth between them and chuckled tiredly. "I guess we do."

* * *

"I'm fine, really," Jay protested as the hospital techs continued to fuss at him, ensuring that his minor injuries were seen to, and his body temperature was where it should be. Down the hall, he could hear Alex cracking a few nervous jokes with the staff, and Sasha seemed to be in a conversation with a family member. He felt a sudden, strong impulse to want to be with them, instead of in an exam bay of his own, but he also didn't want them to see his emotional state.

The attending nurse waved a scanner over his arm, reading the data on his implant. "Says you're on a beta blocker," she noted. "Is that working OK for you right now? Do you need to up the dose rate?"

He shook his head even as he continued to shiver from residual cold and adrenaline. "I don't think so." The meds wouldn't have helped him. What he needed instead was a kind voice. He considered having the ER staff contact his psych, but he had a better idea. "If you don't mind, though, is there a band I can borrow? Mine got lost at the bottom of the bay."

The nurse patted his arm in a motherly way. "Of course. I'll go get one of our loaners."

After handing over the band, the nurse left again, giving him some privacy for his conversation. Tucking in the earpiece, he pulled up his Stream account and selected a smiling face from his list of contacts.

"Lambert! Finally! What the fuck, dude? Are you OK?"

"Hi, Jojo." He smiled just to hear the familiar, strident voice. "I am. More or less. I'm in the ER at Harborview right now, but they'll be letting me go soon, I imagine."

"What the hell happened? I heard some chatter about the rescue mission, but I don't have high enough clearance for them to give me details."

He hesitated; he wasn't sure how much he was allowed to tell her, given that he was also on company NDA. Still, he figured there wasn't much harm in top-level details she could probably already figure out herself. "Basically, the sub crashed while we were going down to investigate the craft. We lost three people: the sub's pilot and two of the company's researchers. I and a couple of the interns barely got out."

"Shit. That's . . . you sound calm about it, though. You in shock? Medicated?"

He shrugged. "My usual meds are all I have in me right now, except for a dose of vitamins and electrolytes. Might be a bit of shock, I guess. I'm definitely shaken up, but I'm actually not as bad as I could be. Kind of a weird mix. It's harder in some ways. I was sent along to keep everyone safe, and I still lost three people under my care. That hasn't hit me yet, though—it doesn't quite seem real. I guess I'm also just glad to be alive." He rubbed a hand over his head. His hair was still damp and crusted with salt residue. Oddly, it reminded him of his days playing around in the water off Kaua'i—though Puget Sound was considerably colder.

"Well, I'm glad you're alive, too. You should take it easy for a couple of days. Maybe talk to your doc—your parents, too."

"I thought I was doing that now," he teased.

"Oh, so I'm your doc?"

"Nah. Parent."

She snorted a laugh. "OK, you really are fine, aren't you? Well, if you start being not fine, you ping me right away, got it?"

"Of course, Jojo. Thank you."

"You're welcome. Now go get some rest. That's an order."

"Yes'm!"

* * *

"You've had a bad shock, Alex. Take all the time you need to recover," Leung said gently. She looked as ragged as he felt. He wondered if she had slept since yesterday's incident; he barely had himself. "I can make sure the work gets done."

Alex shook his head. "It's OK. Honestly, I think I need to work right now. My brain's been buzzing, trying to figure this all out. I need something to do."

"Well, we already have the engineering team getting a salvage effort together, and the tech team is going to study whatever electronics they find. Did you have an idea for something else to work on?"

"I do. I want to take a look at that news drone footage again—maybe see if there's something we or the military missed on our first look at it."

"Can do." She nodded. "I'll have the file sent to you right away."

"Thanks," he said brightly.

"But, Alex," she lowered her voice. "I also need to know if you're OK emotionally. I take the well-being of my employees seriously. You can talk to the grief counselor I brought in, or you can work from home so you can spend time with your family or something."

"I don't have family," he blurted. "Not like that, at least." A cold prickle went over his skin as he realized how true the statement was. He hadn't felt in any way compelled to tell his mother or Jonathan about the accident—not that he could easily have explained it anyway. He did feel a strong need to talk to Gabriel, but that was out of the question. The only two people he felt like talking to at all were the two who had survived the crash with him. They alone knew what had really happened down there, and how close they all had come to losing their lives, just like the other three on the sub had. It was odd that he somehow felt closer to them than he had to the supervisor he'd been working with every day who had died in the catastrophe. He grieved for Dr. Kumi, and even more for the two young sons she'd left behind, but he somehow—selfishly, perhaps—felt glad that if someone had to die, it had been her and the other two, rather than Jay or Sasha.

"Oh. I see." A strange look passed over her features, and she reached for him, mouth opening, but then she stopped. "Well, anyway. Let me know if you need anything. Whatever resources you'd like—personal or for the project—they're yours."

"Thanks, Leung. That means a lot."

As he walked back to his office, he remembered something that might have explained the odd look: Leung had no family, either, at least that he knew of from his years following her career. Thrice divorced, her last marriage had ended before the probe project started. She had no children, either, and given her age, it was unlikely many of her family of origin were still alive. Clearly, she was surrounded by many dear friends and colleagues, but it seemed official family had escaped her much as it had escaped him. The thought made him feel oddly close to her, and for a brief, wild moment, he wondered if she might ever feel the same.

TESSERAE

Denita's eyes kept drifting as Alex was talking. She looked down at her plate, out the window, at the waiter, at her hand . . . anywhere but at him. At first, he thought she was just concentrating on his explanation of the weather patterns on Europa, but now he wasn't so sure.

He broke off his babble. "I'm sorry. I'm probably boring you."

She looked back and smiled insincerely. "No, it's fine. I'm just a little distracted today."

"It's not fine. I have a bad habit of doing this. Most of my friends are big science nerds like me, and we can talk for hours about this stuff. I keep forgetting that not everyone has the same interest in it." The date had been her idea. They had met while sitting next to each other at a performance of their school's spring musical, Into the Woods. *She was there to see her talented sister playing the Baker's Wife; he was there for a friend who played cello in the orchestra pit. They hit it off during intermission and then, during the cast party afterward, ended up making out in the bedroom of the guy who played the Wolf. After being interrupted by said Wolf, they agreed to meet for a proper date the following weekend, and here they were. An hour into dinner, however, it had become clear that they had next to nothing in common aside from physical attraction. She was on the debate team and had dreams of majoring in poli sci at Yale. He had*

73

already been accepted into UW's physics program and was counting down the minutes until he graduated and got to move to Seattle.

"OK, yeah." She winced. "I admit I'm not that into what you're talking about. Maybe we should just call it a night?"

He sighed heavily and signaled for the waiter. "Yeah." He'd been looking forward to the possibility of at least some post-dessert sweetness in her car before they went home, but at this point, he wasn't sure he could perform anyway, however deprived his hormones had insisted he was these days. Somehow, all of his science pals had managed to pair up with each other, leaving him the odd one out. He hadn't been completely starved—he'd lost his virginity last summer to Tanika Rue, and last year's prom night ended with his face in Kieran Hodgson's lap—but those two had already moved on to other boyfriends since then. He'd thought Denita might finally be a break in his too-long dry spell, but apparently not. Trying not to let his disappointment show too much, he paid the bill, and they left.

As they got out to her car, she turned to him. "For what it's worth: I still think you're cute."

He cocked his head in surprise. "Yeah?"

"Yeah." She strode up to him, pushing him back against the car. "You just talk too much."

Alex was subsumed in nervous excitement, thrilled as he was to be explaining his findings to the company. Unfortunately, his jargon-laden patter was coming out far too fast and convoluted for most everyone else to keep up.

"Tessa-what?" Sasha's face was a mask of confusion.

"Tesserae." Alex smiled at her, but squirmed self-consciously. The last thing he wanted was to look like a babbling infant in front of her. "They're, well, they're like . . ." He paused, trying to figure out how better to explain the phenomenon that had caused the alien ship to slip through to their world.

"Breathe, Alex," Leung said, smiling kindly at him. She'd been wonderful to her remaining team in the chaotic days since the sub disaster. In addition to taking even more of an interest in Alex, she had stepped up her attention to

Sasha and Jay, for their bravery and quick thinking in escaping the doomed craft. In scanning the footage from the news drone for any signs of what had happened, Alex lit on the idea of feeding the video through spectral processors, and there, he found the answer.

"Breathing. Got it. Thanks." He gulped a healthy lungful of air, but couldn't help a nervous giggle. He turned back to Sasha, and tried to explain it on her terms. "OK, so. Living things are made up of a mosaic, of sorts, of different cells, right? Well, so is the rest of the universe. Not cells, of course, but the rest of the fabric of reality is structured in a similar way. Some physicists have described it as a foam-like structure, but it's more like a mosaic—just on a very, very small scale. Individual tiles in a mosaic are called tesserae, so I've given that nickname to the phenomena. Anyway, just as individual cells can have unique properties, each individual tile can be unique, too. They can also have different properties as a cluster, and the clusters can be different sizes, too."

"Oh!" Sasha's face lit up in understanding. "So it's something like skin, maybe? With variances in pigment and hair follicles and thickness depending on where on the body you are?"

"Exactly!" He almost cheered. Nothing like finally hitting a point of understanding—especially with someone to whom you were attracted. "Well, as it turns out, in this fabric of space-time, there are these clusters of tiles that are thinner and weaker, so to speak, than the rest of the tiles around them. Because they're weaker, it's possible for an outside force—I don't know what yet—to act on them and sort of push and hold them open. In this case, that means that the space-time barrier between us and some distant point in the universe essentially breaks down. If it happens long enough, matter can pass through."

Jay perked up himself, pushing off from the wall he'd been leaning against, and smiling at Alex. "I think I get it now. An Einstein-Rosen bridge; a wormhole, right?" The security chief had been quiet and subdued since the catastrophe, but also friendly with the two interns. As they recovered from their experience, the trio had talked a lot, and Jay had explained that he was drawn to the XenoNet job in part thanks to his parents: an aerospace lawyer and an infectious-disease expert. He even had considerable tech knowledge, thanks to his work in military operating logistics. Alex's opinion of him, already higher from his help in their escape, was steadily rising the more he discovered.

Alex nodded. "Basically, yeah. That's what stuff like this has been called before, in theoretical terms, at least. Only these tesserae aren't really tunnels, per se. They're more like a self-closing door built into a wall. Put enough of the right kind of force on that door, and it opens. When the force goes away or changes direction, it closes. Same thing here."

"But people have been analyzing this stuff for decades. Why wouldn't they have found these spots before now?" Sasha asked.

"Because when the doors are closed, they look like any other part of reality. It's only when they're open that they can be detected, because that's the only time their properties change. They do open frequently, as far as I can tell, but in most cases, it's only for a couple of seconds, so you have to be looking—and with the right equipment—at exactly the right spot at the right time to catch them."

"Alex," Leung spoke up. The woman's voice was small—as was she—but the room went quiet for her. "How many of these tesserae did you find?"

He flushed. She had been generous with him. As soon as he'd caught the flash of light through which the craft had issued, she'd dumped a ton of resources on him to see if he could find more of the spots. And oh, had he. "Just from a thousand-kilometer-range scan: sixty-seven. There may be more. I don't know. Those are just the ones that opened in the time the scan was running. Most of them were open for less than ten seconds. Only a few were open longer than that."

Leung rubbed her face thoughtfully. "Well, for one thing, I'm thinking there might be a Nobel in your future."

Alex coughed nervously. The quake-smart team he'd been on had been up for a prize a few years ago, losing out to a team that had successfully built an underwater colony near the Virgin Islands. The idea that he might win something just from looking at a bunch of satellite images seemed preposterous.

"Beyond that, though," she continued, "we have to find out more about this phenomenon. Moreover, we need to find out more about what came through the one over the bay. Depending on what we find, it may turn out that these creatures pose a threat to us." She stood up and crossed to Alex, patting his arm in an almost motherly way. "Not to mention: we have no idea what could be on the other side of the rest of these tesserae."

Jay frowned and crossed his arms in front of his chest. "Are we going to need more government or military involvement on this? I know the army still has the site locked down for now while we finish the investigation, but I'm surprised they haven't been more involved."

Leung made a sour face. "It's mostly politics, really. The government actually used to have a dedicated alien-invasion protocol, but that got dissolved back in the '20s, along with a bunch of other agencies that were deemed a waste of money. The contingent of anti-Federalists running Congress right now is doing everything they can to kill all remaining national public services and either shove them off to the states or privatize them entirely. As far as they're concerned, Homeland's only purpose is to keep out terrorists—not aliens—and the military exists only to guard our foreign economic interests and respond in case of a direct military attack. Some of them have even been suggesting that this whole thing is a false flag—a way to convince other representatives to vote against their latest privatization bill."

He groaned and rubbed his face. "But what if we're under attack from this species? Don't they care about that?"

Leung shrugged. "I'm keeping in touch with my contacts about this event, but apparently the people in charge of all the relevant agencies indicated that they want us to take point on this—as with the initial crash investigation. We have more existing knowledge on these subjects than any government agency does, especially since SETI dissolved and they more or less cut ties with NASA. They can scramble military if we do have a sudden, large-scale attack, but it sounded to me like they didn't want to set up a standing team—with the ensuing large cost to taxpayers—without further understanding of what kind of threat we might be facing, or whether we're facing anything at all. After what Alex has discovered about there being more of these spots—these tesserae—they'll probably at least hand us some more funding, but I think they're going to want evidence of more than just a single ship before they get more involved. It does look like this is up to us for now."

Jay sagged back against the wall. "Terrific," he muttered.

She smiled sympathetically. "Assuming we're not going to have more government involvement then, here's my proposal: While the engineering and tech teams are taking apart the craft, you—" she looked at Alex "—need to start cataloguing these tesserae and working up a way to properly map and monitor them. You'll also need a team to help you figure out exactly what caused this one to open for so long, and find out if that phenomenon might happen to any of the others."

"Understood." Alex nodded at her, though his insides were beginning to percolate.

Next, she looked at Jay. "Lambert, I need you to start assembling a proper response team for the local tesserae—

maybe some of your retired army friends or some local police or emergency-service crews? Preferably people with some science knowledge or maybe some with experience managing non-human predators, if you can manage that. If we have another opening like this, we're going to need to move fast—faster than the army can assemble a force—to address any potential threats, but we also need people who can adjust to dealing with combatants that don't look or act human. Once we know more about the phenomenon, I'll see about setting up local teams in other regions if need be. My government contacts are also sharing info with our foreign allies, in case other countries want to start management teams, too. Lucky them: at least they're likely to be able to just start a government agency for it instead of what we're having to do."

"Ma'am." Jay nodded.

"Lastly, I want Sasha and the rest of the bio team working on developing a profile of this species. If I can get clearance to involve other civilians, I'll see if we can get some help from some other anthropologists and such, but that may take some time to get together, and I want to get started on it right away. Anything you can possibly get from this alien or its craft, we need to know about. I want every bit of possible cultural and biological data we can get. If these creatures are hostiles, we'll need to know what they're capable of in case they come back."

"Of course," Sasha said, "but what about our study with the other creatures?"

Leung smiled. "I think for now that can take a back burner. If you'd like, you can keep working with Littlefoot on your own time, but until further notice, everything else you do is going to be about this alien."

"Got it," Sasha acknowledged, though she looked disappointed to be taken away from her scaly little friend.

"There's just one thing," Alex said. "Summer's almost over, so our internships . . ."

". . . as of now no longer exist." Leung smiled.

"Congratulations. You two are now full-time XenoNet employees."

* * *

Every day since the crash, Sasha wished she'd taken more courses in anthropology. Not, of course, that the remains of the creature in front of her could in any way be considered "anthro."

The corpse had been badly burned in a cabin fire when the ship crashed, and had suffered water and salt damage from large amounts of Elliott Bay that had seeped through. Still, there was enough of it left to determine some things. It was insectoid, that much was readily apparent, and somewhat resembled Earth's far-tinier Hymenoptera. However, there were several key differences and some things that initial scans hadn't been able to determine. Under the direction of Leung and with the support of the rest of the bio team, the she decided to do a full autopsy, dissection and all, for which she was currently making a plan.

"Hey, Sasha." Alex's voice echoed from the other side of the room.

"Alex! You can't come in here without—"

"Oh! Sorry." He backed away and grabbed some clean-room gear before he came back in again. For all his cleverness, he was clueless at times. She hoped he hadn't contaminated the corpse. He hovered near the door, face flushed and anxious.

"You can come closer now. It's fine." She smiled at him.

He relaxed. "Oh. Good. Thanks. Sorry about not—I hope I didn't—anyway."

"What can I do for you?" She was growing impatient. Much as she liked the fidgety young man, and had developed some affection for him since the crash, he was still annoying sometimes.

"Right! Ah, I was wondering: have you determined, yet, anything about what environment these creatures are used to?" He stared down at the charred body, and his face went a bit green.

"I thought the engineering team was working on that—deconstructing the craft and such."

"They are. They're taking apart its engines now. But I wanted to see if there was anything else about them you'd come up with."

"Why?"

"I . . ." He looked flustered. "Just curious. I guess."

"Well, your answer is no. Not yet. We're still trying to sort out all the residue from the crash and fire and such. Haven't even got into anatomy yet."

"Oh. OK. Well, if you find out anything, let me know, yeah? I'm setting up shop across from the engineering lab, to help build that monitoring system Leung wants. So I won't be far away if, y'know, you ever want to talk or something."

She smiled thinly. "Sure. I'll keep that in mind."

"Right. Well. Best let you get back to it. And I, uh, have things to do, too. Seeyalaterbye." He dashed out, dumping his clean gear in the bin by the door, and sped back down the hall.

"Alex," she muttered, going back to her work, "sometimes I think you're more alien than this creature is."

Truly, however, that wasn't possible. As she began running a cutting laser over the charred carcass to open it up, she couldn't help a shudder of revulsion. She'd seen plenty of strange and grotesque creatures in her time, and insects, arthropods and the like didn't usually bother her—on the contrary: she most often found them fascinating. An intelligent version like this was, however, more than a little creepy.

"Hideo would've loved you," she murmured. Pain stabbed her chest as she remembered her late supervisor. An entomology expert who worked primarily with the arthropods, he'd have been far better suited to doing this work than she, who had worked primarily with mammals and marsupials, would. Still, she had more hands-on experience than the other two mammal specialists in the department, thanks to her summer cataloguing butterflies, so the job was hers. In any case, Leung seemed to have great faith in her abilities and judgment after the crash. Sasha hoped she'd prove worthy of that faith, and also honor her departed colleague's memory.

As she slowly peeled back the corpse's outer layer—a thin piece of fabric, possibly some sort of clothing—a small, rigid square tumbled out from a protected inside pouch. Her heart skipped. On the square was an image of two more of the creatures: a female, if what she saw curled against its abdomen was an ovipositor, and a juvenile, one so young that it had clearly just finished its transformation from its larval state. With a rush of nausea, she realized the truth: this wasn't just an overgrown bug. It was a person, and one whose mate and child would never see him again.

* * *

Josie nudged Jay with an elbow. "I do have clearance, you know."

"Military clearance, yes," he acknowledged, "but I'm on company NDA, and we're also sending reports to Homeland—not that they seem to care all that much. I can't tell you much more than what you already know from the initial investigation." He sighed heavily. She'd been grilling him nonstop since the moment they sat down, and had bought him a beer to grease the proceedings. Still, he hadn't budged on the details of the salvaged craft, which had been sold to the public as a downed military plane, and didn't plan to. Much as he'd have liked to spill everything he knew to his best friend, the potential threat posed by the alien creatures was still being assessed, and he didn't want to spark any panic.

"Fine," she grumbled. "What *can* you tell me, then?"

He looked around and then lowered his voice. "There's some wonky physics-of-the-universe stuff going on. My friend Alex—"

"The one you have a crush on?"

Jay flushed. "Um. Yes. Well, he's a genius with all that and figured out how the craft got here in the first place. Leung is putting together a team to manage the phenomenon. That's part of why I wanted to talk to you. I need a response team—civilians if possible."

"And you want me on it?"

"I do. There's no one I'd trust more." He left unspoken the desire to have her close by in case he panicked in the field and needed someone who understood to take over for him. He'd gotten through the sub disaster without completely regressing, but this new detail had him worried about his ability to handle the stress.

She sat back in her chair and quaffed the last of her beer. "Fuck. I want to—I *so* want to. I want to find out what the hell all this is and get involved, so I don't have to run out of beer money trying to get you to tell me."

"But?"

"I . . . I can't. My dad would be crushed if I left the military before I made general. He's wanted that for me since I was crawling. I promised my mom just before she died that I'd keep going, make him proud."

"Wouldn't working on a project like this make him proud, too?"

"It might." She shrugged. "But I doubt it. He's been suspicious of private space companies since he tangled with that dude from Dark Matter years ago."

"Kristov Belenko? The guy who runs the moon resort?"

"Yep."

Jay frowned. "I hadn't heard about that. What happened?"

"Well, my dad was originally on the project. He was

doing near-Earth pilot runs then, and Belenko wanted to hire him. It wasn't until he'd totally rearranged his life and was about to sign the contract that Belenko told him he had to lease his ride—like a taxi driver or something. The big paycheck he thought he'd be getting was only going to be about half of what he'd thought, what with all the various fees and such Belenko was charging his employees. Daddy backed out on the deal, and the guy got him blacklisted in the entire industry. He didn't recover until he contracted with the military again, designing the nav systems for the Stingray X."

"This was all before you were born, right?"

"Not quite. I was a toddler at the time. I think that's part of why he was so hardcore into wanting me in the military instead of private industry. He was really upset when the free-marketeers took over the government and started privatizing everything back in the '30s. He's convinced that anyone who does major research or operates public services for a profit instead of the good of humanity is nothing more than a big swindler."

"I don't think Leung's like that, though. Does he?"

"Not really, no, but only because she's been operating primarily from grants and donations so far. If this project is as big as it sounds, the company is probably going to get way more expensive than that can cover. It's inevitable that she's going to have to go wholly private, and well, Daddy won't like that."

Jay went quiet for a moment while he digested what Josie had said. It made sense: The cost of managing the tesserae was going to be far more than XenoNet's existing funding could handle. The company had been working on a few commercial products in its R&D division, plus selling all sorts of branded merchandise to space-travel fans and curious kids, but undoubtedly, they'd need more cash than those could cover. Leung would have to find other ways to keep the company afloat if it turned out that the tesserae were a big problem. She might be able to get a sliver of the military or Homeland budget, but that would have to work its way through Congressional approval, which could literally take years—time they didn't have. "Right. I get it, I do. I hope your dad doesn't think I'm a sellout—"

She snorted a laugh. "Oh, don't worry about that. Ever since you saved me in Pakistan, he thinks you shit titanium."

"Good to know!" He chuckled, too. "Well, I'm sorry that I can't get you in on this, but can you put the word out to the rest of your team?"

"Abso. Will also ping Tito—he left last year to go knock down fires in NorCal. I bet anything he'd like to get involved."

Jay paled at the mention of one of his exes. "I—"

"Oh, right!" Josie bit her lip. "You two didn't exact part on good terms."

"Water under the bridge." He waved a dismissive hand. "That was ages ago. I think he got married after that anyway."

"He did, yeah." She half-smiled. "Husband and three kids, now."

"Not surprised." Jay sighed, mourning opportunities lost to clueless youth. "S'pose that could've been me if I wasn't being such a dick back then."

"True. You were a dick then." Josie winked.

"Hey! You didn't have to agree with me." He pouted, and then flashed a grin. "But, yeah. Go ahead and ping Tito. I can work with him again if he's cool with it."

"He should be, I think. Don't worry, Lambert. You'll get your response team. I promise."

"Great. Thank you." He slung an arm around her broad shoulders and squeezed.

"There's just one thing, though," she said.

"Hm?"

She leaned close, saying quietly, "Are you sure this is good for you? I mean, with your . . ."

"I'm fine, Jojo. My med implant's working, and I don't even see the doc much anymore." Truthfully, his fear of having another breakdown in the field was a constant concern now, and he was very glad he was about to get a solid team that could step in if he did happen to fail. Still, he didn't want Josie to worry about him. After all, it was saving her life that had pushed those buttons for him in the first place. If she wasn't going to be on this job with him, there was no point to worrying her.

She scanned his face, probably seeing the lie, but deciding to leave it be. "If you're sure. I care about you, you know."

"Jojo," he scoffed, "are you going soft on me?"

The sharp kick he got under the table assured him otherwise.

XENOS

Tricia made a face. "But they're so . . . ugly."

Sasha bristled as if the insult had been aimed at her, personally instead of the naked mole rat whose enclosure she stood before. She'd been excited when Tricia had accepted her invitation for a behind-the-scenes tour of the zoo where she volunteered. Grandpa Joey had moved them to the suburbs last month, and it had been hard for her to make friends at the new school. Tricia, one of the few other Latinas, had the locker next to her and had at least chitchatted with her between classes. Hoping that she could make the acquaintance into a real friend, Sasha had suggested the trip to the zoo. So far, however, her potential friend had spent most of the afternoon complaining about the smell or, like now, making judgmental remarks about the animals' relative attractiveness.

"OK, so they're not like big stuffed animals like the red pandas," Sasha said. "So what? They're still fascinating creatures. Did you know that—"

"Ugh. I can't stand looking at them anymore." Tricia turned and started heading back down the path. "They look like giant maggots. They make me want to call an exterminator. Same with those huge spiders you showed me, too. Gross."

Sasha trotted after her. "Spiders aren't vermin. They're not even dangerous—most of them, anyway. They're actually useful since they *eat species that destroy crops or pose other threats. Humans can be really prejudiced about other creatures. We see stuff that doesn't look like us or like the creatures we know as pets, and we automatically think they're evil or something, and that justifies us killing them."*

"What, so I'm racist against bugs, now? Please." Tricia rolled her eyes. "I don't get you, Sasha. You're just weird sometimes. Maybe if you spent less time hanging out with stinky, ugly animals and more time paying attention to your hair and what you're wearing, you might have more friends."

Sasha flushed. Despite Joey's frequent attempts to drill some fashion sense into her, it had just never stuck; she greatly preferred the freedom and durability of loose jeans and plain, long-sleeved shirts. Her hair was usually a tangled mess, and she found makeup both uncomfortable on her skin and a waste of time. Her lack of fashion prowess had been a sore spot since grade school, when Lyla Stanton told her she looked like she slept in a dumpster, and the entire class laughed. Now that she was in high school, she had started trying at least to improve her general grooming—finally realizing that boys were interesting as more than just playmates helped—but with limited success so far. That her efforts weren't paying off stung.

A sudden, heady rush of anger boiled up inside her. "Well, if you're an example of what I should look for in a human friend," she snarled, "I think I'll stick with the mole rats." She turned and stomped away.

The conference room was abuzz with activity—and a lot more people than she'd remembered seeing at the company before. Some of the new faces crowded around Jay. They were decked out in security uniforms similar to his, and all of them had a similar square-jawed, quasi-military look to them. One seemed particularly familiar with the chief; they laughed like old friends.

The engineering team was also present. A couple of them—Jens and Miryam, if she remembered their names correctly from meeting them at the company picnic in July—were nervously picking over fire-scarred chunks of machinery.

Alex and a few of the physics and tech team members huddled in a corner, poring over the display on a small, handheld screen he wielded.

Her own team's work had been completed, more or less. There wasn't a lot she could do with the corpse, but she had noted her findings. The species was clearly intelligent, of course, but also social and emotional. Though she allowed for other possibilities—and wished the government had approved Leung's request for a dedicated anthropologist to help them figure this out—it seemed to her that a member of a species that intended only destruction would not have been sentimental enough to carry family photos with them on an attack run. She had also noted that the creature's outer garments, what was left of them, didn't seem to be combat gear as she understood it. What she didn't note in her report was how unsettled the entire experience had made her. She had worked with plenty of deceased creatures before, but dealing with one that was clearly from an intelligent if alien species was new. Her job had been to assess whether the species posed a threat to Earth; privately, she longed to learn more about them as a people.

Leung strode in, scrolling up her screen and sipping at a cup of coffee. "Good morning, team. Let's get this started, shall we?" She perched on the chair at the far end of the conference table and nodded at Jens. "What did you find?"

He held up the metal piece he'd been staring at. "First, Alex was correct. The craft did have a magnetic component. It looks like it was designed to be a short-range ground-to-space vehicle, with the magnetic drive kicking in once it had cleared atmosphere. We think this component malfunctioned, perhaps due to submersion or some environmental element that wasn't present on its home planet, and that's why the entire craft became magnetized underwater."

Leung nodded. "That makes sense. Anything else?"

"The craft had no weapons systems at all. No projectiles, no lasers—nothing that could be used offensively that we could figure out. Miryam can tell you more about that."

She held up her piece in turn. "This is the most complete item we could retrieve from the craft's cockpit. Everything else was melted from the fire or so waterlogged that it couldn't tell us anything. We're still working on it, but as best we can tell, it's something like a black box—the data recording devices used on aircraft before they started doing continuous Stream uploads. We're working with the tech team to find a way to transfer data from the storage media inside. As best as we can tell, the tech level of this species is similar to developed-world Earth levels around the turn of the century. If they are indeed a threat, we would probably have the upper hand just based on technology alone, so we're probably not in any serious danger."

"I look forward to hearing more if you get that data. Sasha?"

She cleared her throat. Public speaking had never been a strong suit, especially when she was in front of so many people she wanted to impress. Still, she managed to get through her report with a minimum of nervous fidgeting, so she called that a win.

"Then, from what everyone's telling me, these xenos aren't necessarily hostile?" Leung raised an eyebrow.

Sasha nodded. "It's possible we're wrong, so I think we should still be vigilant, but it doesn't seem so. It's probable that this was a military vehicle, and a soldier of some sort piloting it, but he doesn't seem even to have been a scout, much less someone else who was part of a full attack force. Given Alex's initial findings on the tessera, and the fact that the vehicle was short-range, our conclusion is that this was a freak accident for the pilot. He did not expect to end up on our planet."

"That's a relief!" Leung smiled at her. "But I'm glad

we're prepared for more. It's always possible that the disappearance of their craft has the creatures on the other side of this tessera investigating just as much as we are, and they might have interpreted the lost craft as an act of aggression on our part. Even if they don't, I'd rather be safe than sorry, plus we have all the potential threats from the other tesserae to worry about, too. Which brings me to you, Captain."

Jay stepped forward. "Indeed, ma'am. Please allow me to introduce our new response squad." Each of the six new members of the team nodded as he named them and gave a brief description of their qualifications. Most, as Sasha had guessed, had come from military careers, with one member who also had a background in dangerous-predator control in Olympic National Park. She hoped that none of the other tesserae spat forth anything more threatening than the bears and cougars the woman was used to.

Leung smiled at them. "It's great to meet you all. Now let's figure out how mobilizing your team is going to work. Alex?"

"Thank you." He stepped up to the front of the room and the vid window there switched from its view of the lake to a blank screen. Alex fussed with his small screen for a moment, and the window lit up. Spinning in the middle was a crude, three-dimensional map of the planet, speckled all over with little blue circles. "Here it is!" he announced cheerfully. "No name yet, but it's something. It's a real-time display of satellite data scanning the spectral band in which the tesserae appear. If something changes, like so . . ." He poked around again, and the map zoomed in to the Pacific Northwest. One of the circles—a small one, near Crater Lake—lit up in bright red, and an annoying alert chime sounded. "We know about it!"

Jay nodded appreciatively. "That should be useful. I assume the alerts will go out to the whole response team?"

"They'll go out to everyone. The alarm will sound over

the internal PA, and we've set them up to break into every company-networked Stream device in the building, unless the device's owner has opted out of the system. You can also get a connection with a personal device if you like." He held up his arm. A small version of the map showed on his band's screen. "I'm sure the tech team can refine the system further if they can spare the personnel, but we at least have some way of monitoring things now." He switched off the test.

"Well, I'm impressed." Leung smiled. "Looks like all of you have done exactly as I'd hoped. If one of these things opens again, I'm confident we'll be ready for it. There's only one problem."

"Oh?" Jay folded his arms across his chest.

"How we're paying for all this." She got up and started pacing. "I'm still in touch with some government and science-foundation friends of mine about getting more grants for our work, but I'm not sure how much they're going to be able to help. XenoNet's operating budget was planned for little more than new probe missions and studying the xenos they brought back. To fund all these new systems—and our new employees—we're going to have to cut back in some other areas."

Sasha frowned. "Other areas?"

"Well . . . " Leung smiled thinly. "Now that we have access—potentially—to hundreds of other places, I'm not sure the full probe program is all that necessary anymore. We're still running the Omega mission—that's planned to launch in three weeks—but beyond that, I don't know that it makes sense to continue. To that end, I've made some contacts with another company—Dark Matter Technologies—"

"What?" Alex went pale, staring at her. "But Belenko—"

She shrugged. "I know. I don't like it either."

"Belenko . . . Isn't that the guy who runs the moon resort?" Sasha suddenly felt uneasy. Dark Matter's CEO was practically an anachronism: a hardcore profiteer who operated just this side of the law, and didn't care who—or what—he hurt so long as he made money on it. He was also, she remembered with a wave of nausea, a proud sport hunter and traditional carnivore. Not content to get animal protein via the tasty and nutritious bioprinted meat readily available in the developed world, he preferred cuts from actual dead animals—which he enjoyed killing himself when he had the chance. Many indigenous cultures still regarded hunting as a sacred part of their life, and not everyone had easy access to the bioprinted stuff, but people who hunted just because they liked killing things made her livid. She had seen too many innocent creatures come to untimely ends just because some human bullies thought it would be fun or an ego boost to harm something with less power.

"Yes," Leung said. "He's been wanting to look into resource gathering on Jupiter's moons, but he doesn't yet have a craft that can get him there. He's interested in buying Xeno II."

Sasha stared at her. "The one that brought back the arthropods?"

Leung smiled sadly. "In truth, after its journey, it would've taken an awful lot of retrofitting to get back up to deep-space readiness, but it can still do short hops. My original plan was to lend it to NASA for their asteroid-belt project, but, well, we need the money, and Belenko has it." She looked pale and tired; Sasha wondered how much work their boss had had to do in the wake of the crash. Coordinating response plans with the military and Homeland alone must have been a nightmare.

Sasha chewed her lip. The idea that Belenko might go digging around on Europa and do goodness knows what there was disturbing. But the idea that Earth might well be under threat from something far more dangerous than one creepy rich dude was an even scarier prospect. Though she was confident in the teams' assessment that the xeno who had died on their planet wasn't hostile, there was no telling what other threats could be on the horizon. "Well, then. I guess that's what makes the most sense."

"The good part," Leung continued, "is that he's willing to pay us a lot of money for the craft. Between that and making some personnel changes on the probe side, we should have enough not only for a few years of operating budget, but for a few more hires for the tesserae project— maybe a dedicated person to monitor that map, for instance."

"If you'll pardon my candor, ma'am," Jay began.

"I really need to break you of the habit of calling me that," she admonished with a grin. "Please. You have a marvelously level head. What's on your mind?"

"Is this the best use of our resources? This seems like a big gamble with the company's future, when we don't even know whether any of those things will open for long or if what's on the other side is dangerous. Shouldn't we just hand this back to the military and Homeland and let them deal with it?"

She shook her head. "Frankly, I'd love to. The international contacts I've been working with are setting up military-based operations for the tesserae in their area. I just can't seem to convince anyone with clout in D.C. that a handful of physics anomalies with no known threat beyond the original one are worth devoting that much taxpayer money to. Unless we determine the craft is from a hostile race or the other tesserae start sending other dangerous stuff through, they'd rather we just handle it ourselves. They don't understand the science of it the way we do. I'd rather us have the resources and not need them than risk something terrible happening. If that craft had come down in the middle of the city . . . " She made a face. "You all know me: I'm not in this to get rich. I just want to help humanity understand more of the universe. This project will do that. If there's any risk—" She stopped as the alert chime from the tessera map sounded.

"What the—" Alex turned and stared. Sure enough, a bright red circle—in a forested area on the Kitsap peninsula—was flashing.

"Is this another test?" Sasha moved to his side.

He shook his head, his cheeks flushing. His fingers danced over his controls, bringing up live satellite images for the area and zooming in. Even from a distance, something was definitely off. Streaming out of the forest near the tessera's location were half a dozen quadrupeds.

Jay squinted at the map. "Are those deer?" Indeed, they were roughly the same size and shape as blacktail does—plentiful enough in the area.

One of the creatures broke off from the pack. With a graceful leap, it plucked a passing seagull from the air . . . and began chowing down on the helpless bird.

"That," Sasha said, gaping in amazement, "is not a deer."

* * *

Jay couldn't help staring at Alex's flushed face, which sported an enormous grin. The young physicist looked downright exhilarated, if tired and mud-spattered, and he drained half of his glass of raspberry limeade in one gulp. The mission to return the carnivorous xenos back to their home world had been a rousing success. Sasha, the predator specialist, and one of the bio team had tracked and herded the creatures, Jay's small security team held the perimeter, keeping humans and other potential Earth prey out of the creatures' way, and Alex and one of the engineering crew took several readings from the tessera itself. It had all gone smoothly—the tessera closed about 20 minutes after the last creature had been shoved through it—and Jay now had every confidence that this project was not only necessary, but was going to work out perfectly well. Even better, not only had he not had any panic attacks during the event, but being in the middle of it, helping to manage the chaos, had actually spiked his adrenaline in a good way. His doctor had once told him that mild exposure to stressful situations over which he had some control would help him heal. Though he still worried about what would happen if he encountered something more dangerous, the confidence boost he got from coordinating the mission was immensely satisfying.

To celebrate the event, the entire team, filthy as they were, had converged on a pub in Kingston. The only person missing was Tito. Hiring and training him for the team had gone fairly well: they'd mostly avoided talking about their romantic past in favor of talking about the job at hand. Still, it felt somewhat awkward to be more social with the man with whom he was once in love, so they'd stayed at arm's length aside from work. Working with his ex and hearing about his happy life with his husband and their three kids had brought up a lot of other relationship thoughts and feelings, however—ones he hadn't had in a long time. And as the feelings sparked up, they settled on someone with whom he'd become more recently acquainted.

Watching Alex in action as he'd scrambled to get data from the event had been entertaining in itself, and as the evening wore on, his sweat-soaked T-shirt began to cling to his slender body. As much as Jay was in soldier mode and focused on keeping curious humans away from the site, he still couldn't help stealing glances. Now that the job was done, though, he was free to gaze on in earnest at the young man, and so he had. As Alex ran a hand through his messy nest of curls, a small shudder ran through Jay's belly, imagining what else those long, elegant fingers might be good at. But then, as he realized Alex only had eyes for Sasha, who sat across the table from them, his ardor cooled again.

"Dammit," he muttered under his breath and nursed his beer.

"How did I not know that?" Sasha said, staring open-mouthed at Alex. "Your work's now being used in all sorts of new construction."

Alex shrugged. "I just contributed some data mining. The initial idea came from my ex."

Sasha raised an eyebrow. "Ex?"

"Gabriel Jackson. The lead engineer. He was a grad assistant when I was doing some of my undergrad geology classes. When he started up his project, he asked if I'd like to join, and that was that. We started dating after he published, though we broke up in May."

Just like that, the rush in Jay's gut came back, and his mind began racing. His assessment of Alex being straight had been off, and he kicked himself for the incorrect assumption. He tried to ignore the impulse to pursue his interest, knowing how weird things could get when dating a colleague, but his libido had other ideas and kept filling his mind with visions of them.

After another hour or so of chatter, the long day began to catch up with them all, and one by one, they filtered out to catch the ferry back to the Edmonds dock. As everyone gathered their things to go, Jay left the table to visit the restroom, and when he came back out, the rest of the team had already gone. Almost everyone: Alex lingered outside the door, his breath clouding in the misty air.

"Ugh! Fuck my rotten timing." Alex stared at the taillights of a car that pulled out of the parking lot. "I meant to ask Amit for a ride back to the dock."

"I can take you there," Jay offered. "I have my bike, and I'm safe—only had half a beer."

"Nah. I'll just get a drone cab or find a bus stop." Alex shook his head.

"Why spend the money? And really, there's no sense in being alone if we're both going the same way." He met Alex's eyes and smiled slyly, hoping his message was clear.

For a moment, it seemed as if Alex hadn't understood the implication, but then he cocked his head and returned the smile in an equally significant way. "Sure," he said, his voice low and teasing. "I could be convinced to take a ride."

* * *

All through the short ferry crossing, Alex was happy to entertain the familiar feelings. It had been more than a year since had been with anyone except Gabriel, and even though he was still hurting from that and now also thoroughly stuck on Sasha, he thought a fling with the handsome security chief might be just the thing to clear his mind. He was certainly surprised, not to mention flattered, that the guard was even interested in him. In the wake of his breakup, he'd more or less turned his guy-aimed radar completely off; if Jay had been interested in him all along, he would never have noticed. It was also a bonus, he thought, that maybe Jay wasn't into women, meaning Sasha's apparent crush on him couldn't go anywhere. If nothing else, resolving that question was worth it.

So, he was content to return the completely unsubtle flirting while they were on the boat, and even happier to cuddle up closely on the bike again after they disembarked, Jay's wriggling hips doing a lot to spark Alex's imagination.

As they sped down the street on the way to his apartment in Ravenna, however, they passed by the cathedral: a former Catholic church that had survived the great quake and was now the local diocese for Homecoming. Though the building was dark and quiet at this hour, it still reminded him of the reason why he'd lost his boyfriend to begin with. Heart heavy, he felt his interest wane as his mental guilt machine spun back up instead. And, though being so close to Jay's well-built body had given Alex an idea of what Sasha saw in him, he couldn't quite separate the two in his mind, whether Jay was interested in her or not, and that was making him uncomfortable, not aroused.

They pulled up to his building, and Alex dismounted

and tucked the borrowed helmet back in the saddlebag. "Thanks for the ride home." He smiled politely and stuck out his hand. "I guess I owe you another lemon tea."

"Uh, yeah. Sure." Jay shook the hand, but stared at Alex with a bewildered expression.

He took pity on his friend, realizing it was unfair to lead him on. "Jay . . . I'm sorry. I didn't mean to—back there, I was . . ."

Jay shrugged. "It's OK. I assumed that—"

"You assumed right. I just . . . I can't." Alex looked at the ground.

"Can't?"

"Well, it's not 'can't,' per se. Just that I don't think I'd be all that into it, I'm afraid." He heaved a sigh. "I'm just coming off of a long relationship and I'm still preoccupied with that. It wouldn't be fair to you."

"Well, I won't say that I'm not disappointed." Jay smiled sadly.

"Another time, maybe, I might have. I'm just not up for that right now."

"It's fine, truly. Things won't be weird for us at work though, yeah?" Jay tried to catch his eye.

"Oh, no. Not at all." Alex chuckled. "I consider myself professional."

"Good." Jay smiled. "Besides, with all this tesserae stuff, maybe it's not such a great idea for us to get distracted with social things. We have a lot of work to focus on."

"Yeah, you're probably right. Honestly, most of the time, my brain is cortex-deep in equations, so, yeah." Alex stuffed his hands in his pockets.

"Figured. That brain of yours is an impressive machine, after all. Well, I think you're just impressive, period."

Alex looked up again, his mouth open in surprise. "I am?"

"I think so," Jay said sincerely. "Frankly, I think your ex is losing out."

Alex simply stared at him, scanning his face as if seeing yet another alien. He'd figured Jay was just looking for a bit of fun. The idea that there might be something more there was a shock.

Jay shifted uncomfortably under his gaze. "Anyway. Don't feel pressured or anything on my account. I'm good with the friends thing, too. One of the guys on my new team—Tito—is actually an ex from my Army days. It's weird seeing him again, but I'm OK with it. I'm happy to just work with you and hang out now and then. That matters much more to me than anything else. I've enjoyed having you as a friend so far, and I'd like that to continue, if that's fine with you."

Alex finally recovered from the surprise and took a chance, stepping closer for a slightly awkward but comforting hug. "Absolutely. Thanks for understanding."

"See you tomorrow?" Jay gave his arm a squeeze and started the engine again.

"Yep!" Alex waved at him and scurried up the steps and into his building as the cycle sped away.

After a necessary shower, he dove into bed, looking forward to a well-earned night's sleep. His body, however, had other ideas. As had been the case many recent nights, he couldn't help thinking about Sasha and imagining various sordid scenarios. In tonight's parade of mental images, his brain kept insisting on throwing Jay into the picture, both on his own and with Sasha included. When the idea of Sasha with Jay had come up before, he had felt angry and quickly pushed the thought out of his mind. This time, the feelings inspired were almost pleasant, so he let them continue. As the scene began to play, he felt a familiar stirring and snaked a hand down under the sheets to help it along. He couldn't sustain the feeling, however. No sooner had his mind gotten the both of them naked and horizontal than the sense that he himself was a pathetic, intrusive outsider—one who would never belong in a picture of such physical perfection—came crawling back up his spine. With a shiver of revulsion, his ardor faded to nothing. Releasing himself, he rolled over and fell into a fitful, frustrated sleep.

CONNECTIONS

"It's nothing personal. I like you. I think you're a great friend. I just don't like guys at all. Well, I like guys, of course! Just not like that."

"Oh. OK." Jay's stomach, already in knots just from getting up the courage to ask Rico to the dance, threatened to rebel entirely. He tried to stay calm. It had been a long shot anyway, but six months of trying to convince himself that he wasn't falling in love with his friend and ROTC pal had gotten to be too much to bear. He had to at least give it a shot. "I hope you don't mind that I asked, though."

Rico shrugged. "Why would I mind?"

Jay smiled nervously. "I dunno. Just was hoping you wouldn't think I was being weird or something—since we've been friends for so long and all."

"Nah." Rico elbowed him. "Honestly, if I was into dudes, I'd consider it. I mean, you are kinda hot." He winked. "Some guy is gonna be all over that someday, you know."

Somehow, that didn't make Jay feel any better at all.

Not five minutes after Jay got to work—before he'd even finished unloading his backpack and taking over from the night shift—Alex buzzed in.

"Hey!" He strode up to the counter, flashed a sleepy

smile, and set a steaming cup in front of Jay. "They were out of lemon, so it's hot cider. Hope that's OK."

"Cider's fine. Thanks?" He took the cup, but couldn't help sounding confused. "Sorry, I'm not—"

"For the ride," Alex reminded him. "And also because I wanted to try to make up for not following through last night."

"Oh! That's not necessary. I totally get it. I've been on the rebound before, too. I know how it is."

Alex shifted uncomfortably and looked away. "Well, it's more than that, and I think I owe you more of an explanation."

He waved a hand. "Nah. I'm sure it's none of my business anyway." Much as he wanted to keep chatting about personal things with Alex, he felt compelled to try to remain professional, especially since they were actually at work instead of off-duty.

"Actually, it's definitely your business, to be honest." Alex smirked. "In part, at least."

Curiosity overrode professionalism, and he stared. "OK, I'm lost. What do you mean?"

Alex finally looked up again, meeting his eyes. "It's mostly about Sasha."

"I'd wondered about that—I'd noticed you watching her—but you also mentioned your ex-boyfriend, so I didn't know whether you were also, y'know, woman-inclined."

"Right!" Alex brightened. "Well, I'm totally open when it comes to people's gender and such. I have my shallow moments, but I've also found I'm attracted to just about anyone who's nice and has a good brain.

"Ah! Well, I'm basically gay, but the line's fuzzy sometimes," Jay said. "Mostly into guys, but I'm not picky about body config, and I've also been with a few women over the years. They're not usually my thing, but there are a few who spark me now and then. Hooked up with butch lesbian friend once when we were both lonely and coming off of bad relationships. That was weird for both of us, though."

"I can imagine!" Alex grinned back. Then he grew serious again. "Unfortunately, my thing with Gabriel ended badly, so I'm not in guy mode right now. I didn't think I was in anyone mode to be honest, but then I met Sasha, and I think I lost my senses."

"I can understand that. She's not my type, but she is a great person. I can see how you'd like her. I'm sorry, though: I'm still confused about how this relates to me." Jay waved his hands in confusion. "It's not just because I'm a guy, right?"

"No, it's not." Alex smiled wryly and sighed before continuing. "It's just that as much as I have a thing for her, I think she feels the same about you."

"Oh! Oh, wow. I didn't realize that." Apparently Sasha's flirting had gone right over his head. He began wondering what else he'd missed.

"She hasn't been obvious about it," Alex explained, "and she hasn't told me, so I may be wrong. It's just that she just talks about you a lot, and I've seen her checking you out. Hell, at the tessera event, it seemed like she couldn't stop staring at you." Alex waggled his eyebrows. "Not that I can blame her."

"Thanks." Jay flushed and tried to hide his self-consciousness behind a sip of cider.

"Anyway. It's not that I'm worried about you being interested in her, just that I'm guessing she's more into big, buff men like you, so I seriously doubt a squishy, little guy like me would be her thing."

He frowned. "Really? People can surprise you sometimes. I think you're attractive. Maybe she would, too. Why not ask?"

Alex shook his head. "I don't think I could stomach it, knowing she'd probably turn me down. I'm usually good with rejection—who wants to be with someone who doesn't want you, yeah?—but with Sasha, I'm having a hard time getting past it. I will eventually, I'm sure. I'm perfectly capable of being friends with people I've had crushes on. I just don't think I should do anything that would drag that process out. I think being with you would just remind me that I'm not . . . you, and make it harder to get over her."

"That makes sense, I guess." It did seem logical—at least as far as Alex's perspective went. He still couldn't help an inward rush of frustration, though. It was annoying that it was apparently his own fault for winning the DNA lottery since that was keeping him from being able to date the guy he liked.

"So, there it is." Alex let out a breath he'd been holding. "Sorry if this has all been a bit too much personal-angst nonsense for you, but I wanted to be sure you knew it wasn't anything that you'd done wrong. I do like you—a lot—I'm just in a weird headspace right now."

"It's not a problem." Jay smiled and waved his cup. "Though if you want to keep bringing me beverages anyway, I wouldn't argue."

Alex laughed. "I can do that! Anyway, I do need to scramble for now. I'm hoping I can get in to see Leung today before she gets swamped with meetings, so I'm going to go try to catch her as she gets in."

"Yeah, she's due in about 10 minutes, by her usual schedule."

"Perfect. Thanks for understanding!" Alex flashed another impossibly cute grin and bounded off.

Jay finally sat down, cradling the warm cup in his hand, and started looking over the feeds from the security cameras. The one from the south entrance showed the approach of a familiar face. Now, however, a bit more than just the pleasantness of seeing a friend spun through him. For the first time, he seemed to notice that Sasha was, in fact, attractive, despite being somewhat different than what usually interested him. A small but noticeable thrill flashed through his belly.

"Huh," he huffed, surprised at his body's unexpected reaction. "That's new."

* * *

Alex paced nervously outside Leung's office until she arrived.

"Well, good morning to you, too!" She nodded as she came down the hall, lifting her coffee cup in his direction. "I'd have thought you'd be late after yesterday's tessera event."

"Well, I *am* tired, but I wanted to talk to you anyway."

"Of course. Come on in." She swiped her thumb over the pad by the door, and led him in. "What's up?"

He waited until the door had closed and then sat down across from her desk while she unburdened herself of pack and shoes. "Belenko."

Her nose wrinkled. "Oh. Yeah."

"I don't understand. Why would you work with him after all these years? I thought you two hated each other."

She came up next to his chair and leaned against the edge of her desk. "We do, but we're also both practical people. I had something he needed—the probe—he had something I needed—money."

"Aren't you worried about what he'll do with it?"

"I am, yes," she said, "but honestly, we got a bargain out of the deal. What he really wanted at first was getting in on what we're doing—which I refused. He already found out the truth about the craft, but he doesn't know about the tesserae yet. Still, he's smart enough that he'll figure it out eventually. When he does, he's going to be stuck with a fifty-billion-dollar spacecraft that's going to be rendered obsolete by the fact that we can now just walk through a door to get to another planet."

"Well, it's not that easy," Alex said. "At least not as far as we know. We have no idea yet what's causing them to open. Knowing how long they're going to stay that way or being able to keep them open long enough for a human mission is out of the question."

She shrugged. "We can at least send drones through for the ones that stay open long enough for us to arrive there. We don't know whether the tesserae open more than once, but assuming they do, we can program the drones with some version of your monitoring system and tell them to return when the door opens again, laden with data or whatever else we've asked them to gather."

"Like resources," Alex said flatly. Finally he understood. "As soon as he knows, Belenko will want to use the tesserae for mining and who knows what else."

"Exactly. However, he not only just obtained a very expensive and soon-to-be-useless toy, but did so by agreeing not to interfere in our research."

Alex laughed. "OK. I get it now."

"Hey, I'm not stupid, y'know." She nudged his knee with hers.

"Of course not. I was just worried, is all."

"I know you were, Alex. You're a good kid. I'm glad you care." Her voice went soft, and she scanned his face. "Sometimes . . ."

"Sorry?"

She shook her head. "Nothing. Just having a moment of remembering how damn old I am and how much of my life went by without me realizing it. Don't worry yourself about it, though."

He thought about asking her to elaborate, but then the courage to do so left him. "What would you like me to do now? The monitoring system is more or less self-operational. Should I go back to looking at the samples from Aurora?"

"Nope. I want to get on the data mining before Belenko even knows what we're up to. Go ping some of the folks in tech and engineering and get together some of those drones. I want one ready to go the next time a tessera opens."

"OK, on it. I'll—" The tessera-alert alarm cut him off. "Again? What the hell?"

"Go!" she ordered. "We'll talk more later."

* * *

"Incoming!" Sasha called out to Alex as one of the tiny creatures dashed toward the tessera. Chasing the xenos— which looked something like bald shrews—all over the beach had been maddening, and for the first time, she wondered whether it might not make sense to just blanket the whole area with some sort of stun wave and knock them out.

"Dammit!" Alex spat, nearly tripping over the xeno on its mad rush back to its jungle-like home planet. It got through just in time: the steaming air pouring through the portal abruptly cut off, and once again, the only thing visible was the lapping waves of Boundary Bay.

The creature, however, was not the last one. Sasha had been trying to herd a slow-moving pair toward the door, but it closed just as they got there. The tiny creatures came up short at the water's edge, and looked back, wide-eyed expressions painting their little faces. "Aw, crap!" she grumbled and began chasing them again as they skittered along the rocky shore, looking for a place to hide from the huge biped behind them.

"Sasha?" Jay called out from behind her. "Did they get back?"

"No!" Finally, she cornered them in the hollow of a piece of driftwood. "Gotcha!" She picked them up with gloved hands.

As she got a closer look at them, she made note of their features: smaller than Littlefoot; webbed feet; greenish-gray skin with a sparse covering of fine, nearly transparent hair; long noses; and sticky tongues much like an anteater. One of them, to her surprise, also had a small, sealed pouch on its abdomen in which wriggled four tiny lumps. To her even greater surprise, the creature also had seemingly male sex organs.

"What do we do with them now?" Cordy, the former park ranger and the team's predator specialist, rushed up, breathless from her circuit of the area to locate any stragglers.

Sasha shrugged. "Take them back, I guess? We have no idea when this tessera might open again, right?" She glanced over at Alex.

"None whatsoever. I still don't even know what's opening them, much less how to predict it." He fiddled with a handheld spectral scanner. "All I've gotten from any of these so far is that when they open, they show up on an old broadcast spectrum. Other than that, no clue."

"Back to XenoNet it is, then?" Jay slipped his stun pistol back in its holster.

Sasha nodded. "Looks like it, yeah. Sorry, guys," she told the squirming creatures, "you're stuck on Earth for now."

"How are our new guests doing?" Leung grinned at Sasha in their afternoon meeting.

"Jack and Kate? They're fine. The readings Alex got from their home-world's atmosphere said that it's close to Earth-standard. We just added a little extra nitrogen and humidity in their enclosure, so they should survive here until we can get them back home."

"Good to know. I think we might want to study them a bit while we have them here, if you're interested."

"I'd love to!" Sasha beamed. In her spare time, she'd been working with Littlefoot and the arthropods, but most of her exotic-creature contact of the past few weeks had been spent herding various life-forms back where they belonged. Studying samples just wasn't a priority for the company anymore now that tesserae management was so critical, so they hadn't been keeping any of the xenos that had come through. If they were stuck here, however, she might as well spend some time figuring them out. Today's little marsupials were especially fascinating, given their odd anatomy.

Alex spoke up. "I guess I probably should've known about that tessera being about to close. I looked back at my data, and the frequency signal was starting to break up around the time that it closed. If I had been paying closer attention, we might've gotten the critters back home in time."

"I see." Leung folded her arms. "Is this something you can correct for the next event?"

"Well . . . not easily." He glanced around at the team, all of whom looked as exhausted and overworked as he felt. "There's only so much we can do on the ground, even with camera drones and monitoring equipment. We need proper sky- and satellite-level scans to give us a better idea of what we're dealing with. Wide-area IR and Doppler scans, in particular, would help us track down any loose xenos that get through—especially for remote tesserae that take us a while to get to. But my team and I can't easily monitor those if we're also scanning the tessera itself and sending in the short-range probes to get data from the other side. It's just too much for us to deal with all at once." He got up, pacing and rubbing his scruffy chin. "And more than that, we need someone to keep an eye on things back here, in case we ever get more than one tessera opening at the same time. I'd hate for us to be busy with a remote event like this only to have something else— Kingston, for instance—open up and let something carnivorous through without us being there to control it."

"So, what are you proposing?" Jay raised an eyebrow. "Do I need to recruit more security forces?"

"Well, that might not be a bad idea—a full beta team would be nice to have as backup—but beyond that, I was thinking we could use a mission control operator of some sort—a dispatcher, if you will—to give us all the top-level monitoring data while the rest of us are on the ground."

Leung closed her eyes for a moment as she thought. "I agree with you," she finally said. "We need more staff. I'm not sure how we're going to pay for it, but this project is becoming too critical for us not to have a full-scale team to keep an eye on things 24/7. I can't spare anyone from the tech team, and they might find a job like that out of their skillset, but I'll see if I can do some recruiting at the university—maybe get some work-study students—and get it resolved."

Alex sighed in relief. "Thanks. I'm doing the best I can, but we're just overtaxed."

Sasha suddenly got an idea. "As for paying for this . . . Leung, what if we were able to do some research with these xenos that could help us develop more commercial products? Not using them directly, of course—I'd never do that—but seeing if maybe they can give us some insights we haven't gotten from Earth creatures yet: antibodies, that kind of thing."

"Did you have something in mind?" Leung asked.

"Well, yes. When I did some initial anatomy exams on them, I discovered something neat about the xenos we encountered today. They're marsupials, of a sort, but it's the male that carries the offspring."

Alex stared at her. "Like a seahorse?"

She nodded. "Something like that, yes. Anatomically, though, it's different—and different from marsupial pouches, too. Instead of mammary gland, like marsupials have, our little guy has four tiny external umbilicus ports in the pouch. Best as I can tell, after mating, the female deposits early-stage embryos, amniotic sac and all, into his pouch, they attach to their little ports the way Earth's placental mammals implant in the uterine wall, and the pouch seals up while they're growing. After they're born, the female nurses them like any other mammal."

"That's pretty egalitarian," Alex noted. "I like it."

"It is!" She flashed a grin at him. "Aside from the pouches, they're close enough analogues to Earth creatures that we might be able to figure out exactly how it all works and maybe adapt their system for human use. A skin-graft pouch with a port would be a lot simpler, less invasive, and have less chance of rejection than giving someone a transplanted or lab-grown uterus. It also wouldn't come with the pitfalls they had with the external artificial wombs from a couple of decades ago. The developing fetus would have full contact with the host and therefore get all the biochemical and environmental input the artificial wombs lacked."

Jay grinned. "Then it would be easier for men—at least ones without a functional uterus—to be pregnant?"

Sasha nodded enthusiastically. "Yes, definitely. Or women who have uterine abnormalities or who have had a hysterectomy, or—" she gave a kind look to Leung "—women who never had one."

Leung flushed and went quiet. She was open about her status, but she didn't talk about it much. Sasha knew, however, that part of the reason Leung didn't have children was that she had transitioned in a time and place that such ideas were beyond medical science, and she had been too poor then to afford an adoption. In her mid-70s, she was now well beyond an age when parenting a baby, however it was created, would make sense, but she might be interested in helping younger women become pregnant. "That . . . that would be amazing, Sasha," Leung finally said in a quiet voice. "Do you think it's likely?"

She nodded. "We just need to dedicate a few staff members to working on the biotech: copying the tissue's properties and creating a human-analogue print of the pouch. Once it's viable, we can patent it. The money we could get from something like that might be able to fund our tesserae ops for some time."

"Do it," Leung said decisively. "I still want us focused on the tesserae, but if we can get a side business going that helps keep me from having to haggle with alternate funding all the time, I'd be utterly delighted. And you're right. I would love for tech like this to be available to everyone. Make it happen"

* * *

Sasha was sore—delightfully so. When she had first returned to Seattle, she wasn't certain what her employment situation would look like post-internship, so she'd been careful with money. The capoeira classes she'd been taking on and off since high school were an expense she had a hard time justifying when it wasn't Grandpa Joey's money or student aid paying for them. Now that she was fully on at XenoNet, however, she gave in to her longing to get back it. As it was, the job had turned out to be considerably more physical than she expected; chasing rogue xenos around wasn't exactly lab work, and she'd been feeling in less than peak condition for it.

The studio she found, just a few blocks away from her Bisa's building, had seemed like a great choice. Its master, João, was actually Brazilian, as opposed to the woman who taught the class at her undergrad school, and he had a great respect for the practice as both a dance and a martial art. It didn't hurt that he was also stomach-flutteringly attractive. She found herself missing moves and losing her step more than she normally would have because she was more focused on the flexing of his glutes than on where she was putting her own feet. Eventually, however, she fell back into the old, instinctive rhythms, and as they sparred, they matched move for move without missing a beat.

"*Maravilhoso!*" he cheered as they finished. "Well done, Sasha. You haven't forgotten yourself after all."

"*Obrigado!*" She leaned against the wall to catch her breath and sipped generously from her water bottle. "I was worried for a while!"

"How long did you say it had been?"

She shrugged. "A year? A bit more? Something like that. I had to drop the class last fall because I was too

114

bogged down with my thesis, and then the class filled up and I couldn't get back in."

"Well, to me it doesn't look like you've missed anything at all. You have a natural talent. I imagine other masters have told you that the way your body is built helps—being short and compact—but even if it were not for that advantage, you would have skill to burn. If you were to make it a priority, you could be a master someday."

She flushed. Other masters had indeed commented on her skill before, but not to this degree—and certainly not from someone so clearly gifted, himself. "Wish I had the time for that." She sighed. "Work is my big focus for now. But I do feel good for getting back into it, even if I'm just doing a weekly class. I've missed this, so much."

"*Que saudade*, yeah?"

She made a small face. "Huh? I'm sorry, my *Portugués* is terrible—"

He cocked his head. "Oh! I thought—wait. You're not Brazilian?"

"Oh, I am," she said. "Half. My mother's side. Dad's Romanian—hence the last name. I would've had Alvares, but he asked that Mama give me his, and she was love-struck at the time, so she did. Chose the first name he wanted, too, but she did give me Inés for a middle."

"I like Inés! That's the name of one of my favorite aunts."

"I think it was a family name for my mom, too—a couple of generations back, at least. She died when I was young, though, so I didn't get much of the cultural stuff while I was growing up. Tried to at least get a *Portugués* class in college, but their one prof for it died a week before my freshman term started, so I had to take *Español* instead, and never had the time to get back to it later." She stopped, realizing she was babbling, and waved a dismissive hand. "Anyway. Long story there. I won't bore you with it."

He shook his head. "It doesn't sound boring to me. I'd

love to hear about your life. Maybe over dinner, if you'd like?"

Before she could stop it, her grip on the water bottle tightened.

He read the tension and backed away, giving her some breathing room. "If not, that's OK, too. I don't make a habit of hitting on my students. I'm fine just teaching you." He offered a non-threatening grin.

She shook her head. "Not a problem. And yes I'd like to go to dinner. You just caught me by surprise, is all."

"Ah! I see. Well, my brother is head chef at São Paulo Grill—it's just a short walk from here. Great place. Even has a samba band and a dance floor, if you want to get some more culture in."

She couldn't help a laugh. "Honestly, I've never done samba in my life. A creepy white dude in one of my high school classes once asked me if I'd do the 'horizontal samba' with him, and I've never been able to stomach it since!"

He laughed with her. "I can understand that! Well, we don't have to go there. Sushi, maybe?"

"Nah. I'd love to go to your brother's place. And if I get a glass or two of wine in me, I might attempt a samba after all."

Maybe it was the wine—or her attempt at learning the dance—but she didn't at all mind when he asked her back to his apartment. The sex was just as satisfying as the sparring had been—much better than the quick fling with the inept student a few months back. As she lay there afterward, however, she noticed the glow from João's band, which rested on the nightstand nearby. The background image for its home screen showed a charming brown face, a young one: perhaps four, if her guess of the girl's age was correct. An uncomfortable shiver ran through her belly. It was possible the child was a niece or something, but she was at least related because she shared

João's high cheekbones and bright eyes. He hadn't mentioned having a daughter—and his skipping over that information seemed odd, given how she'd told him all about her own family—but it seemed likely.

Sasha had never before dated someone with kids, at least as far as she knew. The apartment, with its single bedroom, clearly wasn't occupied by a child, which likely meant João didn't have custody of her. Not that such scenarios were remotely unusual, but it did remind her of her own remaining parent. She was so young when he left that she didn't remember him at all, but her mother had kept some pictures of him, so she at least knew where she'd gotten her narrow nose and the small dimple in her chin. She wondered whether he at all kept any pictures of her or whether he simply pretended, perhaps even to his new wife, that she didn't exist.

Looking at this girl's face, so like that of the man next to her, Sasha wondered whether, should she ever have her own children, they might look like her or like whoever contributed the other half of their DNA. It was a moot point—her tubal blockers were performing as they should, and she had no intention of disabling them anytime soon—but her curiosity had been sparked.

As she drifted off, she imagined that if she ever had a daughter, she might call her Inés.

ANGEL

Bridget's hands shook so badly that she couldn't read the text on the screen. Closing her eyes, she handed it over to her mother. "Read it for me?"

Her mother laughed. "Of course, child."

"I almost don't want to hear it, though," she moaned. So many of her hopes and dreams were up in the air right now. From the moment she'd shown a talent for computers and electronics when she was just a toddler, her family had been supportive of her education. The one thing they couldn't do, however much they wished, was afford to send her to the best tech schools in America. MIT had accepted her, but had not offered more than rudimentary financial aid. The same was true of many other schools. And though the universities in her home country were world-class, this was the one field where they didn't quite have the specific programs she wanted, nor a ready tech-heavy local industry to start working in after graduation. Her hope rested on the message she'd just gotten from the University of Washington.

Her mother started crying, and Bridget looked over. "What? WHAT?" She snatched the device back.

"We are pleased to inform you," the message read, "that we can extend an offer of full financial support for your degree program in Electrical Engineering . . ."

The sound she made probably frightened the neighbors, but she didn't care.

Bridget yawned. The late nights in the security office were beginning to grind her down. Sure, the job was quiet enough that she spent most of her shift studying or developing hacks for her array of electronic tools and toys instead of managing drunk frat boys and clueless freshmen, but the hours absolutely sucked and didn't dovetail well with her early classes. As an early-autumn squall pounded on the window of her dorm room, the sky seemed impossibly dark for the morning hour, and all she wanted was to roll over and go back to sleep. Not that the other occupant of the bed was interested in that.

"Morning." Dane's breath was hot on her neck, and insistent pressure pushed against her hip.

"Hey," she murmured, turning in his arms. Truth be told, she probably would have gotten more sleep if she hadn't responded to his message about spending the night with him after her shift finished. They'd been dating long enough—eight months now—that sex wasn't always on the agenda when they shared a bed, but he'd been excited after a gaming tournament, and she was full of adrenaline from a medical-emergency call that had ended her shift. Next thing she knew, it was 2 a.m.

He stroked a tangled, lime-green curl from her face and kissed her nose. "When's your first class?"

"Too damned early." She tried to ignore that his other hand was stroking down over the soft expanse of her belly, on its way down to warmer places.

"That's fucked." He pulled his hand back. "I'm sorry for keeping you up late."

She shook her head. "It's OK. It's not you. It's the job. I just can't keep doing those hours."

"Can you quit?"

"Nope. I have to keep a work-study job, or I lose the rest of my aid package." Dane was a clever bloke—he was almost as good with firmware architecture as she was—but he was a spoiled rich boy, too, attending entirely on his parents' money. He didn't understand her obligations, and she found herself reminding him of them far too often. At least he was sympathetic, most of the time.

"Maybe you can find something different?"

"Doubt it. This far into the quarter, everything's full up."

He sighed. "Shit. I'm sorry."

"Eh. Just bad luck. I'll push through it." She found herself missing what his hand had been doing and reached down, putting it back in place. He readily returned to the task, and she closed her eyes, drifting away into the feeling. After a moment, however, he stopped and cocked his head.

"Wait. I just remembered something," he said. "I was going to tell you about it last night, but well, I got distracted."

"What?"

"Sera mentioned it during our game. She'd been updating the financial-aid department's site and noticed a new job listing had been posted. She said she would've applied herself if she didn't already have the job there."

"Oh?"

"Yeah. I don't remember the actual job title, but it was off campus—some local science company or something—and it sounded a bit like what you're doing now, only without the frat rats. Flexible hours, supposedly. You should check it out. Maybe see if you can switch."

"Huh. Maybe I will." She brightened, seeing a bit of hope on the horizon. "Thanks." Then the rhythm of his hand made her forget everything else.

The new job indeed looked great. It offered more pay than she'd get on campus, not to mention resume fodder and a possible work-visa anchor for when she graduated in spring. Much as she missed her family and culture, she found Londonderry deadly boring compared to Seattle—she had no intention of leaving just yet. But the job wasn't anything to do with managing security. As far as she could tell, that position was held by the tall, uniformed man who stood beside her in the lobby.

After checking her in for her appointment, he handed her a screen, on which was an extensive NDA form—longer than any she'd ever seen before—and a thumbprint scanner.

She took the device and scanned paragraph after paragraph of frankly worrisome statements about penalties for disclosure and such: jail time, deportation, and other frightening things. Then she frowned at him. "I thought this was just an interview?"

"It is, Ms. Miller." He smiled kindly. "However, we're dealing with some highly classified data here. In order to properly assess your abilities, we'll need to show you exactly what it is you'd be working on, and we can't have that information get out."

"Right. Fair enough, then." She slid her thumb over the scanner and handed the screen back. "Lead me to the secret UFO research lab!"

The security officer chuckled. "We'll stop by there on the way back."

"What?" She expected him to wink or smirk or in some other way say he'd gotten her joke. He didn't. "Oh, shit," she muttered under her breath and followed him down the corridor.

"Well, first of all," she said matter-of-factly as she poked around on the monitoring system, "your visual displays are about three sizes too small. If you want proper ground-level detail, you'll need some hardcore full-size vid windows for the 2D stuff and projectors for a 3D holo—oh, I can render this map in proper 3D, too, as long as the base data is in a portable format. Also, you'll need live real-time satellite links and some camera drones, preferably something better and faster than the creaky old things you're using for security. Might want to equip them with spectral scanners and some light weapons if you expect to deal with anything dangerous. I can build those if you need them—"

"Uh, Leung?" Alex, the cute young physicist with whom she'd been interviewing, turned to the tiny woman next to him. "I want her. Now."

She had to bite back a crass remark. Instead, she just beamed at him. "Whatever you need me for, Mr. Maloney, I'm all yours."

* * *

Whatever pay rate Leung had set for their new remote-ops coordinator, Alex thought, it wasn't nearly enough. She'd already saved them a lot of time and effort on the first two events she'd helped them manage, and now she was alerting them to a tessera about to close.

"Signal strength is at 60%, Alex," she reported, her delightful accent echoing in his ear. "Might want to get your drone outta the hole soon."

"Thanks, Bridget." He sighed in relief. "You're an angel."

She laughed heartily. "That's me! I'm your guardian angel, keeping an eye on you from the sky."

Sasha came up next to him, flicking sweat-dampened hair from her eyes. "Well, Angel," she teased, "I think that's the last of those lizards, too." The creatures in question, the last of which were scurrying through the tessera, were reptiles about the size of cats, with thick, gray skin patterned like the rocky surface of their planet. They were herbivores, as far as Sasha had been able to tell, and intensely curious if scared of the big humans they had run into. At least that fear made it easy to herd them back home.

"Looks like it, yeah," the mission-control operator

confirmed. "I'm not seeing any other blips on the thermal scan. At least other than the humans. Looks like the civilians are getting testy, though. There's a big active clot of them over by the east perimeter. Might want to send another couple of folks over there to run interference."

"On it. Thanks, Bridget." Jay confirmed.

"Actually, call me Angel," she said with a laugh. "I kind of like the name. Makes me feel all-powerful and stuff."

He returned the laugh. "Angel it is, then!" He gestured to a couple of his teammates. "You heard her. East!" He trotted off that direction, his squad following.

The call itself had been relatively pedestrian—the xenos were no real threat, and their planet was downright boring. Alex hadn't even bothered sending his drones in more than a hundred meters past the tessera's opening because all he could see on the video feed was miles upon miles of salt flats, dotted with a few succulents. The one complication of this event was its location on Earth: smack in the middle of a corn maze on a pumpkin farm in Skagit County. On the Saturday before Halloween, the place was packed. Getting the site clear without spilling the secret had been a nightmare, with confused children begging their parents to explain why they couldn't play, and the adults, already frazzled just from being parents, demanding to know exactly what was going on. The farm's owner, who looked like a kindly granny but swore like a gamer on a frag run, was none too happy at having her revenue stream interrupted by a bunch of strange, armed people saying they were from the government. Alex was starting to wonder whether they needed a proper media liaison to handle the public in situations like this. Jay and his team were able to do some of that wrangling, but it was never easy or smooth.

At least the event was nearing its end, with the xenos all back home and the tessera itself about to close. Alex was more than ready to go home and finish the movie he'd been watching when the call came in. He considered stopping to buy a pumpkin to take home. His mother's religion never allowed for a celebration of the "demonic" holiday, and now that he was an adult, he loved getting into every last bit of it.

"Want to go hit up the pumpkin patch when we're done?" he asked Sasha. She hadn't let on in so many words, but her behavior this week seemed to suggest she'd started seeing someone—and not Jay, as far as he knew. Rather than cool his ridiculous crush on her, the possibility that she was now with someone else had only lit a fire under him, much to his frustration. He couldn't help wanting to take every chance possible to be near her outside work duties.

She knelt on the ground, putting her equipment back into her pack, but looked up at the question. "What?"

"Pumpkins. Want to pick a couple on the way out?"

"Oh! Well . . ."

Jay strode up behind them, holstering his stun gun and tipping back his HUD visor. "Did I hear mention of pumpkins?"

Alex shot him a look, which Jay seemed entirely to miss.

Sasha smiled and stood up. "Yeah. Alex was saying we should go get a few. I like the idea. Maybe we could get a couple of small ones for your reception desk or something. I'm pretty handy at carving them, too. One good thing about growing up in the Midwest—they take their holidays seriously."

Jay grinned. "We had fun with it when I was living in Hawai'i, too, though my uncle always had us kids carving pineapples and oranges instead. The whole front lanai would always smell like an overripe fruit stand by the end of it. I remember one year—DOWN!"

"What the hell?" Alex shouted as Jay's big hand pushed hard on his head, forcing him to the ground. Sasha, also shoved down, crouched next to him. Skittering along the ground—and over their prone bodies—was a herd of the lizards, a dozen strong, each making a sharp, high-pitched noise that Alex assumed was probably a distress call. A split second later, he saw—or, rather, heard—the reason why.

An echoing, unearthly screech split the crisp, fall air. Like the call of a hunting hawk, only with the volume of an air-raid siren, it hurt Alex's ears, and he clamped his hands over them to muffle the sound. A gust of wind and the slap of huge wings made him crane his neck around, trying to see. A shadow passed over him—over all of them—and then so did the creature casting it. With a wingspan topping three meters, and a tip-to-tail length about half again that measure, the xeno was easily the largest living thing that had flown through the Earth's air since the Cretaceous Era. In form, the creature looked something like a stingray, but it was covered with bright red feathers and had a dagger-like beak.

Jay, quick on his feet, had already drawn his weapon and fired a couple of bursts at the creature, but the stun bolts, calibrated for the smaller creatures they'd been herding, had little effect. It quickly soared out of range over the tops of the cornstalks, eyes tracking its prey as they scurried for cover.

"Incoming!" he barked, directing his team as he rushed through the maze trying to get back into range. "Do whatever you have to do! Keep that thing away from the civilians!" A few more staticky bursts sounded, marking the rest of the team's stun attempts, along with a growing cacophony of shouts and screams from the people on the edge of the field.

Sasha scrambled to her feet and ran after him. "We need to herd its prey back to the tessera! It will follow them! Find them!"

Angel, her voice tight with worry, spoke over their coms. "They're scattered, Sasha. They've gone everywhere. All over the field."

The flying creature squalled again, as if angry and

confused at where it was and why its prey were suddenly so much harder to find than on the flat, naked terrain of its home world. Wheeling, it changed direction, heading instead for the crowd.

"No!" Sasha screamed. "It's looking for new prey—it's going for the kids! Get it out of there! Someone bring it down!" More stun bursts echoed, to little effect.

The screams of the terrified children made Alex want to vomit. He looked around, trying to figure out what he could do to help. Out of the corner of his eye, he saw movement. Crouching behind the bag Sasha had dropped was one of the lizards.

"I'm sorry, dude," He whispered. Sneaking up on the creature was easy—its eyes were fixed on the sky. He snatched it up and thrust his hand in the air, waving the screeching lizard."Birdy! Come get your dinner!"

Hearing the distress call of its prey, the bird turned back and dove, aiming for Alex.

"Shit!" Angel moaned. "The tessera's closing! Get it back in, guys! Go! Go! Go!"

The bird was now so close, Alex was certain he could count every feather on its belly. He saw that the sharp beak had a jagged, sawtooth edge. He wondered for a second whether he might lose his hand when the bird tried to snatch its meal from his grip, but he didn't care. Losing a hand would be better than losing someone's toddler. The head lowered, and the beak opened. With a rush of embarrassment, he felt his bladder let go.

A sharp, echoing crack rang out, and Alex was suddenly drenched over more of his body than just his pants. For a second, he thought the blood raining down on him was his own, and he nearly passed out. But then he realized that he could still feel the lizard squirming and biting at his hand. A mighty thump rattled the ground just behind him. He turned. The bird was a wreck of feathers and flesh, and its blood flooded the ground with an almost purplish river. Just beyond the heaving, dying creature, the door to its home world faded and closed.

Alex lost his grip on the lizard, and it bounced down to the ground, to scurry away again. He sat down hard, himself, and looked up at the human who drawing near.

The farmer, her round cheeks crimson and her frizzy gray hair flying around her head, stalked up, holding an enormous rifle. Behind her, Jay, Sasha, and the rest of the team hurried to the scene.

Alex stared at the farmer, bewildered. "What . . . ?"

"My best friend," she said, waving the gun as if it were the most normal thing in the world. "Mom fought in Afghanistan. Brought this home when she left the Marines. Said it would help us keep coyotes and cougars off the farm. Never thought I'd be using it on something like that, whatever the fuck it is. What is it, anyway?"

"Honestly, I have no idea." He was beyond caring about keeping the tessera.

"Guys, the lizards are still everywhere," Sasha noted, her voice hoarse. "We should round them up and take them back to XenoNet so they don't upset our ecosystem."

Jay nodded. "Right. Herding duty!" he called out to his team, and with guidance from Angel, they began looking for the creatures.

Alex looked over his shoulder to the now-dead creature. "What should we do with this one?"

Sasha shrugged. "Well, we'll need to get it back to campus, too. We'll want to study the corpse if we can. I don't know how we're going to get it there, though. It's huge, and all we have is the team's hover."

The farmer laughed, then coughed and wiped her mouth on her sleeve. "Well, I do have a truck."

* * *

Jay grunted and gave a strong shove, and the corpse finally rolled off the truck bed and onto the cart, which was cobbled together from a forklift drone and a discarded piece of shielding from the engineering lab. "Finally! Damn, you're heavy, birdy." He made a face and brushed some dirt and feathers from his uniform.

"Thanks, guys. We can take the body from here." Sasha waved at Jay and Alex as she headed into the building with the rest of the bio team to find space in the xeno lab for the creature's corpse. Leung had met them at the loading dock and quickly spirited the farmer to her office for a debriefing. The rest of the team began filing down the hall toward the locker room.

"Can't wait to get out of this. I feel absolutely gross." Alex, covered in the creature's blood and faintly reeking, made a face and shuddered. "Wish I had a proper change of clothes. Gonna have to see if someone else has something I can borrow for the rest of the day." He began shuffling off after the others.

Jay stayed behind, gulping fresh air while he could. Now that the chaos was over, the adrenaline had faded, and he was shivering.

"Jay? You coming?" Alex called.

"Yeah. Be right there." He tried to hide it, but his voice trembled.

Alex frowned at him, then headed back over. "Are you all right? You look pale. Hope the smell—" he gestured at himself "—isn't making you queasy."

Jay laughed nervously. In truth, Alex did smell, but he didn't care about that. What did bother him was the blood, alien though it was, and the fact that his friend had risked serious injury or worse to try to distract the creature. His head swam, and echoes of losing other friends to catastrophe pounded his brain. "Nah. I'm fine."

Alex's eyes narrowed. "You're not." His gaze flicked down to Jay's forearm.

He followed the glance. He'd have known it anyway, just by how he felt, but the red glow under his skin confirmed it. He had been so confident of late in being able to handle the tessera events without a fuss that he had put off getting his med implant refilled. The stress of today's event had drained the last of the device's reserve, and now he was dealing with the consequences. His head started to swim, and his knees buckled.

"Jay!" Alex caught his arm and guided him as he sat down hard on the edge of the dock. He crouched down, hands on either side of Jay's head and worried eyes scanning his face. "You still awake? Do I need to get some medical help?"

Jay shook his head and tried to breathe deeply and evenly. "No. I'll be OK in a few minutes. Can you—can you stay with me, though?"

"Of course. If you don't mind the smell." Alex smiled and sat down beside him.

Jay chuckled. "I can live with it." Emotion surged in his chest, his nose burned, and his eyes welled up. He wasn't the sort of person who believed tears made a man weak, but all the same, he didn't want Alex to see him cry. He blinked, but that didn't help.

"It's OK," Alex said softly. He draped one arm around Jay's shoulder and took his hand.

The flood started, and Jay sobbed wordlessly for a few moments. Finally, he began to calm, and he stared down at their linked hands. Alex's was covered in tiny, shallow bite marks from where the lizard had struggled to get out of his grip. "I'm supposed to keep you safe," he said, almost to himself.

"You're supposed to keep the *public* safe," Alex countered. "You did that. I'm glad to have you around watching my back, too, but your first job—our job—is to protect the public from whatever might come through those tesserae. With all those little kids around, I should've been the least of your concerns."

Jay nodded. "I know. I did the right thing. I made the right decision. I just wish I could've been a hundred different places at once."

"Well, I'm sure we all wish that." Alex cocked an eyebrow. "Pity cloning's illegal."

Jay smiled wanly, then sobered. "Do you still trust me? I mean, do you still think I'm capable of managing crisis events?"

"Are you kidding? You did fine. No one can manage everything, especially not a surprise situation like that. Don't feel bad. Everyone lived. Well, except the xeno, and I think even Sasha will forgive that." He squeezed Jay's hand. "You're a hell of a soldier. I can't think of anyone else I'd want keeping me safe in the field. Truly."

"Thank you, Alex. That means an awful lot." After a deep breath, he felt his heartbeat finally starting to return to normal. "I think I'm good, now. Thanks for sitting with me."

"Of course."

Jay wrinkled his nose. "You do smell, though."

"Oh, my, yes!" Alex rolled his eyes and stood up. He held out a hand and helped Jay up. "C'mon. I think we could both do with a shower."

* * *

Sasha stifled a yawn. She was exhausted from yesterday's adventurous call—and a rather fun night afterward—and couldn't understand why Leung would want the team in so early this morning. She tipped back in her chair and fiddled with her band, thumbing through a couple of pics João had sent her. Work had kept her busy, but over the few weeks they'd been seeing each other, they'd still managed to warm the bed in his apartment enough times that she was a bit sore now. Not that she cared. In the latest pic he sent, he was shirtless. Tucking her arm under the table to hide the display, she stared down and lost herself in a recent memory.

Just after eight, Leung strode into the conference room, trailed by a young man in a sharply tailored suit. Sasha looked up and found herself jerking to a straighter position. The man wasn't her type—and her attention was certainly focused elsewhere these days—but she could see how others might think him stunning. Alex, in particular, seemed to notice, dropping his band on the table with a clatter and staring with an entirely unsubtle expression of awe. Tall and blond, like a Norse god come down from Asgard, the new arrival had broad shoulders, huge gray eyes, and a wide, professional smile with a slight hint of mischief to it. His silky hair was shoulder-length and styled to look far more casual than it actually was. He radiated strength and poise, almost out of place in the room full of disheveled science nerds. He wore a government-issue band that displayed a department logo Sasha couldn't recognize from where she sat.

"Good morning, everyone," Leung began. "Allow me to introduce the newest member of our team: Remy Bédard. He's been assigned to XenoNet by Homeland Security. Even though we've determined, as best we can, that the xenos who sent the ship that came through the Bay tessera aren't hostile, and haven't even seen another opening of that one, after our disaster in Burlington, the government has decided we at least need a liaison— someone with the authority to scramble other forces if needed. He will also be helping us to coordinate our public responses. After consulting with my government and military contacts, we have decided XenoNet should come clean about the tesserae—not that we could have hidden them now, anyway, with all the vid civilians got yesterday. Managing public expectations is beyond most of us, though, so I'm glad we'll now have help on that count. Remy can tell us more about how that will work, so I'll give the floor to him." She stepped aside.

"Good morning, and I'm pleased to meet you all," the man said warmly, with a Southern accent of a flavor Sasha couldn't quite place. "I hope my presence here won't be obtrusive. I don't want to get in the way of any of the work that you do. I'm here largely as an observer, to keep Homeland apprised of any potential threats so extra help will be fast and easy to get if needed. I will also be gathering data on the tesserae that we can use to compile a heavily filtered public database. People will want to know what they might be facing if a tessera opens near them, so we need to be honest, but we also don't want to give them any details they don't need to know. My plan is to use a color-coded system: red for high-threat xenos, green for low-risk, gray for unpopulated locations, and so on. Several people in counterparts to my position will be stationed at other tessera locations around the globe so that foreign powers can manage things as needed. If you'll direct your attention to the vid window behind me, I have a little presentation on how I'll be integrating into the team, and how your post-event reporting procedures will change." His gaze lit on Alex, and his smile seemed to brighten. "Please feel free to ask me any questions as we go along."

Alex sat up sharply and gazed in rapt attention. Sasha chuckled quietly. He probably had plenty of questions for Remy that had nothing to do with work.

"So, what did you think of him?" Sasha asked as they filed out of the conference room and down the hall.

"Seems competent enough," Jay said. "And I admit I'm glad that Homeland is finally entirely on board. I like knowing that we could have some sort of backup if things go completely awry. Coordinating a military response without a direct government liaison would be a major headache."

"I agree," Sasha said. "I've been furious that the government hasn't been taking this seriously before now. I also like that he has some background in science—not just a form filer or PR flack, at least."

Alex smiled languidly. "I think he's wonderful. He'll be a great addition to the team."

Angel shrugged and made a noncommittal noise. "I got

a weird vibe from him. Maybe it's just the suit. I'm used to working around more-casual people."

Alex's nose wrinkled. "Yeah, the suit does feel a little out of place around here. It's all part of the job, I'm sure, though. I like him. He has a great sense of humor."

Angel read him as easily as Sasha had. "Humor. Yeah. That's definitely the first thing I'd have noticed if I were you."

"Hey!"

"Just teasing." She grinned and nudged him with an elbow. "Not that it matters, since we're working with him, not dating him."

"True." Alex sighed heavily. "We should probably get to know him, though. He's going to want to be involved in every tessera event from here on out."

TRUST

"Please be negative," Sasha begged the small device in her hand as it performed its test. She was three weeks overdue, when her body was usually more regular than an atomic clock. Worse, she couldn't think of which of her recent flings could have caused her current predicament. The week-long homecoming festival had been a blur of fun that had included a roll with one of the guys in her dorm whose name she didn't even know.

She'd had a couple of experiences in high school, but things kicked off once she'd got to college. With a whole new set of guys, many of whom, unlike the high school boys, didn't see her brown skin as either a point against her or a fetish, she had let loose. She felt no shame in her giddy pursuit of pleasure; her Grandpa Joey had made sure to tell her to ignore any messages that might make her feel differently. However, she knew she had been reckless as she went about feeding the needs of her hormones, and it seemed to be coming back to bite her now.

Her tube blockers, implanted two days after her sixteenth birthday, when she could legally consent to them, were still working, according to their status display on her com. However, it wasn't unknown for the tiny devices to dislodge or otherwise fail without sending a warning signal. Doctors recommended having them properly *scanned and serviced as needed every year—something she had neglected to do since the appointment reminder two months ago. The thought that missing that tune-up may have changed her life forever made her queasy. Or maybe that was morning sickness, she considered wildly.*

Exactly what she would do if the test came out positive, she wasn't sure. Theoretically she was open to termination or adoption, however weird and emotionally challenging both might be, but the idea of parenting sent her into a panic. She wasn't even certain she ever wanted to be a parent at all. She absolutely adored baby animals and loved the chance to care for them when she could. Baby humans, however, scared her half to death. The last thing she wanted was to have to quit school and go back to Iowa, to attempt to raise a child alone. She had fought too hard to get out of that stuffy little town and finally make her own path in life. Being set back by a malfunctioning microcontraceptive bot would be horrible.

The device beeped, and her band's screen lit up with the result: negative. She fell back on her bed and laughed until she cried.

João had confirmed, in response to her finally just bluntly asking, that the child whose picture she'd seen their first night was his. The girl lived with her mother in Portland, he said, and he offered to introduce them sometime when she came up to visit him, rather than him going down to see her. The idea of being introduced as "Papa's girlfriend" did freak Sasha out somewhat, and she didn't even want to consider what it might mean eventually to be thought of as someone's stepmother, but she was trying to get past that. In any case, the sex alone had been fantastic, which was flooding the rest of her brain in fun chemicals and thus making her less concerned about the remote possibility of someday playing parent.

Instead, her caretaking instincts had focused on the creatures she'd been researching in her spare time between tessera events. In particular, she'd been working with Littlefoot whenever she had the chance. She still felt the tight bond with him, and he always seemed to be brighter and even healthier when they'd spent more time together. His enclosure had been moved into her office, to make room for the work the bio team had been doing with the other creatures, including the corpse of the large winged predator, and she enjoyed having more of a chance to see him regularly.

"How's he doing today?"

Sasha turned. In her doorway stood Angel, a bright smile on her rosy face and a hand on her generous hip. Today, her riot of shiny curls was pastel blue. She nodded at Littlefoot's enclosure. Since the young student had been hired, the two had become fast friends, and had Sasha not been so distracted by her deepening fling with her capoeira master, she'd have loved to spend more time getting to know the girl with the quick wit and sharp mind. Her appearance in Sasha's office was not unwelcome.

"He's great! You haven't gotten a chance to meet him properly, have you?" She stepped aside so her co-worker could come closer.

"Nope. Not since that first day when I did the big tour and saw him in the lab. Just been too busy. Glad we're having a quiet day so far."

"No kidding!" Sasha agreed. It had been almost 48 hours since the last event, and she was grateful for the downtime. Much as she got a thrill from the exciting missions, she hadn't signed on for such adventures when she took the internship. Being back in her own office, looking through data on the myriad creatures that were housed there, was far more satisfying.

"I hope we don't get any events at all today, not with Alex being unavailable." Angel sidled up to the enclosure and crouched down, smiling at Littlefoot as he rubbed his face on the glass to greet her.

"True. Though I suspect he would probably rather be out on an event than being stuck in that meeting." Sasha was glad *she* hadn't been called into it. Once the information about the tesserae had gone public, Kristov

Belenko had blown a fuse, firing off all sorts of messages and threats to Leung, demanding his company be included in the project. She'd rebuffed him so far, but last week, he'd managed to get some of his government friends convinced to at least hold a meeting with the military and several government agencies, plus other companies in related fields, to lobby for sharing more information and resources, rather than allowing XenoNet to take all the responsibility—and potential profit—of managing the tesserae openings. Leung hadn't called all of her close staff to the meeting, to Sasha's relief, but poor Alex, as well as Remy and a few reps from the physics and bio teams, were currently on their way to a conference room in the Federal building downtown.

"Did you see him this morning before they left?"

Sasha shook her head.

Angel smirked. "It was so funny: He was in a suit. Borrowed it from Jens. It really doesn't fit him, so he looks like a little kid playing dress-up."

Sasha laughed. As much as she liked Alex and considered him a friend, not to mention had immense respect for his intelligence and quick thinking in the field, she did have to admit that sometimes he looked—and acted—young for his age. His usual uniform of vintage T-shirts, sagging jeans, and cardigans made him look more like a bewildered college freshman than a brilliant young man who like she, had recently been awarded his master's. He even seemed younger than Angel herself at times. "I wish I could've seen that. Maybe I'll get to when they come back."

"Any chance I could hold him?" Angel asked, looking up.

"Huh?"

The younger woman laughed. "Sorry. I meant Littlefoot, not Alex."

"Oh!" Sasha joined the giggling. "Right. Of course." Turning, she cleaned her hands and indicated that Angel should clean hers, then opened the top of the enclosure. The team had discovered that the small xeno did just fine with short exposures to Earth's levels of atmospheric gases and slightly colder temperatures, so Sasha took him out to cuddle him when she could. He was friendly with nearly every human he encountered, so long as they didn't make loud or aggressive sounds around him, and seemed to like the attention. Sasha had been surprised by this at first—small creatures were usually afraid of bigger ones, even if they were, as Littlefoot was, near the top of their local food chain. Eventually, the team determined that as the creatures were very social animals in their natural environment, in the absence of more of his kind, Littlefoot had decided humans made a decent proxy. Even though they had seen hundreds more xenos since the tessera events started happening, this one, brought here across a great distance the long way, still served as the team's mascot.

There had been some talk about returning their mascot to his home world, if a tessera to it ever opened, but as of yet, one had not been found. Sasha was secretly glad. As a scientist, she understood the ethical and environmental issues involved with taking creatures out of their habitats for study, but she also understood the importance of being able to study "ambassador" creatures. Although zoos and aquaria were significantly different from how they had been a generation ago, they still served a useful purpose in providing sanctuary for injured animals and captive-breeding programs for endangered ones. Genetic work had even brought a few animals back from extinction, thanks to similar-species gestational carriers; for example, black rhinos now once again roamed the plains of Namibia. Being able to help nonhuman creatures survive and thrive was her life's calling.

More than that, however, she enjoyed getting to know the creatures she worked with, even those of extraterrestrial origin. In addition to Littlefoot, she had bonded with Jack and Kate, the hairless, pouched creatures that had been stranded from another event. Their species apparently very prolific, the pair had already gone on to produce another litter of pups in their time at the center, and the team developing the human-analog pouch technology were delighted to be working with the second batch of new arrivals. Seeing the cute, squirmy little creatures—born with glossy, bright-orange hair, which fell out as they grew older—almost made her broody for a human child. But not quite. For now, Littlefoot was child enough for her.

Working carefully, she drew him out, responding to his chin-rubbing greeting with a few pats, and then handed him to Angel.

"Oh, he's so warm!" she exclaimed as she took him. "I didn't expect that."

Sasha nodded. "He kind of looks like Earth reptiles— his head features definitely resemble a chameleon—but he's actually a mammal. His home environment is much warmer, though, and so is he."

"Wow. It's like petting the world's cutest heating pad." Angel grinned down at the creature. He curled his scaly tail around her hand and chirruped softly. "I should kidnap you and take you home to lie on my lap next time I have cramps."

Sasha snorted a laugh. She'd considered the same thing a time or two herself, including this morning. Not that the arrival of her cycle was unwelcome, given all the sex she'd been having.

Angel looked up. "He's getting even warmer, now. Is that normal?"

Sasha nodded. "The more he relaxes, the warmer he gets. He also starts changing color a bit." She pointed to an area near his snout. The scales there had shifted from their usual dull blue to a much brighter, slightly greenish shade. "When he's truly blissed out, he goes full-on turquoise all over. It's gorgeous."

"Neat!" Angel stroked him a few more times, then put him back in his little home. "I admit, I'm more at home with circuit boards and code than I am with squishy things, but I like this fella."

"Me, too. Wish I had more time to spend with him."

"Sasha?" Jay rapped on the door and poked his head in. She turned. "Yeah?"

"Just heard from Leung. The government people apparently want the rest of us to sit in on the meeting in a conference Stream."

"Terrific," she muttered, her mood instantly darker.

Angel groaned. "I'll go set it up." She hurried down the hall toward the command center, trailed by Jay.

Sasha finished sealing Littlefoot's enclosure and patted the side in farewell. Grabbing her bag, hoping she at least had a hairbrush in there so she wouldn't look on the video feed like the disheveled scientist she actually was, she followed the other two.

Not halfway down the hall, however, she was saved. Her band buzzed and began emitting its tessera-opening alarm. Angel stopped and glanced down at the display on her own device, which showed a tiny 2-D version of the monitoring map. She turned, looking back at Sasha and Jay. "Kingston!" she announced. "Best go take care of the beasties before they chomp all the wildlife."

Sasha almost cheered in relief. Facing carnivorous deer was a far better prospect than facing a room full of soldiers, suits, and obnoxious trillionaires.

* * *

Alex fidgeted. The borrowed suit he wore didn't fit him at all, and he felt nearly strangled by the tie. Still, he would have felt woefully underdressed had he worn his usual clothes, as the conference room in the Federal building was filled with a large assortment of people in business attire and a few in formal military dress.

Next to him, Leung noticed his discomfort. "Relax," she said gently, patting his arm. "I'm going to do most of the talking. You just need to explain your research if they ask."

"I know. I'll be fine." He tried to sound confident, but he didn't feel it. In addition to worrying about stumbling over his words in front of a government committee, he also didn't want to look like a fool in front of Remy. That man, however, seemed perfectly relaxed. He chatted amiably with a colleague from Homeland and greeted each new arrival by name. Every now and then he'd flash a look back at Alex and favor him with a charming, almost teasing smile, and every time that happened, Alex felt himself squirming far more than the suit or nerves could account for.

Then his concern with both the suit and Remy evaporated. Sweeping into the room like a gust of hot air and trailed by an assortment of assistants was Kristov Belenko. A few years older than Leung, the tycoon had had plenty of work done to make himself look not much older than mid-fifties, but his permanent scowl offset any physical attractiveness his features may have had. His dress sense was as loud as he was. His white suit was embedded with small fiber-optic and LED highlights that gleamed bright blue and red as he walked, making him look, Alex thought with a quiet snigger, like a human police car.

"Thompson!" Belenko boomed, greeting the nearest Army official: a major with a stiff, sour look and silver hair pulled into a bun so tight it looked glued in place.

"Belenko!" The major smiled—her first since arriving—and gave him a hearty handshake. "Good to see you here. I'm sure what we're discussing today will be interesting to you."

"Oh, I have no doubt," he said. "I only wish I'd been told about it sooner since this is an area of prime concern for me and my company."

Leung stood up and cleared her throat, and Belenko

seemed finally to notice her. "Jan," he said curtly.

"Kris." She nodded. "I didn't know you'd be here."

He smirked. "Well, I could have sat in on the conference Stream or just read a report, but I figured it'd be better to be here in person. I'm sure I'll have plenty of questions about this little project you've been hiding from me, and it's harder for you to ignore them if they're not just a line of text."

"Indeed." Her voice was tight, and Alex noticed that she was trembling almost imperceptibly. He began to wonder whether she might need more reassurance from him than the other way around.

To his relief, the meeting was fast and far smoother than he had feared, though he kept sneaking glances at his band, keeping up with what the away team was doing on the event that had come up in the middle of the meeting. Belenko was, as expected, an ass about having been kept in the dark about the tesserae, but he shut up quickly after a dressing-down from Remy about the necessity of keeping the events quiet so as not to spook the public. Alex's opinion of the Homeland agent, already high, spiked sharply. The rest of the time was boring, however. It was mostly a lot of dry explanation of the physics behind the phenomenon and their plans for keeping the public informed while also not causing a panic. It was enough of a repeat of the meeting they had with Remy that Alex found himself spending more time staring at the Homeland agent's mouth than listening to what came out of it. As they left the building, he felt almost cheerful.

Eyeing the spring in his step, Leung chuckled as they strolled back to the elevator. "You survived!"

"So did you," Alex teased.

She rolled her eyes and snorted. "Belenko is a blustering fool and an unapologetic narcissist, but he backs down nicely when a bigger dog barks at him." She nodded at Remy, who was a few steps ahead of them, deep in conversation with his colleague. "I'm impressed with that one. Looks like he's just the person we need on our side to help us keep Belenko from making a mess of this."

Alex beamed. "I completely agree."

* * *

Jay was so used to working closely with Alex most days that not having him on the event call made the whole thing feel incomplete. Alex's replacement, Shilo from the beta team, was a perfectly capable, amiable guy, but it wasn't the same. So he was delighted that Alex invited him and Sasha to join the rest of the meeting group for celebratory dim sum at a cheesy hole-in-the-wall downtown. Angel had been invited along, too, but begged off, noting that she was way behind on a class project.

When they arrived, Jay saw that Leung and some of the rest of upper management gathered around the table in one large booth. Alex and Remy filled one side of its neighbor.

"There they are!" Alex cried as he spied Jay and Sasha. He stood up and waved them over. After quickly greeting Leung and the others, the pair strolled up to Alex and Remy's table. Alex switched to the other side of the booth and patted the seat next to him for Sasha. Jay tried not to roll his eyes.

"Hey!" Sasha threw an arm around Alex's shoulders for a quick hug as she sat down. "Looks like you survived it. Nice suit, by the way." She winked.

Alex flushed and fidgeted with the tie.

Jay sidled in next to Remy. "Angel told us how the meeting went. Looks like you did well." He nodded and smiled at his seatmate.

Remy returned the smile. "Thanks! Glad I could shut that windbag up. I go where Homeland tells me, of course, but I admit I'm relieved I don't have to work with him. He makes my skin crawl."

Sasha shuddered. "Mine, too, and I didn't even have to

be in the same room with him."

"Be grateful," Alex said, looking nauseated. "I'm definitely glad Remy's on our side, though. I thought the whole building was going to go up in flames. I don't think Belenko's used to someone being so defiant with him."

Remy grinned. "Eh. He doesn't scare me. My mother's a judge, and I used to work for the DOJ. I have a lot of experience with people who think they're above the law."

"DOJ?" Alex looked impressed. "How did you end up working for Homeland? You said you're originally from Louisiana, I think?"

Remy nodded. "A little town outside Lafayette. Acadian country. I was born there and lived in the area until I was 10. My mother was a lawyer then, but she wanted to work her way toward a federal judge position, plus my dad was tired of the hurricanes, so we packed up and moved to Maryland. I've been around government types most of my life. Bouncing around different agencies just seemed like the thing to do. Been settled at Homeland for a while now, though."

"You have a science background too, right?" Sasha asked.

"Sort of. That's my father's thing. He's into biotech, though from an administrative side. Manages the R&D division for a bionic prosthetics company in Annapolis, now."

The server came by with a cart full of food, and they snagged several plates. Once he'd devoured a couple of buns, Jay continued the grilling of their new teammate. "How are you finding Seattle? Ever been out here before?"

Remy sipped from his bottle of Tsing Tao and nodded. "Once. Before the quake. My mother had a college friend who moved to Redmond, so we visited when I was young. I don't remember a lot, I'm afraid, but I do remember the city looked very different."

Jay nodded. "I remember it, too. I was born in Hawai'i, but we split our time between here and my mom's family's place when I was young and my dad was still working for Boeing. We were in Kaua'i when the quake hit. We lost our condo, and my dad lost some friends and co-workers, but we were otherwise lucky. My sister was a lot more upset about it than I was. She was already in grade school then, and she lost a couple of friends."

"I was just a toddler in Boston that year," Alex said. "When I heard about it later, though, the quake inspired me to get into geophysics."

Remy looked at Sasha. "What about you? I think I remember reading in my briefing that you were born here, yes?"

Jay suddenly noticed that their tablemate had gone quiet during the conversation. "Sasha?" he asked gently.

She smiled sadly. "Yeah. I'm from here." She said no more.

Remy seemed to be oblivious, downing more of his beer, but Jay and Alex exchanged a quick look, and the latter scooted closer to Sasha. For once, Jay didn't mind, and he wished he was sitting closely enough to have helped comfort her, too. Instead, he changed the subject. "Hey, dumplings!" he noted brightly as a cart came by again.

* * *

Sasha closed her eyes. João's hands on her body always felt good, but tonight was exceptional. Every touch, every kiss made her skin light up, and for a brief, half-lucid moment, she wondered if all her time around the tesserae had somehow messed with her molecules. She laughed.

"What's so funny, *gatinha*?" He'd taken to calling her that lately. Even though it irritated her a bit to be compared to a kitten, it was also kind of cute, so she tolerated the nickname.

"Just a work thing. Nothing big. Keep going!"

He returned to his task, and she soon lost herself in

bliss again. When they were done, she got up to use the toilet, leaving him snoozing on the bed. When she returned, he was entirely asleep—so much so that he didn't budge when the message alert on his band chimed. She glanced at the screen—the profile image was his daughter's. She picked up the device to bring it to him, assuming that he'd want to talk to the girl, but as she did, she couldn't help noticing the message that had been sent: "Mama says she misses you and wants to know if you're coming home for Thanksgiving or if you still have to work."

Sasha froze, and the dumplings from earlier threatened to work their way back up her throat. Heart thumping, she scrolled back on the message chain. Everything she saw confirmed what the latest message seemed to suggest: João wasn't, as he had said, divorced, but merely claiming to his family that he had to stay in Seattle while he got his studio going. Suddenly, his weekends in Portland made far more sense. What didn't make sense, however, was for Sasha to stay. After dressing quickly, she slipped out of the apartment without a sound, but when she was finally at the elevator, the tears kicked in.

SHAWNA WALLS

THANKSGIVING

"How can you give thanks if you go to a house where they don't even say grace?"

Alex groaned in frustration. "Oh, come on, Mom. Nobody thinks of the holiday like that these days. It's just a big excuse to hang out with family and eat a lot. Besides, I'm sure if you asked, Aunt Jenna would say a blessing."

"Please, Mom!" Jonathan's small voice echoed from the living room, where he was playing with a toy guitar in between singing and watching his favorite vid program—something about a mouthy purple bird and his friends. "We haven't seen Aunt Jenna and Uncle Taylor in ages. And I want to meet our new cousins."

"Me, too!" Alex chimed in. His mother's sister had recently given birth to twins, bringing her total up to five. Not that he could ever keep their names straight since all of them started with "K."

Their mother sighed and rubbed her eyes. "My sister is a Franciscan, boys. If I visit her, it'll be like supporting her choice to stray from the true church—not to mention her choice to marry outside the faith. Uncle Taylor isn't even a proper Christian."

"So?" Alex set his jaw. He was growing tired of his mother's increasingly dogmatic obsession with religion, and had recently started defying her on the issue. "So what? He's still a good person, and he's still married to your sister. Doesn't your God care about family?"

149

"MY God?" His mother's eyes flashed in anger. "He is everybody's God, whether they want to worship Him or not. Anyone who doesn't . . ."

It was no use. She was gone again. Alex sat down at the kitchen table, staring at the salt shaker as if it might be a switch to open a portal to somewhere else. He only wished he could take Jonathan with him if it was.

"Aunt Jenna invited me for Thanksgiving this year," the message read. "Mom doesn't want to go, but I'd like to. We had a good time when I visited her this summer. Want to come with? I'm sure she'd like to see you again. Kevin's in college now, but Keith and Kim will be there. Besides, I want to hear more about this job of yours, now that it's in the news!"

Alex's thumb hovered over the keypad. A trip to Boston was, unfortunately, out of the question, what with the frequent tessera events, but he couldn't help wanting to see his brother again. He still felt guilty for missing out on the seminary graduation—and for not being able to explain why he couldn't make it.—and if Jonathan was willing to break with his mother's wishes enough to visit her "sinner" of a sister, perhaps there really was a chance of reclaiming at least some of their once-close relationship. Finally, he started typing. "Can't do T-day—work stuff—but maybe we can have lunch sometime this week? Just us. No Mom." He sent the message, then held his breath.

Just when he thought he might turn blue and pass out, another message popped up. "I'd love to! Burger Village on Tuesday?"

Alex spat out the breath and, with it, a nervous laugh.

The aging restaurant was one of the few buildings that had survived the quake. It had more than just miracle value, however: a Boston location of the franchise had been a family favorite hangout when they were small children. Jonathan had still been young enough that his language skills weren't perfect, and every time he said "burger," it came out like "booger"—excellent joke fodder for Alex, who had been heavily into all things gross. His parents had still been in love back then—or at least seemed to be—and though they rolled their eyes at their sons' increasingly disgusting conversation over greasy, salty fast food, they couldn't hide their giggles, either. It had been a magical time; Alex easily remembered how bright and fun his mother had been, instead of how angry and sad she was now. That his brother wanted to meet here was in itself a bit of hope he decided to hold on to.

He had already ordered and sat down when Jonathan arrived. His traditional priest garb earned a few stares, as it always did. "Alex-o!" he called, waving. "Grabbing a Booty Buster, then I'll be over in a sec!"

Alex nodded a response and tried to soothe his nerves by downing about half of his thick marionberry shake. It gave him brain freeze, however, and he cursed under his breath while the ache passed.

Jonathan finally sat down with a tray carrying a sampler of just about everything the place had to offer. "OK! Haven't come here in ages. Forgot how much I missed their fries." He stuffed three in his mouth.

"Same. I've been so busy lately I've barely been eating at all, but I can't remember the last time I was here. There's another location near work, but it's not the same."

"So, tell me about what's been keeping you busy," Jonathan said around a mouthful of onion rings. "I admit I don't understand what the news was talking about."

Alex finished a bite of burger before he began. "Well, you got the basics, yeah? We discovered a series of physics irregularities that could pose a danger to the public, so we're now managing those locations to try to keep people safe."

"Irregularities how? I heard that there might be aliens involved."

Alex nodded. "In some cases, yes. We call them 'xenos.'

They're organisms that originate somewhere other than Earth—like the creatures the probes brought back—but get here through those irregularities."

Jonathan frowned. "Then we're being invaded?"

"No, it's not like that. It's more like . . . hmmm . . . imagine it like gaps in a garden fence. Most of the time, they're only letting through squirrels and stray cats, but sometimes you get a rabbit or a deer that will come eat your azaleas."

"I saw the vid from that farm up in Skagit, though. That didn't look like a deer. Were you there?"

"Yes." Alex shivered; he could still hear the screech of the enormous avian as it bore down on him. "That particular xeno did pose a threat, and we weren't prepared for it. That's why the company has gone public. We want people to know to avoid some of these sites. Sometimes the tesserae—the irregularities—may be far enough away that we can't get there quickly when they open, so we want to be sure people stay safe. We're in the process of putting up barriers and warning signs to keep everyone out. If anything proves dangerous, we'll have guard drones, electrified fields, and so on to keep any visiting xenos from doing harm. We've also found a few that open up to places with dangerous levels of gasses or radiation, and we're sealing those off entirely, so we don't have, say, a park suddenly flooded with clouds of chlorine."

"Wow." Jonathan sat back, taking a bite of his burger.

"Yeah. Wow." Alex couldn't help a smile. "It's a big deal, and I'm right in the middle of it. It's weird."

"I bet!" his brother laughed. "Not exactly what you expected from an internship, huh?"

"Not exactly! I was expecting a cushy lab gig, not getting . . . well, not this, at least."

"Maybe Mom was right. Maybe you shouldn't be working there."

Alex's hand froze in delivering a fried mushroom to his mouth. "I—"

Jonathan shook his head. "Sorry. Didn't mean to bring that up."

"No, it's OK. I'm curious about how she's taking this, actually. I just haven't gotten up the courage to talk to her." Alex ate the mushroom, but its spicy crunchiness was lost on him.

Jonathan shrugged. "She called me as soon as she heard the news. She asked me to talk to you—to get you to quit the job. She thinks this stuff is God's way of telling us not to mess with the universe, to keep ourselves focused on the life He made for us on Earth. She thinks these— tesserae?—she thinks they're doors to Hell and whatever's coming through them are demons God is sending to punish us."

Alex resisted the urge to roll his eyes. "And what do you think?"

His brother started to speak, but paused and stared out the window. A pair of young siblings, dressed up as if they were about to get family portraits done at the studio next door, were dancing in the rain in the parking lot. Their exasperated mothers were trying to keep them from getting their fancy clothes soaked and muddy, but the kids didn't seem to care. Jonathan smiled at the antics. "I remember us doing that," he said, his voice quiet.

Alex watched them and smiled. "Remember the fight over the Santa pics?"

Jonathan chuckled. "I was so mad at you for pulling off his beard!"

"And then you picked up that—what was it? A giant candy cane?—and tried to smack me with it, but just ended up smacking poor Santa."

"Right! And Mom told us we were never going to get any more presents from him as long as we lived." Jonathan dissolved into laughter.

Alex laughed with him—it felt good to do so—but then he sobered. "I guess she was sort of right. I think that was the last Christmas she allowed any secular stuff."

Jonathan sighed and looked away. "Yeah." He shifted in his seat as silence fell over the table.

Alex picked his next words carefully. "Do you—I know you're a priest and everything now—but do you really believe all the stuff the church teaches? Not necessarily the theology, but all the rest of it?"

Jonathan touched his collar, stroking the white tab in the middle. "My faith in God is as strong as it's ever been. I don't think anything can shake that. But I admit that spending all that time in seminary has shown me some of the human side of the church that I dislike. Some of the older clergy, for instance, are still against gender variance and same-gender relationships. And I disagree with their official policy of not ordaining women. I know some amazing nuns and laywomen in the church who would be great priests, but they're not allowed."

"Have you considered, well, leaving Homecoming and going back to garden-variety Catholic?"

Jonathan bit his lip, then shook his head. "I thought about it once, but no. This is where my career is. I feel called to this church. Mom would never allow me to leave it, anyway."

"Allow it?" Alex grumbled. "Jonathan, we're both grown adults now. What Mom will or won't allow is irrelevant."

His brother's eyes narrowed. "Perhaps in practical terms, but *she* isn't irrelevant. Fourth Commandment, yeah? Whatever I may think of her judgment—and I do sometimes question it—I still honor her, as I honor God."

"So . . . does that mean you honor her belief that I shouldn't be working at XenoNet?"

Jonathan closed his eyes and rubbed them. When he spoke again, his voice was tight. "I honor the belief; I don't entirely share it. I'm worried about you, Alex. I'm primarily worried about your safety—this is a dangerous job you've gotten, and I'm afraid of losing you—but I'm also worried about your soul. I do think XenoNet is treading into territory humans weren't meant to. I don't think these tesserae are portals to Lucifer's living room, no, but I do think God might be angry with us somehow."

"I see." Alex felt suddenly heavy, and he slumped back in the booth. He rubbed his belly, where the burger was now sitting uncomfortably. He could honor different beliefs about the unknowable. He could accept that religion was often as much a matter of culture and tradition as theology, and therefore an important part of a person's life and identity. What he couldn't do was tolerate attempts to interfere with science based on human guesses about what a theoretical deity might want.

"That's not why I wanted to see you, though," Jonathan added hastily. "I really did want to spend some time with you—I've missed you—and I'm sad that you can't come to Aunt Jenna's for Thanksgiving. Where you work is your choice, whatever issues I may have with that choice, and I won't try to take it away from you. All I ask is that you consider maybe sometimes looking to the heavens for something other than stars."

* * *

"I'd love to spend Thanksgiving with your family, but I can't. I have to work." Angel felt a nervous tremor through her belly. Since she'd started work at XenoNet, she'd had next to no free time between the job and classes. Something had to give, and of late, that had been her time with her boyfriend, who was not taking things well. He like everyone else, had now heard of what the company was really doing, and had some idea of her role in it, but she'd not been able to tell him nearly as much as he wanted to know. More than that, however, he had grown resentful of her long hours there. As they sat next to each other in the otherwise-empty electronics lab, working on their joint project for a class, he'd grown increasingly agitated.

"Really?" Dane glared at her, his blue eyes seeming icy

in the pale afternoon sun that streamed through the windows. "They're not even giving you the weekend off?"

She shook her head. "It's not that kind of job. I could take holidays off from campus security because classes weren't in session then. The tesserae don't take breaks, though."

"Don't they have someone else who can do it? They have a night-shift person, right?"

"Yes," she acknowledged. "Some of our response team are also trained on the system. They monitor it when I'm in class."

"So why can't they take over for you? Just for a couple of days?" His voice grew softer and he leaned into her. "Please? I miss you." He slid a hand up her thigh, fingers gently sinking into the soft flesh. He bent his head, his lips skimming over her neck.

For a moment, she forgot herself, nice as the touch was. She honestly couldn't remember the last time they'd had sex, and her body, at least, craved the closeness again. Still, she couldn't help the uncomfortable realization: Life with her XenoNet colleagues was considerably more interesting than the life she'd had before. She still kept up with her classes, and looked forward to graduating the following summer, but her social life seemed to be permanently on hold. Dane wasn't the only one she'd been neglecting; she hadn't even spoken to the rest of their gaming group in weeks. The only people she'd stayed in regular contact with were her family—mostly to reassure them that she wasn't in danger, once they, too, learned about her job. "Maybe," she murmured, her will beginning to slip. "I'll ask."

He nearly cheered. "Thank you!" He began nibbling at her neck in earnest.

Desire overtook her, and for several moments, they kissed and caressed, oblivious to any possibility that someone else might enter the room. On hearing a burst of laughter from the hall, however, Angel sat back up again.

"We should go back to my room," she said breathlessly, peeling his hand away from her breast.

"Of course." He smiled at her and squirmed, trying to adjust himself through his jeans.

"I have to pee first, though," she said. "Can you put our stuff away while I go do that?"

He nodded. "Can do."

She hopped up from the table as he began clearing away the spread of circuit boards and assorted wires. "Be right back!"

On her return, she stopped short in the doorway. Dane sat at the table, holding her band, which she had set aside so its signal wouldn't interfere with their work, and staring down at its screen. A telltale alert sound emitted from the device. "What are you doing?" She rushed over to him, snatching the thing from his hand so roughly she left a scratch on his palm.

"Ow!" He barked at the pain. "What the hell, Bridge?"

"You can't see that!" she cried, her voice cracking with alarm. "You can't see any of it." She hurriedly scrolled through the information on the screen. She relaxed slightly; the tessera was a minor one near Everett; its planet's highest life form was a wormlike creature that never left the slimy, bacteria-rich mud of its home environment. Still, adrenaline was making her shake and her anger remained hot. "Don't ever touch my band. Ever." She scolded Dane.

"Oh come on. What's the big deal? It's not like it's a big secret anymore." He sounded exasperated, and a little hurt. He rubbed at the scratch on his hand.

She wrapped the band back around her wrist and began gathering the rest of her things. "There's still a lot you—everyone—doesn't know. A lot I can't talk about. I'm under NDA and a bunch of secret government shit, too. Do you know I actually had to go through an interview with immigration recently? They wanted to make sure I wasn't selling secrets to terrorists or something. Apparently they hadn't heard that the IRA hasn't been active in half a century."

"I'm sorry. Really." At least he sounded sincere.

She sighed. "And I'm sorry for hurting you. That was an accident. But I still can't have you touching my stuff. I could get in huge trouble for it—I could get deported, for fuck's sake." As she calmed, she began to realize how much she was mostly mad at herself for leaving the device where he could get to it. "Do you understand?"

He nodded. "I do."

She came up to him and took his hand, bringing it to her lips for a gentle kiss on the wound. "I have to go now, but I promise you that when I get back, we can pick up where we left off, OK?"

He grumbled slightly, but murmured assent.

She smiled, and kissed his forehead. "And I will ask them about Thanksgiving, too."

* * *

Jay's legs ached from the dash up the snow-dusted hill to the tessera location. Their third event in as many days, this was a relatively new location, and in a hard-to-reach spot on the top of a cliff near Hood Canal. His annoyance with his lack of conditioning, however, was secondary to what he felt about the rapid-fire questions shot at him from the person accompanying him.

"*Merde!* Are they all like this?" Remy sounded breathless, even less happy about the cold-weather hike. For all his carefully sculpted abs and delts, it was obvious the Homeland agent's buff body was achieved in a gym, not by actually using it for anything. Still, however much the man rubbed him the wrong way—and Jay considered whether it might just be a clash in style—he had to respect him. With the agent's deft handcuffing of Belenko at the government meeting, he had earned his keep. Jay tried to think charitably about the man who was poorly dressed for the weather and kept lagging behind the rest of the team.

He laughed and shook his head. "Nope. Some of them are remote, like this one, but some are in easier locations, even smack in the middle of a parking lot."

"The Belle Square one, yes," Remy said, naming a tessera that had emerged from the side of a Starbucks in the middle of Bellevue. He'd insisted on accompanying the alpha team all this week as they visited each tessera location to set up its warning and defense protocols. He said he wanted to get a better idea of what each location was like so he could easily mobilize government resources as needed. What he seemed to really be doing, however, was flirting with Alex every chance he got, which was beginning to make Jay angry. Logically, he knew that Alex's potential love life was none of his business, but he still couldn't help a small part of his baser self feeling as if Alex were his own territory to protect, and therefore bristling at Remy moving in on it.

Remy suddenly looked worried. "Do we know what sort of xenos are at this location?"

Jay shook his head. "No. The only two times it's opened before, it closed again before anything came through. We'd only just managed to suit up by the time it was gone. This is the longest it's ever been open."

"Still not seeing signs of an incursion," Angel's voice chirped over his earpiece. "Signal strength is still steady, though."

Alex, several meters ahead, had already sent a squadron of tiny drones into the rift. He looked down at his screen, monitoring the video and readings they were sending back. "So far I'm seeing only Earth-standard gravity, gasses, et cetera. No signs of life except flora as yet—wait. Whoa!"

"What?" Sasha dashed over to look at his screen. "Oh, wow! Incoming!" She sprinted toward the tessera.

"Let's go, team!" Jay shouted, calling his security force into scramble mode. He flipped down the visor on his helmet, hoping its HUD would quickly feed him the same data Alex was seeing. The new equipment, military headgear Angel had hacked and repurposed, had already proven useful in the field, though using it felt a lot like training games from his exercises in the Army.

Immediately, he saw what had caused the exclamations from Alex and Sasha. Streaming past the drones and through the tessera were half a dozen of the cutest creatures he had ever seen. Sharing roughly the same size and features of Earth's red pandas, they were a bright, almost metallic emerald green and made noises like a cross between a giggling toddler and a forlorn kitten. He tried to shake off the initial reaction of wanting to go cuddle each of them like some sort of living stuffed toy. More than once, a xeno's outward appearance had proven not to be indicative of its temperament or potential for danger. He still had a welt on his neck from last week's sting from something that looked like a beautiful pink hummingbird. He was only glad it hadn't carried more dangerous venom—and that Sasha and Cordy, their predator expert, hadn't berated his poor judgment more than they had.

Jay poured on the speed to crest the hill, Remy huffing as he tried to keep up.

Fortunately, by the time they got to the site, it seemed that for once, the human instinct of thinking something cuddly-looking was innocuous was right. All seven of the xenos that had come through had not attacked, nor, as most prey creatures did, quickly dashed away from the unfamiliar species and back to safety. Instead, they were chittering excitedly and sniffing the humans they had found, as if they were happy to meet new friends.

"Easy there!" Cordy laughed as one of the creatures began nosing around her pack, perhaps trying to find something edible. "Sasha! Any data on these things yet?"

Sasha stared at the scanner in her gloved hand. Another device built by Angel, it used medical scanning technology coupled with animal-anatomy and biochemistry databases to quickly assess each xeno's likely risk of danger. "No known components of venom or poisons. They're mammals. Not emitting any meat-consumption gases, and they have grinding teeth, not fangs. Likely herbivores or low-chain omnivores. I don't—hey!" One of the xenos nosed the device out of her hand. As she juggled to keep control of it, she stepped on the edge of a gopher hole and fell, scraping her exposed wrist on a stone.

"Sasha, you OK?" Alex called, trying to get past his own crowd of xenos to reach her.

"I'm fine, I just—" The xeno that had upset her balance hovered over her, its eyes traveling across her body and alighting on the injury. It made a small dismayed noise and then began rubbing its face all over Sasha's hand and wrist. She pushed herself back. "No!"

Cordy was immediately there, stunner in hand. "Is it smelling the blood?"

Jay had already trained his stunner on the creature. "Do I need to shoot?"

Sasha's eyes were wide, and she trembled, but she shook her head. "No, not yet. I'm fine. I—what the hell?" She stared down at her hand. The portion of her wrist that had been bloodied was rapidly forming new tissue, and within seconds, all that was left of the scrape was a few streaks of drying blood. The xeno nuzzled her hand again, licked it, and then trotted off to see what its friends were investigating on the other side of the clearing. Cordy, stunner still at the ready, followed it.

Jay stared. "What just happened?"

Sasha's eyes didn't leave her wrist. "That can't be possible." She picked up her scanner and aimed it at her own skin. "It's . . . that makes sense, I guess."

"What does?" Jay crouched next to her. Up close, the healed injury was even more miraculous. The skin there looked fresh and healthy. He helped her stand.

"Well, some animals have a coagulating agent in their saliva that helps them heal wounds—that's why they lick them. A creature secreting something like that from their skin or fur wouldn't be out of the question. But what I'm seeing here isn't just coagulation. It's as if whatever substance it had caused the damaged cells to regenerate entirely in a matter of seconds. Like jet-powering stem cells or something. Amazing."

Alex had finally made his way over to them. He gave a low whistle. "No shit. I can only imagine the kind of medicinal uses that could have."

"That's an interesting thought," Jay said. "Do we want to take one of these back as a sample? Study it?"

"No!" Sasha said flatly.

He frowned at her. "Why not? As long as these tesserae keep opening, why shouldn't we try to make the best of it? Think of how useful this substance, whatever it is, would be for combat or disasters. We could save so many lives if we could heal wounds that fast." The ringing of a bomb blast, and the sharp smell of Josie's blood as it coated their uniforms, echoed in his memory.

Sasha shook her head. "These creatures don't belong to us. They don't belong to Earth. They're not for us to use as we will."

"What about Littlefoot? What about Jack and Kate or the others in the lab? Aren't we studying them?"

She huffed in frustration. "Yes, but that's a different story. Littlefoot was a once-in-a-lifetime find. And Jack and Kate got stranded here. If we took one of these xenos now, we'd basically be kidnapping it. If we get to the point that the tesserae stay open longer, or we can find a way to open and close them at will, we could consider doing more extensive on-site study, but keeping one of these things here now would likely mean stranding it on Earth for the rest of its life. We can't do that." She stared down at her hand again. "Even for something like this."

Angel interrupted her. "Well, whatever you decide, it had better be done fast because the tessera is closing. Signal strength is dropping rapidly. If we're going to get these green teddy bears home, best do it."

Remy strolled up to them. "Company and government protocol is returning them to their planets, Lambert. There are all sorts of reasons. You know it makes sense." He came up beside Alex and put a hand on his shoulder. "That's what we agreed on at that committee meeting, remember?"

"Yep." Alex nodded at Remy. "I'm sorry, Jay, but they're right. This is how we're supposed to do things. Let's get them back home, OK?"

Jay had always been a stickler for protocol, but this was rubbing him the wrong way. Or maybe it was Alex leaning into Remy's touch. He started to object, but the sound wouldn't cross his lips. "Fair enough," he finally said and broke off to help the rest of his team.

NEW TERRITORY

"Are you sure you want to do this?" Akena's tanned skin was flushed with arousal, and her breathing was heavy, but she still looked slightly confused.

Jay was slightly confused himself, if he was honest. Up until three weeks ago, he'd been certain he was entirely gay. He'd already had several encounters with other boys and knew that he liked what happened. Ever since he was a kid, he couldn't remember ever having a crush on a girl. Oh, he had plenty of female friends, but none of them lit that spark, deep down in his belly, that he felt when he was around an attractive guy.

None of them except Akena. It probably helped that she was lean and narrow, her hips barely swelling out from her waist, her breasts small enough to have been covered by a decent-sized clamshell. She was also strong and wiry, with well-developed biceps and pecs, and even a hint of a six pack, from her job working at her dad's tire shop. The short spiky hair, the rakish grin, and the way she casually tossed around profanity like it was polite conversation didn't hurt, either. His logical brain figured he was only responding to her for those qualities and had therefore kept her at arm's length—despite her open flirting—since they'd met when she started classes at his school.

But then there was the dream he had about her last week, the

165

dream in which he was perfectly happy to be touching her breasts and slipping a hand down the front of her impossibly small shorts. He'd awakened to a wet spot on his sheets and a jumbled rush of thoughts, and for the next several days, he couldn't stop thinking about her. Eventually, he just gave up trying to figure it out and decided to let his curiosity take flight.

Hence, the date, to which she had readily agreed, and the make out session in the front seat of her dad's tow truck, which she had proposed. Everything they'd done so far had been exciting, much to his surprise, but now things were getting to the point of no return. She hovered over him, fondling the small square package she'd pulled from his backpack. "Are you sure?" she repeated. "Don't want to waste this if you're not."

His fingers were still slippery from where they had played between her legs—the warm, damp place that now called to him like a homing beacon. Heat rushed to his groin.

"I'm sure," he said throatily and took the condom from her hand.

It had been some time since Alex told Jay about Sasha's supposed interest in him, but more and more, he was beginning to believe his friend's perception. Though it had seemed to fall off for a while—she hadn't said anything, but he suspected she'd been seeing someone—in the past few days, her attention had come back to him with a rush. He wondered if it had something to do with the tense voice convo she'd had on their way back from an event a few weeks ago. He had tried not to listen in, but he'd overheard "married," "forget it," and something about being lied to. Whatever the reason, she'd gone from staring at her band every minute she had free to being glued to Jay's side instead. She seemed to take every excuse to be close to him—sitting next to him on the hover when they were going back and forth to missions, catching him in the cafeteria and sitting next to him for lunch, and, when she wasn't otherwise busy, hanging around the security office chatting with him about inconsequentials.

It all might've been unconscious, Jay considered. Sasha

didn't seem to be the type to play coy and wait for someone else to make a move, even if she was rebounding. He supposed if she really was interested, she'd simply say so, not dance around the issue. So, until that happened, he assumed the known status quo: nursing his refusing-to-fade crush on Alex, Alex nursing his own on Sasha, and Remy trying to flirt with Alex. It was all complicated enough that he had decided to ignore the whole mess in favor of concentrating on their jobs, which were getting more complicated with each new tessera.

Today's debut, in the wilds of Discovery Park near a large quake rift, was no exception. Cordy was out for the day with her sick fourth grader, and Hansen, the beta team's xeno expert, was in Minnesota for his sister's wedding. This left Sasha as the team's sole source of intelligence on the behavior of the intruding xenos. She was normally good at it, but was tired today, and she made a rare judgment error in sussing out the xeno, a doglike creature that, despite being an herbivore, still had a mouthful of strong teeth. The pack leader, apparently deciding she'd gotten too close to one of his pups, had attacked her. A burst from Jay's stunner stopped the attack, but not before it had done damage. The creature's sharp incisors had torn through several layers of uniform and clothing and left deep wounds in her upper arm.

While the rest of the team finished wrangling the xenos through to their home world, Jay took Sasha back to the hover to attend to the wound, only wishing he'd had some of the cell-regeneration substance secreted by those green creatures.

"I'm fine," she protested. "I've had plenty of animal bites and scratches in my time. I know how to do my own first aid. I can handle this." She tried to wave him away, but since she was using the injured arm for the gesture, she instead managed to fling blood on his tac vest.

He raised an eyebrow. "Oh?"

"Uh . . ." She flushed crimson.

"C'mon. I've had field medicine training. I know what I'm doing, too. Remember, my job is to keep you science sorts safe. I'd be shirking my duty if I didn't fix this." He gave her the same look his mom had always used on him. Luckily, Ele Lambert's patented Stare of Doom worked.

Sasha sighed heavily. "All right. Fine." Wincing, she clambered up into the hover, and sat there fidgeting while Jay rummaged through the hover's onboard med kit for supplies. "Honestly, though, this isn't any worse than the mauling I once got from a coyote." She pulled aside the collar of her shirt; the top of a parallel series of shallow-but-ragged scars showed just below her collarbone—faint enough that he had missed them when he'd seen her stripped down during the sub catastrophe. Truly, the old scar didn't look that bad, and neither did the bite on her arm. Assuming the creature that had attacked them didn't carry venom or disease—and she had expressed confidence that it didn't—she'd be fine after patching up.

"You should see the scars I got from Pakistan," he said wryly as he began cleaning the wound and slathering it in antibiotic gel. "Had shrapnel bits stuck just about everywhere. They missed anything vital, but it looks like I have a map of West Seattle on one side of my ass."

"I'd like to see that someday," she said. Then the flush on her cheeks deepened, and she stammered. "I—I mean, not that I'm . . ."

He met her eyes. In all the time that he'd known her, Sasha had never once seemed like a flighty adolescent. Yet now, it was as if she'd dropped 15 years and was gazing open-mouthed at some teen-dream pop star—almost as ridiculous as Alex's mooning about over her, though that had started to taper off lately. It was, Jay thought with a start, absolutely adorable, and he couldn't help smiling. "Not that you're what?" he prodded.

She rolled her eyes. "You know what I mean."

"Do I?" He began sealing the edges of her wound with a squirt of surgipaste.

She squirmed and tried to change the subject. "Ow! Watch it with that stuff. It stings."

He didn't take the bait. "Oh, so now you're complaining, when you were all Tough Sasha a minute ago?" She went quiet and looked away. Finally, he took pity on her. "OK, I'll let it go."

She shook her head. "No, it's fine. I think my subconscious has started speaking for me, is all."

"How so?" He pasted an absorbent bandage over the wound, put the kit away, and perched next to her.

She smiled shyly at him. "OK, so maybe it's obvious— in which case you probably think I'm a dipshit—but I have a thing for you. A minor thing, but still. I know it's messed up, since we work so closely together and all, so I've been trying to ignore it. I don't exactly have a great track record with keeping relationships professional." She winced—Jay assumed there was recent pain behind that. "So, well, there you have it. I hope you don't think there's something horribly wrong with me now."

He shook his head. "No. Not at all. I'm flattered. Thank you. And, well, you're not the only one with a work crush."

She perked up. "Oh?"

"Well, that's where it gets complicated." He smiled tightly and stared down at his fingernails. "It's not for me to name names, but I will say that I'm interested in someone else, who's also interested in you."

She frowned. "In me?"

"Like I said, not my place to give away someone else's secret, but I'm guessing you could figure it out if you thought about it enough. It's not like he's been all that subtle on his end." He chuckled.

"It's a he! Well, that narrows it down a bit. Wait. It's a he. Oh, fuck me for being clueless. I didn't even think about that. Are you—?" She fidgeted. "Because it would be just like me to crush out on a gay dude."

"Close but not entirely," he said. "I identify as gay as

shorthand, but I'm not exclusive. I'm not attracted to, well, the heels-and-makeup set, if that makes sense, but I do find the occasional woman attractive, and I've dated a couple over the years. Also dated a couple of non-binary folks and trans guys who passed on body mods. I'm OK with whatever bits someone has, basically. I just find myself mostly attracted to people who are somewhere in the neighborhood of M rather than F."

"OK, got it." She sighed in relief. "I'm pretty much straight, for what that's worth. Fooled around with my roomie in undergrad when she was coming off a bad relationship and wanted to see if she liked it, but it didn't do anything for either of us." She rubbed her chin thoughtfully. "So does that mean that mystery guy is straight and that's the problem?"

Jay shook his head. "He's not straight, actually, but I think the bigger problem is that I don't think I'm even on his radar."

"And I'm guessing he's not on mine, if I don't know who this is," she said. "I suppose I'm not on yours, either, though."

He grinned significantly. "I didn't say that, now, did I?"

"Oh!" Her eyes went wide.

He held up a hand. "I want to be honest with you. Aside from the work thing making it unwise, I'm not sure it's a good idea anyway. I don't want to sound like I don't like you. I think you're a wonderful person, and yes, I do find you attractive. In a different situation, I might have asked you out already. Unfortunately, I'm also annoyingly stuck on our mystery guy, and he's stuck on you, and I'm not sure it would be fair to any of us if you and I got together while my mind is still being a dorkass kid with a crush on the local hot nerd."

Sasha raised an eyebrow. "Hot nerd?"

Jay shrugged and flushed. "I know. It's probably weird for a big soldier type like me, but I have a thing for brainy people. Always have. I—"

A commotion from the copse of trees just ahead of them caught their attention.

"Hey, guys!" Alex called out, leading the rest of the delegation back from the site. "We're wrapped up here. Critters are home, tessera is closed. Dunno about you two, but I could kill for a beer and a bowl of pho. Any takers?"

Sasha looked up at the new arrival and grinned in sudden recognition. She glanced over at Jay, and he couldn't help the guilty expression on his face. "Well," she said slyly, "speak of the nerdy devil himself."

* * *

Though most of their recent tessera events hadn't been dangerous, Alex had learned from their Burlington event not to count his chickens—or his xenos, as the case was— so he asked again whether Angel saw anything else on her readouts. A new tessera, this one on the south rim of Crater Lake, always made him nervous. As beautiful as the location was—the deep snow in the area lending a festive feel as December approached—he was still on alert.

"Going by my IR and radar sweep, we're clean," she assured him. "So long as none of them decide to come back through, you're good."

Jay directed his team to load up and strolled up behind them. "Almost sad to see these go. Pretty things."

"They were," Alex agreed. Though Jay had nicknamed the xenos butterflies, they were more like some sort of bird, as Sasha had noted, and about the size of the average crow. Their most unusual feature, however, was that they were nearly transparent, huge wings and all. They'd come through the tessera in a giant swarm but had stayed nearby, flitting around the trees. Good thing, too, since it had taken the team an hour and a half just to get here, even with their high-speed hover piloted by Hotchkiss, one of Jay's ex-Army team members.

Fortunately, the tessera had stayed open for a long

time—nearly five hours—giving the crew plenty of time to round up the xenos, and for Alex to send one of his remote-controlled drones through to the other side, to gather data about the planet that the creatures called home. The pictures he'd gotten of the place so far were stunning, and he was hoping he'd have more time to collect samples.

Finally, he heeded the warning about the tessera's imminent close and called his bot home. It zoomed through the opening and came to rest nearby, idling quietly as Alex began shutting it down.

"Got dusty there, didn't you?" he told the object. He brushed at the glittery layer of fine soil that had accumulated on its trek. As he did, he noticed something odd about its composition.

Sasha noticed it, too, and peered closely at the drone. "Why is that dust so shiny?"

"I'm not sure." Alex frowned. Training his scanner at a particularly thick patch of the dust, he got his answer. "Oh. Oh, crap."

"What?" Jay looked over his shoulder. "What are you seeing?"

"That explains what I saw on the images my little friend sent back." Alex shook his head. "I guess I shouldn't be surprised: infinite universe, infinite possibilities, and all that." He grinned up at them, then nodded toward the closing tessera. "That planet over there—or at least this part of it? The top layer of dirt is all powdered platinum."

Sasha gaped at him. "Really?"

Alex nodded. "And, if I'm not mistaken, those veins I saw in some of the other rocks are probably also precious metals. That place would be worth a fortune in mining."

"Pity the tessera's closing. We could make back the entire company's yearly budget from a few buckets of dirt," Jay said.

Sasha shook her head. "Not worth it. It's not our planet to mine, and we have no idea how doing so might affect the ecosystem. Our glass butterflies wouldn't be the only species—probably not even the dominant one—and stripping their habitat could cause catastrophic issues we have no real way of controlling."

Alex nodded. Her heart was a big part of the reason he was so fond of her; she managed to play conscience for all of them. "It's just as well, yeah. For what it's worth, I did send a bounceback signal while the drone was there. Depending on where the planet is, we should be able to pick it up soon so we know where it is if we want to go there in the future."

The tessera finally closed, and they packed up to head back to the hover.

"You know, this—and those green teddies—make me wonder," Jay said thoughtfully as they climbed in for the journey back home. "We're not the only crew with an interest in what happens on these missions. That meeting you had with Belenko hasn't stopped him hammering on us for more information. I'm guessing he wants to know if there might be commercial opportunities. If there are, he might be able to change some government minds about our zero-impact protocol."

Alex made a sour face. "Well, as far as I'm concerned, he's never going to know about what I've found so far. He's certainly not going to know about this one."

"What do you mean?" Sasha frowned at him. "He already managed to win access to more data than we feed to the public. He's probably going to have everything before long."

"Well, everything that gets registered in our databases, at least." Alex grinned. "How about we let our platinum planet be our little secret, yeah?"

Sasha favored him with a broad smile. "I like the way you think."

Alex only hoped that someday, the way he thought wasn't the only thing she liked about him. Unfortunately, he was far from confident about that. If anything, she seemed to be even more besotted by Jay these days, and to his frustration, Jay was inexplicably returning her flirting more often.

As they sat together on the hover back to base, he watched them, trying to figure out exactly how he felt about the situation. They were touching each other readily now: Jay plucked a bit of leaf debris from Sasha's hair; she returned the favor by laying a light finger near a smudge of dirt on his uniform. He offered her a bite of his energy bar; she let him take a swig from her water bottle. It was maddening, and Alex felt like a third wheel—like an audience member, watching someone else's romance unfold in front of him. He'd even been kicking himself these days for not taking up Jay's offer of a fling a few months back. At least then he could've felt like he'd been involved somehow, instead of being an outsider.

His com buzzed, saving him from having to think about it anymore. Without looking at his band, he thumbed the earpiece. "Yo."

"Alex?" Remy's velvety voice purred in his ear. In half a second, he had his screen out so he could see as well as hear him.

"Sorry about that. How can I help you?"

"I was observing the remote coordination of your mission, but I haven't seen a full report of the tessera come in yet. Are you still working on it?"

"We are, yeah. You saw the creatures, right?"

He nodded. "I just need the full planet data for my file. Homeland wants as much info as we can give them for each of these."

"Of course. I'll write it up and have it to you later this afternoon."

"Thanks, Alex. I look forward to it." He smiled warmly and ended the call.

Alex's toes began to tingle, and he squirmed. He glanced back up: Sasha and Jay were watching something on his screen and giggling at some private joke. Suddenly, he found that he didn't care. They could go off and do whatever they wanted as far as he was concerned. He had someone else to think about now: someone with fluffy blonde hair and a divine accent.

* * *

Sasha was convinced Jay had told her a tall tale. Thinking back to some of their initial interactions, she could see how Alex might been interested in her at one point. Now, however, it was as if he didn't know her at all. In fact, he seemed to be spending less and less time not just with her, but with Jay and the rest of the field team. He was distracted on each mission, antsy to get back to campus.

Eventually, she discovered why.

With the winter solstice just days away, the sun set early at this latitude. By the time she left work, the building's energy-efficiency systems had already turned off most of the lights. All that illuminated the security desk—and the man behind it—were a few localized task lights, a string of decorative holiday lights threaded across the front of the desk, and the glow from the array of vid displays. It was enough, however, that she could see the glittering on his cheeks. As she drew closer, she saw that he had been crying.

She approached his desk cautiously. "Jay?"

He glanced up, startled, and began brushing hastily at his face. "Sasha! Hi. Long day?"

"A bit, yeah. Been compiling more reports on Jack and Kate and their offspring for the team that's creating the pregnancy pouches. Wanted to finish before I left." She hesitated, but curiosity took over. "Are you all right? You look upset."

"Fine. I'm fine." He glanced down at his arm, then forced a smile.

"Pardon my candor, but: bullshit. I may not know humans as well as I do other creatures, but I can still read basic body language for distress." She softened her voice. "You don't have to tell me if you don't want to."

He went quiet for a moment. Then he beckoned her to step behind his desk. "This should explain it."

She scooted behind his chair and looked over his shoulder as he brought up a security cam feed. There, clear as day: Alex was leaning back against his desk, eyes closed and mouth open, and kneeling in front of him was a man, his distinctive blonde locks bouncing on his shoulders as his head bobbed.

"Oh." Sasha managed to say as Jay turned off the feed again.

"I was just about to pack up for the day—Monica is due in for the evening shift in about 10 minutes—when I saw that." He rushed to explain, "Please don't think I'm a creep or something. I know I should've just shut off the feed immediately, but I felt—I felt like I was frozen. I only watched for a few seconds."

Sasha patted his shoulder. "It's OK. I get it. I know you're not like that. And, well . . . Alex isn't exactly being discreet. He knows he has a cam right outside his office."

Jay grimaced. "He should know that, yeah. But from what I can tell, he's a bit . . . distracted."

She had to laugh.

He chuckled bitterly. "I have no idea why I was crying, though. How ridiculous is that?"

She shrugged. "Well, it's a shock, isn't it? I suppose we could have guessed that they might hook up, but I admit I had no idea. Honestly, I wouldn't have suspected a guy like that would be into someone like Alex anyway."

"Yeah. People can surprise you. I feel stupid for caring, though. I know Alex and I decided getting together was a bad idea, but I guess I still held out hope it might happen."

Sasha frowned. "Wait. Decided? What?"

"Oh. That's a long story." Jay waved a helpless hand.

A strange feeling crept up her spine, and a rush of boldness opened her mouth. "Well, I don't have anything else planned tonight. Want to tell me the story over dinner?"

He cocked his head, scanning her face. "OK. Yeah."

By the time they had finished a couple of plates of koorma and rice, Sasha had been thoroughly briefed on the history of Jay's love life. She finally understood why he and his teammate Tito kept each other at arm's length, why he hadn't dated in such a long time, and was tight-lipped about his personal life. He had been hesitant to tell her about his PTSD issues, and stressed that he was in no danger of being incapacitated in the field. She in turn reassured him that she trusted him completely; they had faced some dangerous xenos already, and he'd never once flinched.

After Jay spent nearly half an hour explaining his crush on Alex, she found she almost understood it. She had been pestered by enough emotionally stunted geniuses while in college that she had automatically dropped him in the same box; she saw now that doing so had been unfair. Alex may have been awkward, but he wasn't at all the boundary-ignoring sort—someone looking more for a nameless ego boost than for a real partner. She now almost regretted not picking up on his interest in her before it was too late. But late it was, unfortunately, and even so, she wouldn't have dated him for fear of breaking Jay's heart the way she now saw Alex had done by hooking up with Remy.

There was still one possible bright side left, she thought. With Alex now clearly into someone else, Jay no longer had a reason to avoid *her*, aside from possible workplace weirdness. As he seemed perfectly fine working with the ex he once thought he might marry, maybe he'd at least be interested in something casual—something that might help take his mind off Alex and wash away her own last traces of bitterness over João's deception. She shifted her body language accordingly.

"I guess it's all moot," Jay finally said, draining the last of his beer. "I'm an adult. I just need to get over this and get back to baseline. I'll find some way to stop obsessing about him."

"At some point, yeah." She locked her eyes on his and smiled significantly. "Maybe some point soon?"

Jay paused, then returned the smile. He met her gaze evenly, and his voice dropped. "Could be." He sucked a stray drop of beer from his lower lip. Sasha had to suppress a strong urge to do that for him. "You said you live with your great-grandmother, yeah?" he asked.

"Yeah." Sasha found she couldn't breathe right.

"I live alone," he said, leaning forward. "Maybe you should tell her you won't be home tonight."

KEEPING WARM

"I love you, you know."

Alex whipped his head around, and stared at Gabriel's face, looking for any indication that he might just be joking or talking to the wall or to himself or to his cup of coffee—anything but actually aiming those words at him. He looked dead serious, however. "Me?" Alex blurted anyway.

"Yes, you." Gabriel smiled and approached his workstation. "Of course you. Who else have I been dating for the past four months?"

"No one. That I know of, at least." Alex couldn't stop staring, certain his face must be crimson. He had had plenty of dates and plenty of flings. He'd even had a few relationships with people he'd occasionally referred to as boyfriend or girlfriend before they fizzled out. But this? No. No one had ever said those words. At least not like that. Not with the open smile and the warm tone, both sincere. If he was honest with himself, he couldn't remember the last time his mother or brother had said that to him, either. His mom constantly reminded him of God's love for him, but said next to nothing about her own.

A tense look passed over Gabriel's face, and he ran a hand over his fuzzy head. "Did I say the wrong thing? I don't want you to feel pressured. It's just that I've liked being with you so far and I'd like to be more serious about it. Maybe we could even—I know this is fast—but maybe we could move in together?"

Alex found himself trembling, and he dropped the screen he had been studying. He bent over, and picked it up. When he straightened up, he met Gabriel's gaze and smiled in a way he hoped didn't look as nervous or awkward as he felt. "Well," he said, "my apartment does feel kind of lonely."

Alex wriggled uncomfortably: a thick strand of blonde hair had managed to park itself on his face as he held its sleeping owner from behind. After Gabriel, he was so unused to sharing a bed with someone who wasn't close to bald that he'd forgotten how long hair had to be worked around. Blowing lightly at the strand so as not to wake Remy, he managed to dislodge it. Only now his nose itched. With a wave of annoyance, he also realized that he had to pee. Moving slowly, he managed to extricate himself with little more from his lover than a snuffle. He tiptoed quickly down the hall, biting his lip when the floor creaked, and dashed into the bathroom.

As he was washing his hands, he stared at himself in the mirror. His wild curls were tangled more than usual from having a pair of strong hands woven into them, and his lower lip was swollen from where Remy had been sucking and biting it. A few other dark marks, in various states of fading, spotted his neck and chest, and one nipple was bright pink from being bitten. He hadn't been into getting rough before, but for some reason, the manhandling was hitting all his buttons these days. Remy could have suggested breaking out restraints and a crop, and Alex would have agreed.

At the moment, however, he was on a downswing after their evening's session, so instead he was just slightly sore and tired—and thoughtful, remembering how things had started in the first place.

"Finished that mission report, yet?" Remy had poked his head into Alex's office. It was early evening. Most of the team had gone home already and Alex was tired and his hair was still damp from the tessera event. This one involved an aquatic creature, and the resulting scuffle with the xeno as they herded it back to its home had left him drenched with at least a gallon of Lake Sammamish.

"Almost. Just double-checking that my drones recorded their data correctly. One of them got wet, so I was afraid its Stream connection may have been interrupted during the upload."

"Ah, makes sense." Remy's eyes traveled over Alex, and he smiled warmly. "Hey, do you have any plans for the evening—when you're done?"

Alex cocked his head. Remy's body language had changed, and so did the energy between them. "Not especially. Why?" He tried not to hope.

"There's that new pub down by the train station. Want to get a beer or two and maybe some dinner?"

Alex felt a surge in his chest. "I'd love to. Sure!"

"Good. I've been wanting to talk to you about how we catalogue the drone data, but haven't had the chance, yet."

Alex's shoulders sagged again. "Yeah, of course."

Only half a beer and a plate of appetizers later, Alex realized that work wasn't at all what his new co-worker wanted to talk about. After a dinner laden with personal-life chatter and not-at-all-subtle innuendo Remy led him back to his car—a beautiful vintage Mustang so old that it still had a combustion engine, albeit one converted to biodiesel—and proceeded to do things that took his mind off work entirely.

Now, even though it had only been two weeks, it seemed like they'd been dating for months. Remy had started sleeping at his place over the weekend—his own place was a tiny pod only suited for a single occupant—and hadn't really left. This was not how flings were supposed to go, at least in Alex's experience, and he found himself downright baffled, if also delighted.

On the surface, Remy didn't seem like someone he'd be compatible with. He seemed to have a fair amount of science knowledge, thanks most likely to his dad's profession, but clearly didn't understand most of the higher-level physics stuff when Alex started going off on the topic. Their conversations on those therefore tended to be stunted. They had similar tastes in food and music, but that wasn't much to go on. Even with the differences, though, it felt amazing to be together. On rare occasions, he still found himself longing for Sasha or wondering what might have been with Jay, but for the most part, all conscious thought in terms of his love life was focused on the person who was snoozing away in his bed.

This wasn't like Gabriel, he knew that much. There, they had an incredibly tight and symbiotic relationship formed over work, and a deeper emotional connection formed when Alex, deep into a bottle of rum, spilled his guts about his mother one night. Gabriel was a caretaker—he'd had a sister with a chronic illness, and was used to being needed—and Alex was only too happy to let himself be cared for. Their relationship, brief as it was, had done a great deal to heal him emotionally, which was why the breakup still stung so hard. He knew he needed someone he could bond with like that again. Was Remy that person?

Before he could fumble for an answer to that question, a sharp electronic ping sounded from the bedroom.

"Dammit." He was already exhausted from a busy day at a tessera site near Chehalis. Another event so soon made his bones ache just thinking about it. XenoNet's beta team wasn't due to go on shift for another two hours. Alpha team was still on call.

He hurried into the bedroom and started grabbing fresh clothing from his closet while his lover sat up, rubbing his eyes.

"Again?" Remy grumbled. "Where is it now?" He fumbled for his band. The sheet slipped away as he did, and Alex's breath caught as he stared at the thin trail of dark-blond hair leading to places he longed to revisit. "Oh. Snoqualmie. Nothing big, then." He fell back on the bed, though the sheets stayed where they were.

Alex glanced at his own screen on the nightstand to confirm. This event was a reopen: a tessera that had, thank goodness, proven on its debut opening a while back not to be terribly dangerous. The dominant life-form in that area of the alien planet was a slow-moving marsupial that preferred eating the bugs and fungus from its much-warmer home world. The chances of one of them wanting to venture into the chilly drizzle of a Seattle December were small.

He stared again at Remy, wondering if he could somehow get away with crawling back into bed instead of going out in the cold and damp to stare through a hole in reality. He sighed heavily and forced himself to look away and start pulling on his boxers. He had an obligation, and his sense of duty was too strong to ignore it. They might not have been as important to him these days as Remy was, but he still felt a deep sense of loyalty and friendship with Sasha, Jay, Angel, and the rest of the team, not to mention Leung. He couldn't—wouldn't—ditch this call. "It's nothing big, no, but I should be there anyway. Never know when something might change."

"I understand. Any chance of bringing me some croissants when you come back? I think that little bakery in Issaquah stays open until midnight."

"Of course." Now that Remy had mentioned food, his own stomach rumbled. Dinner was four hours ago, and he'd burned a lot of calories in their romp afterward. There was no time to deal with that now, however. Perhaps he could bum an energy bar off Tito, who always seemed to have a supply in his pack for handing to his kids when he got home. He finished dressing and knelt on the edge of the bed, leaning over to drop a kiss on Remy's cheek before he fell asleep again. "Sleep well," he whispered.

"Come home soon, *m'cher*," he murmured and rolled back over.

The word echoed in Alex's mind as he made for the

door. *Cher.* Dear. A term of affection. Whatever this was between them, it had now gone beyond casual.

* * *

Sasha was well satisfied. For a guy who had said he was mostly gay, Jay was certainly not unskilled with body parts most often found on women. It had been so long since she'd been with someone who wasn't a stranger that it felt odd to be so familiar while they were both naked. In between kissing and groping and the primal noises such things elicited, they made little jokes about work, the tesserae, and some of the frankly silly xenos they'd encountered. She was pleasantly surprised by how funny Jay was when he wasn't in soldier mode, and she found herself relaxing more than usual. The result was some of the best, most gratifying sex she'd ever had. For his part, Jay seemed content, too. Sasha apologized once for not being Alex—for not even being a guy—and he shushed her immediately. He said that if he didn't want to be with her, he wouldn't have taken her home that first night—much less the four nights since.

She hadn't noticed his apartment much before—her mind being on other things—but as she lay next to him in his small bed now, two weeks into it, her mind buzzed too much to fall asleep. She should've been tired from the tessera event they'd had earlier in the evening, but the mild chaos—and the terrific sex when they got back—had energized her. She glanced around the moonlit room, taking in the ephemera of the man who slept by her side.

It wasn't nearly as military-issue as she might have imagined. It was messier, for one. The surfing trophies on a shelf were a surprise, as was the framed print of a mid-1980s pop star whose name she couldn't remember. On the nightstand was a glowing picture frame, its display shifting every few seconds to reveal animated pictures of friends and family. Someone who must have been his sister—they looked nearly identical, though Jay was younger—stood in the middle of a cold, white landscape while wind whipped her dark hair. A huge gaggle of family gathered, the children fidgeting impatiently, on the front lawn of a large home somewhere in Hawai'i. There was even a still photo from his parents' wedding; the pair looked just as charming and kind as their son. There were also several pictures from his army days, and she was excited to see that he looked just as good in military uniform as he did in his security kit.

She felt like a voyeur, seeing more about Jay than he had thus far divulged, and the intimacy felt strange. Stranger still was that for once, she didn't mind. When men she'd been sleeping with got too close, she usually felt like peeling her skin off to escape. Now, she felt comfortable, even safe. As the long day and the post-coital buzz finally began to shut down her brain, she rolled over to nestle into Jay's side. He drowsily fitted an arm around her shoulders. With a deep sigh, Sasha let the sound of his heartbeat lull her to sleep.

* * *

"Happy, happy!" Josie crowed, throwing her strong arms around Jay for a breath-stealing hug.

"You, too, Jojo," he squeaked and sucked in a breath when she finally released him.

"Usual?" Colin called from the bar. "Or maybe something more seasonal? I have a pot of spiced cider on."

"That sounds good." A cold, damp weather system had set into the area. Though it didn't bring snow with it—no white Christmas expected this year—it still was a penetrating chill, and the idea of being warmed by something other than alcohol sounded nice. What he really wanted to be warmed by—Sasha's soft, sweet embrace—wasn't possible tonight since she was spending Christmas Eve with her great-grandmother.

"Beer for me," Josie said. "Cider makes me piss like a stallion." She led Jay to their usual corner booth. "No Kalikimaka in Kaua'i this year?"

He shook his head. "There's still too much going on with the tesserae. We have site security and a full beta team now, but I don't feel comfortable leaving while they're still green."

"Aw, that sucks. When did you last see your parents?"

He thought for a moment. It had been a while, and he missed them. He considered asking them to fly up soon. Of course, that might necessitate another conversation like the one he was just about to have, and he wasn't sure he was up for that just yet. "Last December. Lucia came up from Antarctica, and Dad took us all snorkeling off Molokai."

She laughed. "Now there's a festive way to spend Christmas!"

"What about you? Doing anything with your dad?" She was living on base again, but she'd been visiting him regularly. Both kept insisting Jay come out for one of her father's massive barbecue meals, but he hadn't found the time.

She shrugged. "He wanted to go to Vegas this year, so it's just me. I thought about going back to visit the cousins in K.C., but nah. They're all raising herds of babies and toddlers right now, and I have no desire to be barfed on or bitten, even if the little monsters are damned adorable to look at."

"Understandable." Jay had to admit that the idea of being surrounded by adorable children didn't sound bad to him at all. He had recently met Tito's three children, and his heart ached, knowing that they theoretically could have been his, had he not made such big mistakes all those years ago. "I do still want kids myself someday, though."

"Of course. I always figured you'd be a great parent. You're the most patient person I've ever met. Think you'd do adoption or surrogate?"

He flushed. That was a question he thought he'd resolved years ago. There was always the off chance that he might have partnered up with a guy who had pregnancy-capable anatomy and interest in using it for that purpose, but he'd otherwise assumed that any children he'd have would likely have DNA belonging at least to one person other than himself and his partner. Now, however, the reality hit him. He knew Sasha had tube-blocking nanos installed—that was a discussion they'd had early on—and he didn't know whether she'd ever want to disable them and become pregnant someday. Still, it *was* possible that he could directly make a baby with the person he was now dating. The thought made him chuckle.

Josie frowned at him. "What? Did I say something funny?"

"No. It's just . . . Let's say that if things go well, I might end up passing on my genes naturally."

She stared at him, a rare expression of confusion written on her face. "What the fuck does that mean?"

"I'm seeing someone." He couldn't meet her eye, but as he stared at the table, he smiled anyway.

She brightened. "Oh! Found yourself a boy with ovaries, did you?"

He shook his head. "Nope. A woman."

Josie fell silent, then burst into a gale of laughs that echoed throughout the bar. "You're shitting me, right?"

"Not at all." He caught her eye and grinned.

"I'll be damned. Congrats, I guess! How long has it been since you visited the other side of the fence?"

"Six years? Something like that. The munitions specialist we were stationed in Ankara with. The redhead. Trace?"

"Oh, right. The one who kept trying to ask me out. Finally had to tell her I'm only into long hair and short skirts. Broke her heart, I think. I didn't realize you'd gone there. That's when you were rebounding from Tito, right?"

Jay nodded. "Yep. She sort of reminded me of a guy I had a crush on in high school, and we got shitfaced one night, and next thing you know . . . She told me the next morning that I reminded her why she didn't usually date guys."

"Ouch."

He shrugged. "It was fine. It wasn't bad, just awkward. And since then, I'd just never found a woman I was all that into."

"Until—what's this one's name?" Josie asked.

"Sasha. She's a bit more your type than what I'm attracted to, but something about her . . ." He trailed off, thinking about exactly how attracted he was.

"Well, I admit I'm surprised, but I'm happy for you. If she likes you, then she's got good taste in people, at least."

He smiled at the flattery. "Thanks."

"So when do I get to meet her? Or are you not yet at that stage?"

"Not yet. We've been working together for months, but the more-than-friends thing is still new."

"Ah, so that's where you found her. I didn't think you'd been going out enough lately to have found someone outside of work."

He laughed bitterly. "True. But yeah. She's one of the company's xenobiologists, on the alpha team that I go out on tesserae events with. She was involved in that sub accident with the alien craft."

Josie sat up straighter. "Oh, *that* Sasha! I remember seeing her on some news vids. Short-and-curvy gal?" He nodded. "Damn. I can see why you'd be into her, mostly gay or no. She could turn a straight lady." She waggled her eyebrows.

He flushed. "She's attractive, yeah. It's more than that for me, though. She's incredibly smart, compassionate, fun, open-hearted . . . I just like her all the way around."

Josie winked. "I bet you do."

He stuck out his tongue, and she laughed.

Colin brought over their beverages, and Jay started sipping at the fragrant, sweet cider. Something about the spicy scent—the hint of cloves—reminded him of Sasha, and he couldn't help a warm smile. "So, there you have it. Yes, I'm dating a woman now. I have no idea whether it's going to go anywhere, but I do have a good feeling about it. At the very least, she's someone I can see being a close friend for a long time. It's nice. Not that I don't love you, of course, but . . ."

"Hey, the more friends the better, if you ask me." Josie shrugged. "Does this mean things with Physics Boy aren't happening?"

Jay made a face. "Unfortunately, no. He hooked up with someone else—that's kind of how the thing with Sasha happened. We started talking about Alex, then went back to my place and—"

"Began bumping crotch tackle."

Jay rolled his eyes and kicked her under the table. "You're hopeless, you know that?"

"I know. But that's why you love me." She kicked him back. "Now that we have your love life out of the way, I gotta tell you about this new gal I met last week."

"Oh, do!" Jay sat back and let both cider and conversation make him thoroughly warm.

POACHERS

People were always reminding Sasha not to get too emotionally invested in the animals she worked with. She was there to gather information on them, not bond with them. They weren't humans, and in many cases, a human attempting to bond with them might interfere with their own social behavior and skew the data. Even worse for the ones in the wild, they might lose their fear of humans entirely, which could lead to their demise.

Still, though she could control how she behaved around the creatures, she couldn't control how she felt about them. Her own experiences trying to understand and interact with humans always seemed to come up short. With animals, everything made so much more sense. They were more emotionally and socially complex than most people thought, but their actions were driven by simple impulses: food, shelter, reproduction, safety, and so on. Sure, they cared about status and physical attributes, but they hadn't made the whole mess nearly as complicated as humans had. It was therefore a comfort to simply observe, as she had been lately, a pack of wolves rearing the season's pups.

"Sasha, stay there." James, her supervisor, looked wary as she walked up to him at the blind the team was using for observation of a birthing den.

Dread washed through her chest. "Is something wrong?"

"I'm sorry," he said. "There must have been poachers or sport hunters around—"

She pushed past him. The team had given the female wolf a number—563—but Sasha had been calling her Artemis. She lay prone on the ground near the den, blood staining her fur from neck to tail where the buckshot had peppered her. Her three-day-old pups— all five of them—lay near her body, stiff and silent from lack of their mother's milk.

Sasha rubbed her eyes. The meeting Leung had called was painfully early, and she had had a late night. Not that the reason for it was necessarily a bad one. Like most people there, she had welcomed in the new year, but then she had stayed up even later, enjoying celebrations of a more physical nature. She glanced across the room at Jay. He too looked tired, though he hid it better under his military demeanor. A crass piece of her mind started murmuring about standing at attention, and she giggled to herself.

Even with the nice memory, though, things had started to feel weird. They'd only gotten together a few times since their initial encounter, but Jay had started asking her to stay longer when she was there, and was making a point of cooking breakfast for her on the mornings after. Their pillow talk had also gone from lighthearted and flirty to something more intense. He told her more about his experiences in Pakistan; she told him about the quake and losing her mother and grandfather. When they were alone, curled up together in bed, it seemed normal and natural to share such intimacy, but here, in the uncomfortably bright lights of a conference room, she felt off. She had considered Jay a good friend for months, and had certainly been attracted to him all this time, but they were still co-workers. He was head of security for her employer. He held her life in his hands when they were at a dangerous tessera event. Lovers or not, they had to interact professionally when they were working.

Not that Alex and Remy seemed to have thought along those lines. Sasha couldn't help staring. They sat close together at the end of the table, positioned such that it was obvious they were holding hands under the table. Over the weeks that he'd been with the company, Remy had proven to be perfectly competent and friendly, if rather aloof now and then. Alex was clearly besotted and happy. Aside from the heartbreak the men's new relationship had caused Jay, there was no reason for her to have any negative feelings, yet she did. She wondered idly if that made her a hypocrite, considering that she too was sleeping with a co-worker. Jay glanced over at her as they waited for Leung to arrive. He flashed a warm, flirty smile, and Sasha found it actually made her want to turn away. She returned it, however, and then tried to focus on finishing waking up well enough to pay attention to the impending meeting.

She noted with some curiosity that there weren't many people in the room this morning. Usually staff meetings encompassed an entire department or even all of them. This time, the only people present were the core alpha response team, plus Angel and Remy. She took a deep draught of her latte and settled in to wait and see.

Leung strode in moments later, head down over a screen. Her body language was tense and upset, and going by the rumpled hair and yesterday's clothes, she hadn't slept at all.

"Hello, everyone," she said, her voice gravelly with tiredness. "I'm sorry to have to get you up so early, especially on a holiday. I'm not pleased about it, myself, but there's something serious we need to discuss. Here, let me show you first." She drew her hand across the screen and slid its display to the vid window at the end of the room. What appeared there made Sasha want to vomit.

The surroundings were familiar and beautiful. The site for this tessera was perched high on a cliff overlooking Hood Canal, and yesterday's snow lay thick on ground and foliage alike. But there the beauty ended. Bright blood had soaked through the snow and spattered the undergrowth, and scattered among the white-dusted ferns were the remains of at least a dozen of the gentle, healing xenos the team had encountered there. All of them had been decapitated. All had been skinned. Were it not for a few tufts of green fur littering the snowy ground, it wouldn't have been certain even which species they were.

"Poachers?" Sasha managed to croak.

Leung nodded. "Seems like it, yes. Best as I can tell, it happened overnight. A hiker stumbled across the scene this morning and messaged the tip box listed on the tessera marker. I have some experts—and thank you, Angel, for helping me with that research—looking at all the usual black-market sources for exotic-animal parts. Nothing has come up yet, but it's clear that was the goal. A few members of beta team have already gone up to secure the site and handle the corpses. I'll be sending you folks up there, too, to do some investigation. Before we do that, though, I'd like us to brainstorm a bit to figure out how it happened."

Angel, her own face a mask of nausea and exhaustion, spoke up. "Jason went home already—he was asleep on his feet, the poor dude—but he told me that there weren't any event notifications at all on his monitoring shift last night. We went back over the logs this morning before he left, and I didn't see any indication that he'd missed something."

Alex was now sitting bolt upright, both hands now above the table and fidgeting with his earpiece. "It makes no sense. It's possible there was a flash opening—we've had some that lasted less than half a second, which our scanners barely picked up—but I can't imagine how so many of the xenos would have gotten through to Earth in such a short time."

"There's no way any of them were left behind when the tessera closed after the first event," Jay noted. "Only seven came through that time, and both ground and satellite scans came up negative for unfamiliar life-forms when it closed. We saw no stragglers."

"Right," Sasha said. "Unless they have some manner of cloaking themselves from IR or other scans—which doesn't seem at all likely to me—we got them all back home."

"What about some left behind from an earlier event, before we started monitoring?" Leung asked.

Sasha shook her head. "Not possible. Even if they could cloak somehow, their home world's atmosphere is slightly higher in oxygen. They would have passed out and probably died from our poor air. They couldn't have been roaming the area alive this whole time."

Leung ran a hand through her hair and sighed. "So we're left with two possibilities, neither of which makes any sense to me. Either our monitoring system failed—and Angel kicked off a full diagnostic cycle just before we came in here to be absolutely sure—or somehow, the tesserae, or at least this one, are changing such that we're not picking up their signals anymore."

Alex pushed his chair back. "I can't see that happening. We know they change frequency each time they open, and we don't yet know where their opening signals are originating from, but the openings still show up in the spectra we're covering."

"Right. Well, I'm blocked." Leung looked around the room. "Anyone else have any ideas?"

Cordy spoke up. "No answers, I'm afraid, but I do have another question. If *we* didn't know about an opening event, how would the poachers have known about it? In my experience, they don't like to wait around for their prey. There's too much risk of getting caught."

"For that matter," Alex added, "how would they have known that this particular tessera opened to a world with something they'd want?" He turned to Remy. "Our public-facing information on the tesserae only lists location and classifies them according to potential danger, right? We haven't posted anything specific about the worlds or the xenos that come through. Only the events that happened with public witnesses should have any of that information."

"Yes, you're right." Remy said, then looked back at Leung. "And only three of my contacts at the agency have full access to the data. All of them have extremely high clearance. It's possible there's been an accidental leak, but otherwise, the only thing I can think of is that we have a mole—someone who would sell tessera information to people who shouldn't have it. Maybe it's also someone who could sabotage the monitoring system to keep it from signaling an event."

Sasha's stomach roiled again. She glanced around. Everyone in the room was someone she now considered a friend. She was still somewhat wary of Remy, but that was for personal reasons, not professional ones. He had proven himself trustworthy and reliable as far as his job was concerned. He and everyone else there had also passed the rigorous background checks Jay ran on each new employee. She didn't know all of the beta team as well since they worked opposite shifts, but she still trusted them—or at least was confident in Jay's trust. The idea that any of them, or even any of the employees not on a response team, could do this made her want to curl in on herself and disappear.

"I'm afraid you might be right." Leung sat down heavily in a chair. "I hate to ask this, but. . . Jay, would you please set up an internal investigation?"

He nodded. "Of course. I'll do everything I can."

"Thank you. In the meantime," she said to the rest of the group, "I'd like you to suit up and head out to the site to relieve the beta team and start investigating. Perhaps these poachers left behind something that will at least give us a clue as to who they are."

"Ms. Leung?"

"Yes, Remy?"

"Do you want me to notify my Homeland contacts? Or maybe military or local police? They might be able to help."

Leung shook her head. "Not yet. If we have a mole, I'd rather keep that information as internal as possible. That also means keeping this entire event quiet for now. No discussing it with anyone outside this room who isn't on one of the response teams. Believe me, when we find this person—and we will—they are going to wish they'd never set foot in this building."

* * *

Jay wondered what it was that Sasha, sitting across from him on the hover, found so fascinating out the window. Ever since the meeting, she'd been uncharacteristically quiet and withdrawn, suiting up for the mission with barely a word to anyone. Since the weather outside the vehicle was wall-to-wall drizzle and fog, he couldn't imagine she'd be watching the scenery.

He nudged her leg with the tip of his boot. "You in there?"

She glanced at him and then at Alex, who sat next to him, furiously typing on his band's screen. He also hadn't been all that communicative with anyone else. She smiled weakly. "I am. Sorry."

"Upset about the xenos?" Given her affinity for the creatures they encountered—even some of the more dangerous ones fascinated her—he figured she might well have been disturbed by the images of the ones that had been skinned.

She nodded. "It's more than that, though. I'm not sure I can put my finger on it." She glanced around the hover. The rest of the alpha team were chatting, nibbling energy bars, or checking their kit. Some looked slightly down or agitated, Cordy especially, but most were about as calmly alert as they ever were on an unexpected tessera event. "I just . . . I don't like the idea that XenoNet could have someone who would help something like this happen."

He winced. "Yeah. Me, neither." Most of the people he shared the vehicle with were ones he'd known for years through other places: the military, mostly, but also a couple of acquaintances from his college days, and some friends who had come highly recommended by Josie. He trusted them—more than that, he trusted the background checks he'd run on them—so he wasn't worried. It was possible that one of the other XenoNet employees—maybe someone angry about the company's shift away from the probe program—could be involved, though. It wasn't unknown for someone with an otherwise clean background to encounter something that hit a nerve and sent them down a dark path.

One of his old surfing buddies from Kaua'i had done that. Chase had been a straight-A student all through high school and had plans of going to Stanford for an electrical-engineering degree. When his dad died two months after his graduation, thanks to a drunk driver, Chase lost it. He stalked the driver while he was out on bail and beat him bloody, earning himself five years in prison and a lost scholarship.

Jay had already started piecing together a list of people he should talk to as part of his investigation. He could see a few of them who might have done something like this—especially ones whose pay had been stagnated and needed the money. Sid in engineering? Mariah, who had helped build the probes' telemetry systems? He didn't think so, but it could have been anyone. He sighed heavily as he realized how much work he had to do.

At least, he comforted himself, he was doing this with someone he liked so much. Sasha had turned back to the gray expanse outside the window, but even with her subdued expression, he still felt giddy looking at her. A year ago—hell, six months ago—if someone had told him that he was going to fall so hard for a woman, he would have laughed and questioned whether they'd been diving too deeply into a stash of weed. Now, the possibility that he was really doing this loomed large. It was more than slightly weird, so much so that he still questioned whether he should have told Josie about it. She'd been perfectly fine with it so far, but still needled him now and again. He wasn't planning to tell anyone else right away, however, since he didn't want office gossip to detract from the importance of what was happening with the company. Chatter had already started about Alex and Remy, helped along by their entirely unsubtle PDA.

Jay glanced over at Alex's screen and quickly wished he hadn't. Remy had sent Alex a media message: an animated pic of him blowing a kiss Jay rolled his eyes. Attracted as he had been to Alex—and still was, if he was being totally honest with himself—the way he was behaving with this new paramour was cringe-worthy.

But Alex was young and in love. Jay well remembered that feeling and understood how it could cloud a person's judgment. His eyes settled back on Sasha. She reached up to push a lock of hair behind her ear, and he suddenly had a memory of doing something similar for her when she was lying next to him on his bed, her eyelids fluttering as she started to drift off to sleep. His breath felt tight in his chest, and he smiled involuntarily. Maybe the feeling of being young and in love was more recent than he thought.

Jay was glad that the weather had let up by the time the hover touched ground at the tessera site. The rain had washed away a lot of the snow and blood. Only pink patches remained in the shadows and hollows around the trees. The beta team was happy for the relief; they had done a great deal of work in cataloguing the condition of the site and packing up the xeno corpses to return to cold storage at XenoNet. Leung had pointed out that they might as well let the biology team have at the remains of the unfortunate creatures if they were already deceased and not easily returnable to their home world. After giving the new team a sitrep, the betas clambered aboard their own hover with their cargo, messaged a quick farewell, and sped off.

"Let's spread out, folks," Jay told his crew. "I know Beta said they didn't find anything, but we have fresh eyes, clear ground, and daylight. Time to go over it all again."

"Aye, Cap'n." Alex grinned up at him. He'd already started unloading his small cadre of drones, each configured with various scanners. Sasha and Cordy moved off into the brush, looking for trails that might indicate where the xenos had scattered to hide and where they'd been captured. The rest of the team fanned out, eyes and devices set for anything that looked like it didn't belong on a remote cliff a hundred kilometers from the nearest town. Only Tito remained behind.

"Mind if I tag along with you on this one?" he asked.

"Uh. Sure." Jay frowned in confusion. "I mean, I don't mind. I'm heading to the east perimeter."

"Suits me. Lead on."

As they combed the territory, Jay couldn't help a wash of curiosity. "Can I ask why you wanted to come with me?" He and Tito had been working together well since he was hired for the team, but they'd still kept their distance from each other. Working closely with someone you had dated for two years was awkward.

"Just wanted to talk a bit, if you're all right with that."

Jay shrugged. "Feel free."

Tito sighed and rubbed his face. "Yusuf and I are getting a divorce."

Startled, Jay turned to stare at his ex. "Really? I thought you and he were happy."

"I thought we were, too, but I guess he's been worn down by managing the kids while I'm off on tessera events so much these days. He ended up having an affair with Jackie's violin teacher. They think they're in love and want to move in together. Or, I should be more precise, the teacher wants to move into my house. Yusuf has asked me to leave. Even worse, he's asking for primary custody, with just rudimentary visitation, because I can't guarantee I'll be there if the kids need me."

"Holy shit. I'm so sorry to hear that. That's awful."

"I offered to quit the job—go back to firefighting or even do something else entirely, something with a steady schedule—but Yusuf said that wasn't enough. He said it was too late for me to change things and we just need to move on."

"Tito, I don't know what to say. That's not fair of him at all."

Tito shrugged. "I guess what's done is done. Now I have to figure out how to stitch my life back together again."

Jay wanted to give him a reassuring hug, but didn't know how he'd take it. "Well, if there's anything I can do to help, let me know. I know things between us didn't end great, and I apologize for being such a callous ass back then, but I do care about you. I don't like seeing you hurt."

"Actually," Tito said, slowing down to look at him, "there *is* one thing. Any chance you have a couch I could crash on for a while until I can get a place of my own?"

Jay stopped, and his arm dropped away. "Well, I'm not sure . . ." He glanced across the clearing they had stopped at. On the other side, Sasha and Cordy were crouched down, picking through a blackberry bramble. It wasn't like they had anything official yet, but with all the nights Sasha had spent with him already, she might soon be more of a fixture at his apartment, which already felt cramped with the two of them. "Thing is," he finally said, "I'm sort of . . . seeing someone."

"Oh!" Tito backed away a few inches. "I had no idea. Anyone I know, or is it a non-work someone?"

"Um, if you don't mind, I'd rather not say. We're keeping things fairly quiet for now." But he couldn't stop looking at Sasha, and Tito followed his gaze.

"Wait. What?" Both of the people over there were women, and as far as Tito had known when they were dating, Jay wasn't into that.

Jay quickly turned back and cleared his throat. "Like I say, we're keeping things quiet. Please."

"I'll be damned." Tito chuckled. "You *have* changed, bro."

Jay opened his mouth to protest, and to correct the apparent misconception about him, but they were interrupted by a shout from the two women in question. The com link in his ear flashed to life, and Sasha's voice echoed in his head.

"We found something, guys," she said breathlessly. "You're going to want to see this."

SPIES AND LIES

Angel remembered the first time she learned about the Troubles. She had grown up while Ireland had been at peace for generations, so the revelation from her teacher that her homeland had once been involved in some truly awful things—neighbor killing neighbor; atrocities she couldn't even imagine without feeling faint—was a shock.

She came home from school crying, and her mother enfolded her in strong, soft arms. "Angel, my sweet girl," she purred soothingly. "I wish I could tell you that the world wasn't like that anymore, but it is. It always has been. It always will be. We can try to push the hate away, but it will always rot the hearts of some people."

"Are they just bad people, Mama?" Until today, the "bad people" she knew about were villains in the vids and stories she liked. The idea that there were real villains in the world was beyond her.

"I wish it wasn't so, but yes." Her mother twisted a loose strand of hair back into the braid it had emerged from. "Love can change many sour hearts, but it can't change all. It's better that you know these things now, because you'll need to be wary of that sourness in people."

"But I just want to have friends," she protested with all of her six-year-old's logic.

Her mother smiled, her ruddy cheeks glowing in the warm

afternoon sun. "You can! You can have many, many friends. There are many people in this world who will be kind and generous and peaceful. Many people will spend the last of their money to buy you food or open their home to you if you need shelter. Many will comfort you with their arms and words even if they have nothing else to give. There are many people who truly believe in helping and doing good, especially for those who are in need. It is my deepest hope that you will be one of those people. But you still have to be careful because sometimes the bad people will seem like good ones at first. Sometimes, they are very good at making others think they are not bad, or at least not as bad as they really are. Those people, my child, are the ones you need to run away from, as fast and as far as your legs will carry you."

There was fear in her heart, yes—what she was facing now was something more complex and dangerous than anything else she'd experienced in her 22 years so far—but there was also anger. A lot of it. Still, as furious as Angel was, it didn't remotely match the look of murderous rage that twisted the face of her boss as she paced around her office.

"That son of a snake!" Leung spat as she looked over the piece of equipment that had been recovered from the tessera site. Hoping to preserve its integrity, Angel took it back from her while the woman continued to vent— spewing something in Mandarin that probably translated to wishing death and destruction on their foe's entire genetic line. She slipped back into English, still furious. "How? How the hell would he have known the details about this tessera?"

Alex shrugged. "I don't know. I'm sorry. Angel and I are going to work on reverse-engineering the device. Maybe it has some data on its firmware that can give us more of a clue."

Angel toyed with the thing. It was elegant. A small, titanium cube no bigger than a box of raisins, it bore a simple embedded screen and a telltale "DMT" logo on the other side: Dark Matter Technologies. Alex had sent her an image scan of the device while he and the team were on the hover back to campus, and she had examined it in virtual mode while waiting for its tangible version to arrive. As best as she could tell—and Alex confirmed that he was thinking the same thing—the device was a signal interrupter of some sort. While operational, it probably sent out a form of spectral white noise that blocked the tessera's opening signal from scanners outside its range while transmitting the signal to another location. Accordingly, the device specifically ensured that someone other than XenoNet was notified that the tessera was open.

Leung finally sat down. Her face was almost gray with exhaustion. "Could there be more of these devices at other tessera locations?"

Alex shrugged. "Maybe."

"Honestly, I don't think so. Not yet, at least," Angel added. "I don't yet know how long this device was in place before it was used, but I'm guessing it hasn't been more than a week or so. Its battery likely doesn't have more active time, and it doesn't have any visible solar pickups for charging. We've had plenty of events in that time, including some flashes, and most of the local tesserae are showing up on our monitor just fine. It may also be that this tessera was the only one he was interested in, for getting something valuable enough on the black market to risk being caught."

"But Belenko's always been interested in mining and other non-living resources, hasn't he?" Alex asked. "I'd think he'd be more likely to try to send a mining drone through a tessera to see if he could get something useful out of the planet itself."

Leung shook her head. "Not necessarily. Without knowing for sure how long the tessera would be open, he probably wouldn't want to risk losing equipment that expensive. With the xenos, all he had to do was find a way to lure them through to where a few of his crew could slaughter them. Quick and dirty."

"Dirty is right," Angel muttered. "Pardon my unprofessional language, but fuck this guy. Fuck his whole company."

Leung nodded grimly. "Language definitely pardoned."

Alex looked at his hands and took a deep breath. "I do want to bring up one thing." He squirmed uncomfortably. "What if this wasn't Belenko? What if this device is something one of his employees made without his knowledge? Or maybe it's a prototype of something innocuous that got sent out to third parties for beta review and got hacked or modified."

Leung rubbed her face. "Knowing Belenko, I'm almost certain he's behind this, but I have to concede that it's a possibility. Much as I'd like to confront him—"

"You and everyone else," Alex interjected. "I don't think I've ever seen Sasha so furious. I thought she was going to hijack the hover and land it in his living room."

Angel had to laugh. Sasha, of whom she'd grown fond, was a kind and fun person, but she had an angry streak. Someone attacking her beloved xenos would've been signing their own death warrant if she'd had her way.

Leung smiled, too, a welcome sight on her tired face. "I can imagine. As I was saying, though, it's best that we proceed with caution. The last thing we want to do is get ourselves in legal hot water by acting too rashly. Besides, we still have our own internal investigation to do. We still don't know how Belenko—or whoever did this—got the tessera information to begin with. That's a critical piece of the puzzle."

Angel's mood clouded even more as she realized the truth of Leung's words. A sick feeling that the investigation might eventually end up in her direction had been gnawing at her since the poaching was discovered. As far as she knew, Dane hadn't seen anything of value in the few moments he'd had access to her band, and she also didn't think he'd be the type to engage in such awful things. If nothing else, his family was very rich; he'd have no monetary incentive to do Belenko's dirty work. Still, she had to admit that there was always a possibility. He was upset enough with her these days because of her long hours that he could have done it out of spite. Though the thought made her heartsick, she had already started working on a way to investigate her boyfriend without him realizing it. And, she thought with a fresh wave of nausea, without her boss realizing the mistake she'd made and firing her—or worse. This close to getting her degree, the idea of being deported sounded like a nightmare. "Well, I'll do everything I can," she assured Leung. "I'll get as much out of this thing as possible, and I'll keep my ear out for any office chatter that might tell us who our mole is."

"Thank you," Leung said. "I admit, this whole thing could have been worse if I didn't have amazing people on my staff, you two chief among them. I'm confident that if we have a bad apple, it's only one."

"I hope so," Alex said, "for everyone's sake—especially the xenos."

* * *

Sasha sat in her office, parked in front of Littlefoot's enclosure and making silly faces at him.

"How is he these days?"

She jerked up and turned to see who had appeared in her doorway. "Oh. Hi, Jay." She turned back, placing her hand on the glass. Littlefoot rubbed his chin there and thumped a back foot. "He's good. I haven't had much time to work with him lately, though. I've missed him." The creature did another little dance, one that was a greeting specifically for Jay.

"Hey, dude!" Jay grinned and waved. Sasha knew he liked the little xeno, but he certainly didn't have the same deep feelings for him that she did. Bonding with animals was easy. Bonding with a human was a different story. Humans were harder to trust.

She pushed her chair back and looked up at Jay. "How goes the investigation?"

His nose wrinkled. "Nothing so far. Angel wrote a quick program to scan all internal Stream data logs, looking for anything that might tie someone to Dark Matter or even just to the device we found. There's a lot to go through—10 years of archives, some in obsolete formats—so it's going to take a while. I'm exhausted, anyway, so I'm going to let that scan run overnight and get some food and rest. You should probably do that, too." He approached her and stroked a hand down her messy hair. "If you want to come back to my place again, I'll cook. I think I have supplies for some yakisoba."

Unexpectedly, she tensed under his gentle touch and pulled away. "Don't."

"Whoa." Jay stepped back. "Are you OK?"

An uncomfortable shiver ran through her. "I'm sorry. I didn't mean to react like that. I'm just on edge tonight."

"Understandable. I'm sure dinner would help, though."

She shook her head. "No, it wouldn't. At least not . . ." She trailed off into a heavy sigh. Rubbing her hands across her face seemed to pull the picture into sudden focus. "Listen, Jay. You know I like you. I think you're a great friend, and I love working with you."

His face fell. "Shit. This is one of those conversations, isn't it?"

She looked away. He was right: it was. She couldn't nail down exactly why, but she definitely did not want to go back to his apartment. She wasn't even sure she wanted to go back to her Bisa's place. The only thing that appealed to her, apart from spending the entire evening playing with Littlefoot, was getting in a round of capoeira practice at the new studio she'd been attending. While its master wasn't as skilled as João, and also not Brazilian, she was entirely professional and not remotely Sasha's type. "I'm sorry, Jay. I'm sorry if I gave you the wrong impression or something."

He shrugged, though it was clear from his face that something had broken inside him. "It's not because I'm primarily into guys, is it?"

"Oh, no. Not at all. I think that's perfectly fine. No, it's just . . . I'm upset by this whole mole thing, and I need some distance for a while. There's nothing wrong with you—please don't think I don't like you—I just don't feel all that good about humans in general right now." She stood up and took his hand. "No weirdness, OK? I do like you."

He tried to smile, but a couple of tears slipped down his face. "It's OK. I understand. I do. It just hurts a bit right now. I'll get past it soon enough. I promise, no weirdness from me."

"Thank you." She stood up to slide her arms around his waist and press a gentle kiss on his damp cheek. Something inside her still loved his touch, and was telling her that she was making a huge mistake, but the fear was too much. She had to let go.

"Dammit!" Sasha grumbled. The chord wasn't working for her, and her fingertips felt raw. She'd been so busy with work recently that she hadn't picked up her guitar in more than a month, and her calluses had smoothed out. Still, she felt stubborn, so she kept trying.

"I hate to interrupt, but is there a reason you've been playing that same chord for an hour?"

Her head swiveled around. Her Bisa had come in from her studio, apron spattered with paint and a dripping brush tucked behind one ear. She'd nearly forgotten that there was someone else nearby who might be bothered by her attempts at a suspended F minor. She stood up and set the guitar back on its stand. "I'm sorry!"

Bisa smiled. "Oh, keep playing if you like. Just maybe a couple of different chords?"

"Sure thing. Of course. Sorry if I'm out of it tonight. It's been a hard day." With a twitch, Sasha realized that it was long past dinner time, and she'd only had a glass of juice. She'd been so used to having dinner with Jay that she'd forgotten she needed to feed herself tonight.

"So I had gathered. I'm surprised you're here, though. Thought you'd be spending the night with that friend of yours again." Bisa winked knowingly.

Sasha smiled weakly. "Not tonight, I'm afraid." She hadn't told her much about Jay, but it had been obvious why she hadn't been sleeping at home.

Bisa frowned. "And not again, if the look on your face is right."

Sasha looked away and bit her lip.

"That's what I thought. Into the kitchen with you." Bisa stowed the paintbrush in a pocket of the apron and began taking it off.

"What?"

"Kitchen. I'm hungry. We're making pancakes." She grabbed Sasha's arm and steered her toward the kitchen.

Sasha wasn't much of a cook—and neither was Bisa, if she was terribly honest—but between the two of them, they managed to put together a couple of hearty stacks of steaming pancakes. They sat down at the kitchen table to dig into the buttery, maple-soaked softness.

"Ah! That's hitting the spot." A blissful smile spread across Bisa's lined face. "Seems silly, I know, for a girl who grew up in Brazil, but American-style pancakes were always a treat for me. My *papai* made them for us every weekend in tourist season while my mother worked the souvenir shop below our apartment."

Sasha had a sudden, sharp memory of her mother doing something similar when she was young. She had been so young when the quake happened that she had few clear memories of her. This was one she hadn't accessed in years. "My mama did that, too. I think."

"I'm sure she did. I did it for your *vovò*, and he did it for her. I wasn't much of a traditional grandmother, I'm afraid, but that was one thing that we enjoyed as a family while your mother was growing up. There were other things, too. We celebrated *Carnivàle*, even though Papai was the last Catholic in our family. I passed down some songs that my grandparents had sung. That sort of thing."

The sweet stickiness in Sasha's mouth suddenly took on greater depth than it might otherwise have. She felt her nose tingle with an impending rush of tears. "I had no idea."

"I'm sure you didn't. Did you have any other family traditions with Joey?"

Sasha nodded. "We did all the usual seasonal holiday stuff—it's impossible not to in Iowa—but none of it was all that personal. He bought an artificial Christmas tree the year I turned six, and that got hauled out of the closet every year. He took me to the park for Easter egg hunts. He threw me a nice birthday party at a pizza parlor when I turned 10. But I can't say that any of it felt like it mattered. It was done because it was expected, not because it meant anything to us. There was rarely anything emotional or unique to just us about it." She took another bite, savoring it, and continued. "I think doing those things with me reminded him too much of doing them with Vovò Juan and my mother. I know I look a lot like her, so he probably kept having memories of her every time we did something they had done as a family."

Bisa nodded. "Undoubtedly. They did all those things here rather than in Iowa, but I'm sure it was still painful for him."

"You know, he didn't even have any pictures of them up in the house."

Bisa's eyes grew wide. "None?"

Sasha shook her head. "I once found a box in his closet with a bunch of old things: some baby shoes of hers, a blanket, some of her toys, pictures of his and Vovò's wedding. There was also old flash drive in there. I took it to a vintage electronics dealer, and she pulled off thousands of pictures and video of Vovò and my mother and put them on my Stream account. Every night before bed, I'd look through them, seeing what their lives were like back then. It felt weird, though, like I was looking at something I wasn't supposed to. And I guess I probably wasn't, if Grandpa had all that stuff packed away and never showed it to me."

"Oh, child." Bisa stood up and put her arms around Sasha. "I'm so sorry you didn't have the family you were supposed to."

Sasha accepted the hug and sniffled a bit as a few tears came out. "It's OK. You can't miss what you've never had, right? I got used to being more or less on my own. It's not a huge deal, I don't think."

Bisa stood back, a stern look on her face as she stared down at Sasha. "No. It *is* a big deal. It's a very big deal. Some people are happy to be alone—I've been living on my own since I divorced your Bisavò, and I'm happy this way—but children shouldn't be forced to live like that. I know Joey didn't mean to hurt you, but it did happen. You're adrift, Meniña, like a boat. You don't have an anchor."

Sasha was quiet as Bisa sat down and continued eating. True, she had envied the children she grew up with. Most of them had large families. The few who did not still had many family friends who filled spaces that absent cousins and grandparents would have. Except for contact with her Bisa, she had next to nothing: just Joey and a couple of people he worked with in his accounting office. She had tried hitching herself to the families of some of the other kids, but they had never truly welcomed her in as one of them. After a while, she simply gave up and set about being her own best friend and family, aside from the animals she made friends with everywhere she went. She was too convinced that everyone else in her life would be temporary to do otherwise.

"Oh," she blurted, and a fresh wave of tears started flowing.

"What?"

She sighed. "I think I know why I'm here tonight instead of with my friend."

"Things getting too serious for you?" Bisa smiled knowingly.

Sasha nodded. "Yeah. Jay—that's his name—is a good friend from work. We've spent a lot of time together on tessera events, and we've gotten close. That's . . . not how things usually go when I'm, well, *with* someone. I'm just there to have some fun, and that's it. I haven't even thought about getting serious. The thing I had with João got weird for me even before I found out about him still being married. I didn't feel comfortable dating someone who already had a child—it was too much for me. Jay's the first person I've been with that started out as such a close friend, and we're only getting closer."

"And that's making you scared."

"Yeah. There's some other work stuff I can't tell you about that's pushing those buttons right now, which isn't helping. I told him tonight I just needed some distance. I think I broke his heart."

"Ouch. Can you get it back? Or do you even want to?"

Sasha shrugged. "I don't know—on both counts. I don't know what it would feel like to actually be in love with someone, so I don't know if I'm anywhere close. It's probably moot, anyway. Work is getting absolutely chaotic, and it's probably best if I just drop the whole thing for now." She dug back into her pancakes, willing their fluffiness to take her mind off the subject entirely.

Bisa gave her a sad smile. "Well, whatever you decide, just remember this: make sure it's absolutely your decision, and not something you're doing for someone else or because you have old demons nipping at your heels. From what you've been telling me, your Grandpa Joey cut himself off from love—including loving you—because he was afraid of feeling anything. He was afraid of how bad he would hurt if he lost someone he loved again. Don't repeat his mistake."

* * *

Jay couldn't imagine facing even Josie with this, much less anyone else, but there was one person he thought might make a difference—or at least take his mind off the sudden, unexpected way Sasha had dumped him.

Things have changed, he typed to Tito. *You can stay at my place after all.*

LOVE: SICK

What Jay had always loved the most about Tito was his sense of humor. He had a knack for finding a laugh in any situation, no matter how awkward or dire. Crawling through the mud on a training exercise? He made pig noises. Condom broke before they could even put it on? He started singing a cheesy pop song about broken hearts. So when they were about to be shipped off in totally different directions, Jay figured Tito might laugh that off, too. He was wrong. Their last night together, spent in a cold, damp corner of the compound, Tito broke down crying right after they had finished. Jay held him, and petted his soft, dark hair, and tried to be funny for both of them.

"Hey, we can always do vid calls. Think about it: personal, made-to-order porn!"

Tito looked up, his eyes red and swollen. "Porn? That's what you're thinking of right now?"

Jay pulled back. "Uh. No, not—I'm sorry. That was crass."

"It's OK. I know you didn't mean to be. I'm surprised you're taking this so well, though. I can't imagine being away from you for two years. Isn't it going to bother you, too?"

"Of course!" Jay thought he was telling the truth, but as he said the words, he realized they weren't honest at all. He liked Tito— probably loved him, in fact—but his boyfriend had always been on

215

the clingy side, which was becoming uncomfortable. At 22, they were both only starting military careers that would likely take them all over the world. Surely he couldn't have expected them to settle down and start raising kids already. Jay knew he wanted that someday— maybe even with Tito—but now? No. Not for a long time. Still, he wasn't about to hurt the man any further with such a revelation at this moment.

"We'll be in touch, though, right?" Jay tried to reassure him. "All the time, whenever we can. It's not like we're being shipped to some remote chunk of tundra somewhere."

Tito sniffled, then nodded. "You're right. And we can see each other in person whenever we get leave."

"Exactly. It'll be fine. We'll be fine. I'm sure of it."

He'd seen Tito once after their breakup. They were both stationed in Pakistan when the war broke out, but in different places: Jay to his remote-ops bunker in the South, Tito following drones with human-transport vehicles to rescue civilians stranded in the war zones. After Jay's bunker was bombed, the whole unit wrapped operations and prepared to send everyone home. He passed Tito's seat on the transport plane and gave him a quick, friendly smile, but was greeted only with a frown before the other man turned away.

Working with Tito now—seeing again the man he'd once loved after so many years—brought back old memories for Jay: mostly good ones, but some painful ones, too. He felt as if karma had dealt him his due, with Sasha breaking his heart much the same as he had broken Tito's. Perhaps guilt over that was why Tito currently lay in his bed, curled up next to him, an arm thrown over Jay's chest and smiling in his sleep.

Unfortunately, hooking up with his ex had done precisely nothing to make him feel better, and the knowledge that he'd probably just compounded Tito's pain made it even worse.

He glanced at the glowing screen on his nightstand:

23:15. Too late to message Josie: she'd be zonked out for the usual early wake on base. But Hawai'i was two hours behind. He picked up the screen and rolled over to keep its light from disturbing Tito as he tapped out a message: *Mom? You awake? I could use some advice.*

* * *

"What's wrong?" The roses Dane held were still perky, but his face no longer was.

Angel shook her head. "Nothing, babe. They're beautiful." She took the flowers and smelled them, letting the heady scent calm her mind. Weeks into her investigation had so far turned up nothing—no tracks left by anyone at the company who could have been the mole. More and more, the evidence was pointing to someone outside of it—and one person in particular.

Though it felt horribly unethical to do so, she had followed her suspicions, and hacked into Dane's personal Stream account, looking, she hoped, for something that would clear him, rather than provide evidence that he was involved. What she found was, frustratingly, neither. The most she was able to track down were electronic breadcrumbs left from deleted messages with an unknown third party—messages that had happened while she was in class or at work. All of his other communication was accounted for: With her, his family, their gaming group, professors and classmates and other assorted acquaintances. None of it was the least bit incriminating. One thing that did give her some hope was timestamps on several pictures and video from an all-night gaming session that had happened the night before the dead xenos were discovered. At least, she thought hopefully, he wasn't one of the poachers. The deleted messages themselves could also have been something innocuous—advertising, a wrong account contact, the tenacious ex-girlfriend who had pestered him for months after their breakup—but she had no way of knowing for sure without seeing them in their entirety.

Her hacking skills were good, but not good enough to get into the automatic logging of all message data that lurked in official Stream archives. For that—and for the sake of court admissibility for anything she might find—she would need government clearance. And for government clearance, she'd need to tell Leung about leaving her band where Dane could get to it.

She was therefore back at square one: Hoping that the rest of the investigation would turn up something—anything—that would place suspicion on someone other than her boyfriend—and her.

Dane smiled at her again. "I'm glad you like them."

"I do. Thank you," she said, with a smile she hoped looked sincere. "Happy Valentine's Day."

* * *

Once again, Alex was sore. Once again, he didn't care. Remy disengaged and rose to tidy up and get a drink. Amazed that his lover could even walk following their frantic clinch after a Valentine's-Day dinner, Alex flopped back on the couch. He mopped with his shirt at the thin sheen of sweat—and spots of other things—on his chest and tried to catch his breath.

His band, sitting on the coffee table where it had been dropped as they came through the door, barely even crossing the threshold before they started disrobing, chirped noisily for an incoming message. He considered ignoring it—it wasn't a tessera alert, after all—but conscience and curiosity got the better of him. He picked up the device and ran his thumb down the edge. It locked into its flat position and lit up, the message alert on top. It was from Dave, a member of the beta team's security force. Alex sat up.

Couldn't think of anyone else to ping at this hour, figured you might be able to handle this. Just talked to my sister in Klamath Falls. She went up to Crater yesterday and ran across a small box near the tessera site. Looks like the one your team found at Hood Canal.

His heart thumping wildly, Alex touched the screen to expand the attached image. Sure enough, the box was another signal-intercept device, the same DMT logo on its side. Whoever wanted to exploit the planets the tesserae connected to had chosen another target. The only problem was, as far as almost everyone knew, there was nothing at all about Crater remotely of interest to someone seeking to make quick cash. The glass-butterfly xenos were pretty, but of no real value except as a novelty pet, and one that likely had a short lifespan, which lowered its potential worth. The planet itself, however, was a different story.

He tried to blame his sudden shakiness on coming down after his romp, but he knew better. There were only three people who knew about Crater's real value in the alien planet's bedrock full of precious metals: him, Jay, and Sasha. The horrible realization that one of his friends must be the mole made his head spin.

Alex sat in Leung's office, picking at his ragged cuticles and trying to pretend that he hadn't said it.

"Are you absolutely sure?" Leung leaned in. Her face was pale, and her mouth trembled.

"Not completely, but nothing else makes sense." Alex fidgeted. "There's absolutely no way Sasha would have allowed the slaughter of the xenos at Hood Canal, so it can't be her. And Jay has access to all the background-check information. He could have easily falsified his own somehow."

Leung rubbed her eyes. "But it doesn't make sense. Why would he do it? I knew Jay's father when he worked at Boeing; he helped me with the patents for some of my work. He's a stand-up guy, so I'd imagine his kids probably would be, too. And, to be perfectly blunt, Jay's family isn't exactly hurting for money. Besides his military pension, if he needed cash, he could hit them up. Why would he do this, if not for that?"

Alex shrugged. "I honestly don't know. He said something once about how we should be more open about the tesserae and more willing to keep the xenos here for study. He was insistent about keeping one of them for the cell-regeneration stuff. Maybe he thinks like Belenko—that humans should be using the planets for resources we need. Though, hell, for all I know, maybe Belenko's blackmailing him somehow. Maybe there's something in his old military record he doesn't want getting out."

"It could be anything, I suppose." She sat back in her chair and stared at the ceiling for a moment. Finally, she sighed and stood up. "OK. The best thing to do for now is to put him on paid leave while we investigate. I'll make Monica Shibak the temporary security chief and alpha-team lead, and I'll talk to Angel about making sure he doesn't have remote access to anything while we're looking into it."

"Makes sense." Actually, none of it made sense, but Alex was at a loss to say anything else.

Leung approached him and laid a gentle hand on his shoulder. "Thank you for coming to me with this. I know you, Jay, and Sasha have become close friends since the sub accident. I'm sure it wasn't easy to tell me your suspicions."

Alex smiled tightly and tried to accept the comfort. "No, it wasn't. Not at all."

* * *

It was no use arguing, Jay knew. In Leung's position, he probably would have done the same. It was kind of her at least to put him on leave, instead of firing him outright or even having him arrested, but it still hurt—a lot. As he shuffled to the parking garage, a bin of his belongings tucked under his arm, he couldn't help crying out of frustration and humiliation.

What was even worse than being suspected for the poaching, however, was not knowing who was really behind it. Alex was right in what he had told Leung: the three of them were the only ones who knew about the resource-heavy planet. There was a remote possibility that one of them had still had a live com and Angel had overheard their conversation when Alex's probe returned, laden with platinum dust; but that was unlikely, and Angel had been far too angry about the poaching to have been involved. He agreed that Sasha would never have done it, and he knew he hadn't, so that left Alex. He was clever enough to have diverted suspicion from himself by naming Jay, that much was apparent. Jay also knew that even with his salary, Alex had trouble affording his apartment after his ex had moved out, so he could see money being a motive. But it was Alex's idea in the first place to keep their platinum planet a secret; it didn't seem at all likely that he would have sabotaged that. Still, it was a possibility Jay had to consider: that the man he'd nursed a crush on for so long had not only sold secrets to another company, but was framing him for it.

As he began loading up the saddlebags on his bike, a sound echoing up from the level below caught his attention. He immediately recognized Remy's honeyed voice, chatting merrily away in Cajun-accented French on his com. There was enough distance, and Jay's command of the language was rusty enough, that he couldn't get more than every third word, but a couple phrases did catch his attention.

"Le garde est un vache," Remy told his caller, and laughed. *"Pas de problème pour nous."*

Jay shuddered from head to toe. No, Alex would not have sold company secrets, but in a moment of weakness, he might have let information about it fall into the hands of his charming new boyfriend. Dropping the bin beside his bike, he took off at a run for the stairs down.

"You!" he shouted as soon as he burst through the door.

Remy turned, dropping his screen in the process. "What the hell?"

Jay rushed up, getting in the agent's face and backing him up against his car. "Who were you talking to?"

"That's absolutely none of your business. And shouldn't you be off campus by now? Do I need to call someone to have you arrested?"

"I heard what you said, Remy."

The Homeland agent looked him over and snorted. "Oh, so the island boy magically speaks French now?"

Jay felt his face go hot. "Does 'Lambert' sound Hawaiian to you? I'm half Belgian, you ignorant ass."

Remy suddenly paled. Then he straightened, composing himself. "Whatever you think you heard, you're wrong. And even if I had done anything, what would you do about it? Leung thinks you're the one responsible. Who else are you going to tell? Alex? Like he'd believe you over me."

Jay balled up a fist. He'd never before struck someone in anger, but the temptation now was so great he thought he might well pound that smug, perfect face into a squishy mess.

Remy noticed. "I wouldn't if I were you. One punch, and you'd lose Alex forever—and a lot more than him, too."

Jay glanced down. The glow under his forearm had turned yellow. The device had sensed his emotional state and done what it was supposed to do: release a flood of his beta-blocking medication. Calm washed through him, and he relaxed his fist.

Remy smiled. "There's a good boy." He put a hand to Jay's chest and pushed him aside. "Why don't you just run along home like a good little soldier, hm?"

Jay stood back and watched as the vile man got into his

car, started the loud combustion engine, and pulled away. Remy was right. Alex would never believe him if he tried to explain what his lover had done.

Sasha, on the other hand . . .

* * *

The person standing at the entrance to her Bisa's apartment building was not someone she would have expected this late in the evening, and, under the circumstances, not who she would have wanted to see, either.

"Fuck off, Jay!" she shouted over the intercom.

He winced and looked up at the camera. "Sasha, please. I didn't do it—you have to know that—but I know who did. Please let me in."

Bisa came up behind her and peered over her shoulder at the screen. "Who's this?"

Sasha turned. "This is my former friend. The one who did the awful thing at work I can't tell you about."

Bisa raised an eyebrow. "Isn't this also the guy you were seeing for a while? He's a handsome devil, that's for certain."

Sasha grumbled. "He's ugly as far as I'm concerned."

Bisa rolled her eyes. "Meniña, look at him. Handsome or not, that is not the face of someone who is lying to you. If you don't let him in, I will."

Sasha stared at the screen. She had to admit that Bisa had a point. Jay's eyes were red and puffy, and he sniffled even as she watched. Someone cold-hearted enough to be involved in such horrible things wouldn't be crying about getting caught. Though a small voice told her to stay wary, she authorized the entry.

By the time Jay was done explaining, she was not only convinced of his innocence, but her baser self was reminding her that she missed other things about him, too.

Jay sighed and rested his head on her shoulder. She let

223

him, allowing herself the enjoyment of the closeness. "I wish we could convince Alex, but I know Remy was right. He's in a love fog right now. He won't listen to anyone. And he and Leung are tight enough that I don't want to talk to her and risk coming between them unless I have absolute proof. I just don't know what else to do."

"Well, I still have full access to everything, so I could do some poking around myself," Sasha noted, "but I think Leung knows that we were seeing each other. Unless I could come up with something blatant, she probably would assume I'm just trying to point the finger somewhere else to save you."

Jay let out a weak whimper.

She brightened as the idea came to her. "Although, there is one other person who would probably understand."

"Oh?"

"Angel. She's never liked Remy, so she'd probably be perfectly happy to help us get enough evidence on him to convince Leung and have probable cause for an arrest—something he wouldn't be able to weasel out of."

"Ah! Of course." Jay finally smiled for the first time that evening. It was good to see.

"I should go contact her." Sasha moved to grab her band, which was resting on an end table nearby.

Jay pulled her back down. "I wouldn't. Not yet. If Remy's been doing this for months, he probably put spy hacks in place, to make sure no one was onto him."

She frowned. "Even on our personal accounts?"

He nodded. "Anything that ever connected to the internal Stream would likely be affected. Angel would know how to root those out, too, but I'd recommend talking to her in person, first."

"OK," Sasha agreed. She glanced up at the clock. It was late, but Angel, being a young college student, might still be awake. "Her dorm's probably locked down for the night, but I could still go try to find her room anyway."

Jay shook his head. "Not worth it. The only thing she'd be able to do is scan the internal Stream right away, and an after-hours login like that might trip the spy hack. She'd probably tell you the same thing: It's safer to wait until you see her at work tomorrow."

Sasha grumbled. She was wired, now, and wanted to do something—anything—to help bring Remy down. Still, Jay's concerns made sense. "I'll pull her aside first thing tomorrow and see what we can come up with, then."

"Thank you. Frankly, I feel like I'm dodging a big bullet right now. I'm just glad Leung didn't have me thrown in jail or something."

"Really!" Sasha smiled at him and stroked his arm. "Listen . . . my bed's small, but if you don't want to be alone tonight, I could—"

Jay shook his head and sat up. "I can't."

Sasha frowned. "Can't?"

"I . . . uh. It's complicated. Though I don't even know if he's there. I'm sure he's heard by now about what I got accused of, so . . ."

"What? Who's heard?"

He smiled sheepishly. "Tito. A couple of weeks ago he told me that he and his husband were splitting up and asked to stay at my place while he looked for an apartment. I told him I couldn't do it. That was while you and I were . . . and I thought . . . well, anyway. But then you said you needed space."

Sasha stared. "Oh. So are you and he . . .?"

Jay ran a hand over his head. "Honestly? I have no idea. I don't know if this is just a rebound fling for him—or me—or what. I at least need to go home tonight so I can talk to him and try to convince him that I'm not a criminal. Exactly what's going to come after that conversation, I don't know. I wish I could be clearer about it, but . . ."

"I get it. Complicated." Sasha sighed. It was probably best that he not stay the night anyway. It wouldn't be fair to him, especially with the crisis he was currently in, if she got cold feet yet again. "Go home, then. I'll talk to Angel tomorrow, and we'll be in touch. I promise, I'm going to do everything I can to see that Remy gets his ass handed to him."

* * *

"What the festering fuck? I knew Remy was lodged so far up his own ass he could use his kidneys for bongos, but even I never expected this kind of thing from that little cocksnot."

Despite herself, and the secrecy required for this conversation, Sasha had to grin. Among the young woman's many talents, she had a facility for profanity. Still, the outburst had drawn stares from others milling about the central communications space. "Sssh!" Sasha hissed. "We need to go somewhere quiet so I can explain."

"Of course." Angel grabbed her portable monitor and the half-empty latte on her desk. "Courtyard. No one's going to be there until lunch."

It was cold and damp in the green space between the buildings, and Sasha shivered, even with two layers of shirts and a hoodie. Angel had been right: the place was deserted. The only evidence of someone else's presence was a tiny security camera embedded on one side of the building. Angel disabled it after a few seconds with the small device on her lap. "OK. I looped the last 10 minutes of footage from that cam. Monica won't notice a thing. So. What's this about Remy being a massive turdwaffle? I should never have trusted that guy."

"I wish Alex had felt the same" Sasha sighed. "Jay said he doesn't know the details, but he confronted Remy in the parking garage last night, and it was obvious he was involved. Problem is, we have no hard evidence, so it would be Jay's word against Remy's. If he were anyone except a liaison from Homeland, I'm sure Jay would come out in favor, but having that level of clearance means he's going to be hard to catch."

"So we need something tangible we can take to Leung—and then to the FBI or something."

"Right."

"Easy enough. Give me just a minute." Angel's fingers flew over the screen. In a couple of seconds, it started playing footage from a garage cam. Unfortunately, it was several meters from where Jay and Remy stood, and though it was obvious they were arguing, the audio pickup caught nothing distinct. "Damn. I'd been hoping it would be this easy. Not so much. Well, there's more I can do. I can hack into his personal Stream account and trace who he's been talking to, which should help."

Sasha shook her head. "I don't want to risk us getting busted for illegal surveillance—we wouldn't be able to use that as evidence legally anyway. We need to do this above-board however we can."

"Noted," Angel said. "Still should be easy, though. I have authorized access to every internal com, data, and security system. You can thank Jay for that, since he enlisted my help with the initial investigation. All I need to do now is tweak the code I wrote to focus on Remy's activities and add some French to its keyword search. If he talked about this at all while he was on campus, I'll find it."

Sasha finally relaxed. "Thank you, Angel."

"Of course. I do have one question, though."

"Yeah?"

A look of concern crossed Angel's face. "What's going to happen with Alex? I mean, assuming we get proof that his boyfriend is a criminal. The poor guy's going to be gutted. You think he'll go supernova?"

"Honestly, I don't know. I consider Alex a good friend, but since he started dating Remy, we haven't spent much time together at all, except during tessera events. I've always seen him as an overgrown kid, but I know that's probably not fair. He might get angry at us for attacking Remy, but he may get angry at Remy instead. I just don't know." She closed her eyes and sighed. "I care about him a lot. I'm afraid of breaking his heart with this."

"Understandable. But you still might want to be the one to deliver the bad news, at least."

Sasha frowned. "Why me?"

"Because of that huge crush he had on you for about forever."

Sasha snorted. "Did everyone know about that except me?"

Angel nodded and grinned. "Sorry. He wasn't all that subtle. Not that Jay was all that subtle about wanting into Alex's pants, either. Could tell he was busted up when Remy came along."

"That much I knew about," Sasha said.

Angel nodded. "Intimately, I imagine." Sasha flushed to her toes. The other woman nudged her with a shoulder. "No worries. I'm observant, but I don't gossip."

"It's all moot, anyway." Sasha fixed her gaze on the ground. "We're not seeing each other now."

Angel frowned. "Oh? Why not?"

"Long story, and it's not entirely mine to tell."

"Got it. None of my concern. In any case: Yeah, I think you might want to try to build a bridge back to Alex if you can. When all this starts going down, he's going to need a friend, and it probably should be you."

"You're right. I'm having a hard time not being angry with him, though. How could he be so close to Remy and not know what he was doing?"

Angel shrugged. "Love makes people stupid."

HEALING THE BREAK

Not that such violence was ever justified, Alex knew, but he couldn't help thinking that the fact that his cheek was hot and stinging was at least partly his fault.

"How dare you!" his mother repeated. She raised her hand again, but this time let it fall, trembling, to her side. "How dare you question my judgment after what your father did to me—to us!"

"I'm sorry, Mom." She was right. Trying to excuse his own lack of judgment by throwing his parents' divorce back in her face had been a bad idea. "But really, it's not that big of a deal."

"No? And I suppose you think Carly did nothing wrong when she started sleeping with a married father twice her age."

"That's different."

"How?"

"Well, Kelsey isn't married—just engaged. And hardly a parent, either. I'm only two years younger."

"And technically underage, I'll remind you. We had an agreement when you got into college early that you wouldn't start acting like the older students."

"I'm not underage, though. Not legally. Plus we're both college students. Kelsey's not taking advantage of some naïve high schooler."

She sighed, and passed a hand over her face. "Dear Father in heaven," she muttered quietly, "save my child from himself."

He felt confident that he was being honest, at least about Kelsey's intentions toward him, but he did have to admit that perhaps his own judgment wasn't as sound as he'd like to think. His mother was right: sleeping with someone who was engaged to someone else, however rocky their relationship, was unethical. No matter how hot he found Kelsey, he shouldn't have taken the offer they gave after that long midterm study session. He reached out and patted his mother's arm. "Look, I get that this is upsetting you, and I understand why. If it'll make you feel better, I'll break it off."

She looked up, her eyes red-rimmed. "It would, Alex." She raised her hand again, but this time the touch on his cheek was soft. "I'm sorry I slapped you. You just . . . you look so much like your father sometimes, and I'm always afraid you're going to turn out like him."

He would never have told his mother—or Jonathan— exactly how shitty his judgment had been this time. On balance, the choices he'd made in his romantic life hadn't been all that bad, but there were definitely some unwise moves. Even dating Gabriel hadn't been a great idea since Gabe was technically in a position of authority over him when it started, and therefore should have known better than hitting on Alex. It wasn't like Alex had had the best model of a healthy relationship, considering how badly his parents had screwed that up, but even so, there were some basic ground rules that in the heat of attraction, he often forgot to heed.

On the surface, hooking up with Remy hadn't been a bad idea. There was an age gap—Remy was 10 years older—but it hadn't seemed terribly big. The Homeland agent also had a far more powerful job and all the authority that came with it, but he never seemed inclined to pull rank that way. They had several differences in interests and lifestyle and such, but most of the time, Alex didn't care that Remy had no idea what he was talking about in terms of his job. What he should have noticed, he realized in hindsight, was how Remy had refused to let

Alex see more of his own life. He'd never once had Alex over to his own apartment. Never once introduced Alex to any of his friends, much less family. Hell, he'd barely allowed Alex in his car, and that was only a few times to take him to dinner at some swanky restaurant, where Alex felt out of place and underdressed. It was the same kind of secretive behavior as his freshman fling Kelsey, before he found out about the fiancé back in Kelsey's hometown of Atlanta. All the signs were there—it was the same sneaking around his father had done with his dental assistant—but Alex had stubbornly ignored them in favor of feeding his id-level instincts.

This time, the things he should have noticed were far more serious than someone cheating on a partner. This time, innocent xenos had died, and the government was investigating XenoNet from top to bottom. Not that he trusted them anymore. They hadn't noticed that one of their own was giving out secrets and putting the public at risk in the process.

He had immediately offered his resignation to Leung, but she was having none of it. Instead, she encouraged him to deliver the news to Remy himself, and so, accompanied by a couple of stern-looking FBI agents, he was on his way down the hall to do just that. He was terrified—his legs felt like they'd been replaced with water balloons—but fury about what his lover had done drove him on.

Remy looked up at the doorway on his arrival. "Well, hello! How are you, *cher*? I didn't—" He broke off as he saw the agents trailing Alex. "What the hell?" His face reddened, and he stood up, backing away.

Alex rolled his eyes. "Really? You know exactly what this is. All I want to know is why."

Remy sputtered for a moment as the agents started toward him, one of them readying handcuffs, the other calmly reciting his rights. "This is ridiculous! That stupid security chief did this. You know that!"

Alex shook his head. "No, Remy. Jay didn't do anything wrong, and I should have trusted him, not you."

"*Cher*, please!" His voice rose with panic. "He must have planted some evidence. I had nothing to do with this!"

"No?" Alex reached into his pocket, tossing a small, DMT-logoed box on Remy's desk. "What's this, then? And why was it in your car?"

Remy's expression changed as he realized he no longer could get away with lying. Instead, he sagged, held up only by the agent who was fastening the cuffs around his wrists. "Alex, I'm sorry. Don't be angry with me."

"Are you kidding me? Why not?" Alex folded his arms across his chest.

"I did this because I had to!" Remy's eyes were now wide, his expression full of worry. "Belenko was . . . he was blackmailing me."

Alex raised an eyebrow. "Uh huh. And how, exactly?"

Remy hung his head. "Because I lied. I lied when I first started working for the government. I faked a background check to get hired on at the DOJ, because a real one would have shown my juvenile record."

Alex gestured for him to continue.

Remy sighed heavily. "I robbed a convenience store when I was 15. My mother managed to get me out of it with only public service, and then had the record sealed. Any civilian job wouldn't have been able to unseal it, but the government ones would have. I was . . . I was trying to impress a boyfriend by getting a big, important job like that, so I had a friend fake the background check for me. My whole career—DOJ, Homeland—it's all been based on that. When I stood up to Belenko in that meeting, he decided to try to take me down, so he dug into my history and found that. He's been threatening to expose me the whole time. I had no choice but to do what he wanted." He looked away, his face fallen, and his eyes welling up.

For a moment, Alex felt sorry for him, but the feeling

quickly passed. He straightened up. "There's always a choice, Remy. Always. And you made the wrong one this time." So, Alex thought bitterly, had he.

The next two weeks he stayed at home, with Leung's blessing, spending most of the time playing games and eating ice cream in his underwear while ignoring a stream of messages from everyone. Eventually, he gave in to Angel's gentle chiding that perhaps he should come back to work.

So now he was back on the Monday morning that Remy and Belenko were arraigned, watching the news stream on the vid window in his office and feeling like vomiting.

"Sources say that Belenko's assistant, a Monaco national whose name has not been released, was the point of contact for the Homeland agent." The woman giving the voiceover on the news footage seemed almost cheery about it. "The agent stole the secrets from a company employee he had been dating . . ."

Alex waved his hand, killing the feed and returning the vid window to its usual view of a marina on Lake Washington. It was a beautiful, late-February day—one of the first clear ones in weeks—but he felt as dark as the skies usually were all winter.

"Alex?"

He started and twisted around, nearly pulling a neck muscle. Standing in his doorway, her brow wrinkled with concern, was Sasha. She'd sent him a dozen messages while he was on leave—as had everyone else—but he'd answered none of them. She was, in fact, the last person he wanted to see right now. As humiliated as he was, having his former crush trying to be nice to him burned a new hole in his stomach. "Hi," he said flatly and turned back to staring out the window.

"Can I come in?" Without waiting, she edged gingerly into the room.

His first instinct was to tell her to go away—he even wondered if he should say something mean to make her leave—but something about her voice and body language changed his mind. He shrugged and made a wounded-puppy noise.

She crossed the rest of the distance and leaned against the edge of his desk. "How are you holding up?"

"How do you think? I fucked over the entire company because I was thinking with my dick instead of my brain."

"Alex, it wasn't your fault. You didn't know Remy was doing this. How could you?"

"I should have known. It was obvious."

"Really?" She raised an eyebrow. "If it was so obvious, why didn't any of the rest of us figure it out when we were trying to find the mole?"

He looked up at her. She did have a point.

"Honestly, we all thought the same thing that you did: that because he was with Homeland, there was no way he could've been doing something that put the public at risk. We all assumed that he had been vetted so thoroughly that he wasn't capable of this."

"But I was closer to him," Alex protested. "I should have figured it out."

Sasha closed the distance between them. "Alex, no one blames you. No one. Leung doesn't. I don't. Even Jay doesn't."

"He should. I accused him of being the mole!"

"Oh, Alex." She shook her head and reached out a hand. "Come here," she said gently. "If you want to, that is."

He stared at her hand for a moment, wondering if it might suddenly grow long claws and slash open his throat. He thought that might be preferable to the affectionate contact she was offering. But the well of need inside him was deep and empty, and it overrode his self-loathing. He stood up and took her hand.

She pulled him in, wrapping strong, warm arms around

him. "Alex, you sweet boy," she murmured into his messy hair. "We all still love you."

He sobbed into her shoulder for what felt like an eternity.

* * *

Jay's apartment felt uncomfortably empty. He'd lived alone for years, and never once had it bothered him. Having spent most of his life with his loud sister in the room next door, and then stuffed into barracks with other soldiers like human sausages in a can, he'd never considered having space entirely to himself a problem. And it wasn't, until he had gotten used to having other people there. First Sasha, for several weeks of what had felt at the time like perfect bliss, and then Tito.

Now they were both gone. Though Sasha had warmed back up to him considerably since Remy and Belenko had been brought to justice, she hadn't shown any signs of wanting to rekindle what they'd had. And as soon as Yusuf had come to the door, crying about his husband leaving and begging him to come home, he was gone, too. That part was for the best, he knew. His mother had given him some sound advice about trying to steer clear of anyone going through a divorce, and he did feel some relief when he no longer had to think about telling Tito he wanted to break it off—again.

Still, the bed felt cold and far too big for just him, and it made trying to get to sleep each night a difficult task. One thing that had helped, though he felt some shame about it, was a souvenir that Sasha had inadvertently left behind at his place: an old T-shirt that she often slept in, which still smelled strongly of her. He kept it in the bed and held it close to his face, wishing that its owner was there instead.

Tonight, however, even the shirt wasn't helping. It only reminded him of what he really wished he had. He laughed bitterly to himself. It was so strange, that he had first been angry with Sasha for being the object of Alex's affections and then ended up dating her instead. His crush on Alex had waned as soon as the relationship with Remy had started, and he still felt sour enough about it that thinking of Alex stung. Even worse, he had noticed in the past several days that Sasha and Alex had returned to the closeness they had had before Remy had ever come into their lives. She seemed to have forgiven him the lapse in judgment and was a rock of strength, something for which he seemed grateful. Jay knew that he should have been offering such comfort, too, to help soothe Alex's guilt about pointing the finger at him, but under the circumstances, he simply couldn't muster it. Both people he had most recently been sorely in love with were now thick as thieves, and he felt left out. He knew it was immature to feel this way, but he couldn't help it.

Frustrated, he let the shirt drop to the floor beside the bed and rolled over, hoping that his brain would stop churning so he could sleep. Snippets of an old childhood song came to him, and he murmured the words, thinking of his mother singing them when he was restless and couldn't sleep. The song was about parents expressing love for their child, telling him that they loved him and would always be there for him. It had certainly proven true most of his life. Though he didn't see them often these days, he'd always had a good relationship with his parents and loved them deeply. Perhaps, he had once considered, that was why he fell in love so easily. He was used to giving and receiving love as freely as had been the case with his family, and he expected that to happen with others, too, even if it was clear they weren't willing or able to give it.

Things were different now. He was an adult, and no one was obligated to love and care for him anymore. He had to earn that love, and even doing so wasn't a guarantee that he'd get to keep it. Still, the song was a comfort, and as he began to fall asleep, he mumbled the familiar last words, "So fear the dark no longer, child, for we will be your light."

* * *

Alex was exhausted and caked in sticky, foul-smelling mud. They'd all gotten filthy from trudging through a soggy cow pasture to chase the xenos—six-legged, rabbit-like things that were incredibly fast—back to their home world.

"I'll be glad to see the back side of that tessera." Jay sighed and wiped dirt off his face as they hiked back to where the hover was parked.

"What was that about your back side?" Sasha grinned and lobbed over a chunk of mud, which he dodged.

Alex barked a laugh, which felt so good he almost kept laughing. Things did seem like they were back to normal again. Remy and Belenko had been sentenced and were now in prison, and the new agent Homeland had assigned, a jovial older woman named Lisa, already felt like an old teammate. In the middle of it all, the tesserae just kept opening, as if nothing had gone awry. It was almost, Alex thought, back to how things were before Remy had showed up to begin with. Sasha's gentle comfort had brought back in full force the crush he'd nursed on her since the day they met. Unfortunately, she still seemed just as distracted by Jay, and knowing now—thanks to Angel accidentally blabbing it to him one day—that they had hooked up at some point when he was seeing Remy just made it worse. They weren't together now, that much he could tell, but they had been growing closer again in recent weeks, and now hovered around each other like hummingbirds at a feeder. It made his gut ache just to watch them.

And yet there was something else to their interactions—something that made him want to see more, not less. Sasha asked Jay to help clear the dirt from her back, and Alex found himself staring—and his blood rising—as Jay's hands brushed at her. But, he realized with a start, it wasn't that he didn't want Jay touching Sasha. He just didn't want Jay to be the *only* one doing that.

His mind drifted back to his undergrad days and the truly wild parties thrown by the cocky senior two doors down. On one of those nights, things got heated with Jamilla, one of the girls from his geomechanics class, and her boyfriend, Kevin. Kevin was rather new to the whole guy thing, but he was an eager enough learner, and Alex was certainly willing to teach him. There was next to no room on the narrow bed in his dorm, but they somehow all managed to fit on it. And the things that happened on that bed were amazing indeed. Watching Kevin pleasing Jamilla while Alex was introducing him to the finer points of sharing the same anatomy was mind-blowing, even without the potent weed they'd all been smoking. It had only happened the once—the couple had split up a month later for unrelated reasons—but it was, Alex had always thought, one of the highlights of his sexual history.

Remembering it now, the faces in his mind's video playback started to change. The look of bliss on Jamila's face became a look of bliss on Sasha's. The happy noises Kevin made sounded like Jay. But Alex stayed the same, and if anything, the pleasure was far, far greater.

Jay must have felt the stare because he looked up, laughing softly from a silly pun Sasha had just thrown out. A sharp look of concern crossed his face. "Alex? You OK? You look flushed."

"I am," Alex purred. Then, as he realized where he was, he coughed and straightened up, shifting away from them and trying to hide the obvious evidence of what his brain had been up to. "Oh! Yeah. Just a bit warm, is all. Summer heat always gets me." He laughed lightly.

"Alex. It's April." Sasha raised an eyebrow. "And it just started raining. Again."

He glanced around. "Oh. Well, humidity, too. That

must be it." He smiled uncomfortably and hoped he didn't look like a serial killer.

"Ah. I see." She shook her head and went back to trying to clean her uniform.

Jay was more tuned to Alex's body language. He glanced down, seeing what the younger man had been trying to hide. He cocked his head and smiled thoughtfully as he looked between Alex and Sasha. "Yeah," he said. "It's definitely a little warm in here."

*　*　*

It was getting messy, this business with Jay and Alex, so much so that Sasha wished she could simply find the love switch in her brain and shut it off for good so she didn't risk getting distracted in the field. Either she was staring at Jay and trying to forget how he looked naked, or she was watching Alex and coming to realize what Jay had seen in him. Unfortunately, her growing interest in Alex only made things more complicated.

Her Bisa had been singularly unhelpful with advice so far, telling her only that she was still young and still had time to decide what to do. Without anyone else to talk to—well, anyone who wasn't her boss or directly involved in the problem, at least—Sasha moped around, trying to figure it all out.

Finally, one morning as she sat in the break room down the hall from her lab, nursing a cup of coffee and ruing her confused state, an angel appeared. This angel, however, was wearing dark sunglasses and rubbing her forehead with a whimper. Her hair today was a bright violet, but looked unbrushed.

Angel waved weakly before she poked at the bevbot on the counter. "How goes, Sash? I'm hung over like nobody's business, so please speak quietly."

"Uh-oh." Sasha smiled "Should I ask?"

"Oh, you can ask. I just probably don't remember

enough to answer. This is the last time I let Dane's sister take me to that strip club, though. I mean, yeah, the guys were hot, but the drinks were also really cheap. And really strong. Ugh. I am never—I swear, never—touching tequila again." She sat down heavily in the chair opposite Sasha and wrapped her hands around the warm, steaming mug.

Sasha stifled a chuckle. She well remembered her own early college days and a few too many nights out that ended up in mornings like this. Having met Dane's sister once while visiting Angel on campus, she understood how the boisterous young woman could be a party magnet. "I feel your pain," she said sympathetically. "Rum's my nemesis. A trip to Curaçao one summer break completely wrecked my brain."

"Meds. I need meds." Angel dragged her bag up onto the table and began rummaging through it. "What the—? How the hell did . . ." From the bottom of her bag, she fished out a man's hot-pink G-string.

Now Sasha did have to laugh. "That's . . . impressive? Sure Dane's going to be OK with you having it?"

Angel hurriedly stuffed the mystery garment back into the bag. "Well, it's his sister who took me out, so I suppose he can blame her. Not that it matters. I wouldn't cheat on him, but otherwise, I do what I want. If he doesn't like it, I'll find a guy who does. Ooh! And maybe that one." She glanced through the room's open door, where Alex was strolling by, chatting with one of the engineering team and looking considerably more chipper than he had in weeks.

"Wait. Alex?" Sasha felt an uncomfortable rush of jealousy. "You have a thing for Alex?"

"Yeah. Absolutely." Angel laughed. "Dude is cuter than a basketful of kittens."

"Uh." Sasha squirmed, but couldn't find any other words. Maybe there weren't any. It wasn't as if she and Alex were anything but friends, technically.

Angel shrugged. "Not that he'd be interested in me,

anyway. There are only a couple of people he would remotely be into right now, after that mess with Remy."

Sasha went quiet for a moment. Obviously, she was one of those people. Jay was probably the other. With two people now expressing interest in Alex, she suddenly realized she'd been looking at him all wrong. Where she'd only seen a slightly naïve kid was actually a brilliant young man. Baby-faced, sure, and a couple of years younger than she was. Also not exactly possessed of the best instincts about people. Still, he was hardly the overgrown adolescent she'd originally thought. And, as she recalled noticing a time or two when they were suiting up for an event, definitely not built like an adolescent, either. A thrill ran through her, and for the first time, she considered dipping a toe in that potentially stormy sea. Doing so, however, would likely send Jay into—understandable, she knew—fits.

Angel pushed her shades back on her head, training bleary eyes on her. "Did I say something wrong?"

"Oh. No." Sasha shook her head. "Just . . . ah . . . thinking about Alex." She smiled shyly.

"So you know what I mean, then, yeah? Basket of kittens. Totally."

Sasha sighed. "I do know what you mean. More than you might realize. Only it's complicated."

Angel went wide-eyed and leaned in. "OK, there's a story here. Tell."

Sasha bit her lip, wondering where to start, but after several minutes, she'd poured it all out.

"I don't get the problem, though." Angel shook her head. "Why choose?"

"What?"

"I mean it. Who says you can't be with both of them—and them with each other, for that matter? What, have you never heard of poly relationships?"

"Well, yeah, but I . . ." Sasha felt a warm feeling growing in her chest. "I've never really been relationship oriented at all, so I haven't exactly considered having more than one."

Angel shrugged. "Maybe you should."

Sasha frowned and chewed on her lip. "I just don't know if I could do that. It sounds like a potential minefield. I've dated around, of course, and sometimes was seeing a few different guys, but that was just casual. No emotional stuff involved or anything. Just flings. Getting serious about it . . . I don't know that I'm capable of it. That's part of why I stopped seeing Jay. Getting freaked out about getting close to one person was bad enough. Not sure I could manage two."

"Well, it's not for everyone," Angel acknowledged. "Some people are just wired to only do the one-at-a-time thing, and some people just get too jealous and possessive. And some people of course aren't into relationships at all. Maybe you're one of them. But I have a cousin who was in a poly quad when she was in college in London. They split up after graduation, but for about a year or so, it was all four of them all sharing a house and a bed. She seemed chuffed enough about it."

Sasha went quiet for a moment as she mulled the information. The idea of getting serious about anyone at all terrified her, but she couldn't deny how she felt about Jay, and the more time she spent with Alex, the more she began to understand what Jay saw in him.

"If you ask me," Angel continued, "I think it's silly how you're all chasing each other in circles like some kind of fucked-up dog-tail relationship. At least one of you ought to just stop and let yourself get caught and see what happens."

"Maybe." Sasha was still unsure. "I mean, I don't know how the guys would feel about that."

"Well, why don't you at least give it a try? Go out on a date, all three of you. Something fun, no pressure, whatever."

"Like a concert, maybe?"

"Bingo. Perfect situation. You go, hear some good music, and have fun. If it works, cool, and if it doesn't, you're still friends, right?"

"Right, sure. Of course." Sasha began warming to the idea. "Let me think about it."

"Good. Because really? If you don't go snap up those boys, someone else will. Maybe even me!"

UNITY

"Is it serious with this boy?" His mother sounded almost giddy. "Do I need to start thinking about what to wear to a wedding?"

Alex laughed nervously. He'd only been dating Gabriel for five months, but the two had known each other for so long before then that it felt as though they'd invested much more time. Though he didn't expect they would jump into marriage right away, the possibility, especially now that they were moving in together, was definitely there. "Well, don't go shopping yet," he cautioned. "We're still just seeing if we can stand being under each other's feet all the time."

"Yes, of course. I'm not completely comfortable with that, you know, but I understand why. Your father and I lived together for a time, too, though in hindsight, maybe we shouldn't have. Perhaps he'd have been more willing to stay true to his vows."

Alex made a noncommittal noise. Truthfully, he'd been somewhat surprised when his mother hadn't batted an eye when, after going on his first date several years ago, he confessed to her that he was also interested in dating guys. Given her investment in her religion, he almost expected her to start chanting early-century anti-gay slogans at him. That she accepted that part of himself, if not celebrated it, was one of the few pleasant surprises he'd had from her.

"So when are you moving?"

"Next month, as soon as my dorm contract and his lease are up. We're getting a place near campus. It's small, but it'll be fine for just the two of us."

"Sounds nice. I'll be sure to get you some household things if you need them. I'm getting a raise this quarter, so I'm happy to help." She beamed. She'd always worked steadily, but had never had a lot of money; scraping together enough funds to send her son to an out-of-state college had drained her savings.

"You don't have to do that, Mom. We'll be fine. Gabriel's getting hired on as adjunct faculty soon, so we'll manage."

"Faculty. So he's at your school, then?"

"Yes. Remember I said I met him in a class last year?"

"Right! Eastern history, was it?"

Alex shook his head. "No, that was Marcy. Gabriel was the TA for my geomechanics class."

"Geomechanics? He's in a science field?" She frowned.

Alex got a creeping feeling up his spine. "Yes. My field, mostly. We're doing the same thing. He's the head of that quake-smart project I've been working on."

"But he's not doing your space stuff, right? Because I don't want you dating anyone who will keep encouraging your interest in that field. Geology is fine. I don't mind you studying rocks and volcanoes as long as they're here on Earth and not on some other planet."

Alex bit his lip. His hopes that his mother would fully support his relationship were now crumbling like one of the quake-devastated building models he and Gabriel had built last year. "No. Don't worry. He's not interested in that stuff at all," he lied.

Alex tapped lightly on the half-open door. "Leung? Hey."

She turned, smiling at him. "Please, come in! Must admit, I'm happy to have some one-on-one time with you. We really should have another proper boss-employee talk one of these days—I want to pick your brain about getting some better galactic mapping displays for our tesserae locations. But that's not why you made the appointment today, is it?"

"It's not," he said shyly. He came in, closing the door behind him, and sat down in the low, soft chair opposite her desk. "Actually, it's something a little more, well, personal."

"Oh?" A look of concern crossed her face. "Are you well? Having family issues? If you need to take more time off, no problem at all, though I'm sure the team would miss having you around."

He laughed nervously. "Well, they might, yeah. And it's not family issues."

"Oh, good. So what can I help you with?" She leaned forward, giving him her full attention.

"So, just to get it out of the way, first: given how terribly my, um, thing with Remy ended up, are you against employee fraternization?"

"Not on principle." She shrugged. "That was a special case, and seeing how everyone else has behaved in the wake of that has increased my trust in my team. Homeland scolded me about you and Remy, but after I reminded them that he was their employee and therefore their responsibility, they shut up. If I thought anyone was capable of being unprofessional in relation to how they deal with each other, I wouldn't keep them on. Obviously, I can't allow any dating between supervisors and the people who report to them, but peers, or people across different teams, not a problem." She grinned slyly. "I assume you have someone in mind?"

He flushed. "Ah, yes. Well. That's where it gets weirder." He sat back, trying to figure out how to explain it. "See, uh, Sasha asked me out this morning."

"I'd wondered about that! You two seem close lately. But I'm not seeing the weird part."

"Well, I'm not the only one she asked out."

"What, was she hedging her bets?"

Alex smiled. "No, not like that. Um. She asked out both me and Jay. For the same night. Same date."

Her eyes went wide. "Oh! And this is a proper date, I

take it? Not just friendly stuff?"

"Yeah, no. We've all gone out after missions and stuff before. This is definitely a real date."

"How does Jay feel about this?"

"He's all for it. And so am I. But we all wanted to make sure you were OK with it before it went any further. Just in case, you know, it ended up getting complicated or something. And—" he flashed her a grin "—since I work with you the most directly, I got picked to talk to you about it."

Leung was quiet for a moment, then shrugged. "As I see it, you're all three adults, you're all three level-headed, sensible, and professional people—and I think you've learned your lesson about bad judgment. Even if this doesn't work out in some way that makes you all happy, I think you'll still work together well enough not to affect missions. So, if you were looking for my stamp of approval, you have it."

"Great!" He let out the breath he didn't realize he'd been holding. "Thank you so much."

"Of course." She leaned over, "You're a sweet kid. I know you've been through a lot, so whatever I can do to help you be happy here is all my pleasure."

Alex froze. In at least the last 10 years, he could never remember his mother having said anything like that, and hearing the words now, from someone for whom he had enormous respect, was deeply moving. He found himself looking at his boss in a whole new light—as a person, more, not just as the genius entrepreneur he'd always looked up to. He realized that he'd always felt that way about her; maybe, in his yearning for the relationship he should have had with his mother, he looked to someone else who could accept all of him, not just the parts she approved of.

"Thank you," he said again. "You have no idea how much that means to me." Abruptly, he stood up. If he stayed any longer, she was going to see him cry, and that would be even more awkward than this already had been.

"Of course. But if this does work out, I demand an invite to the wedding!" She winked.

His head spun at the very thought.

* * *

The breeze across the light-rail platform carried a chill, running up her skirt—a rare item for her and unpractical in this weather—but Sasha didn't mind. She was high on the evening. The concert had been fantastic, as had the meal and nightcap they'd enjoyed at a nearby pub afterward. More than anything else, the company was the most exciting part, and it was doing a lot to keep her warm. Still, the breeze made her shiver slightly, and Jay noticed.

"Y'OK?" He slipped an arm around her shoulders. "You can borrow my jacket."

She shook her head and smiled. "I'm fine, Jay, but thanks." His body heat took away the edge of the breeze—and started heating her up in other ways.

Alex walked at Jay's other side, though Sasha guessed it wasn't just because of the chill. He and Jay had been close most of the night, chatting endlessly about their mutual interests in odd music and—to Sasha's amusement—flirting. Intellectually, Sasha knew most people might feel jealous about that, but watching them interact like that only gave her a fuzzy, happy feeling in her belly. And, to her pleasant surprise, plenty of other feelings south of there.

Jay glanced up at the schedule display. "I thought there was supposed to be a midnight train."

Alex followed his gaze. "It's five minutes past, so we just missed it. Explains why we're alone here, I guess. Next one's in ten."

"Fair enough. I think I need to sit for a while, though. All that dancing wore me out." Sasha sat down on a bench under an awning, hugging herself for warmth. Alex plopped down next to her, and Jay next to him, draping an arm over the back of the bench—around Alex's shoulders, with his fingertips brushing her arm. She glanced between the two of them. "This has been nice," she said quietly. "I'm glad Angel suggested it."

"Oh, is that who we blame?" Alex asked archly.

"Blame? I'd say credit," Jay shot back with a grin. "We should've done this ages ago."

Sasha nodded. "I agree." A prickly flush crept up her cheeks, and she took a chance. "So . . . do we want to do this again sometime?"

Alex went quiet in thought. After the mess with Remy, Sasha couldn't blame him if he was reticent about getting involved again, even—or maybe especially—if this new situation was so different.

"You don't have to decide right now," Jay told him gently. "I'm fine either way. You know how I feel, though."

Alex smiled. "I do. Truthfully . . ." He slouched, rubbing his face. "It would be so nice," he murmured, almost to himself. He sat up again and took a breath. "OK, so the thing is . . . I don't come without baggage. I have some fairly complicated family issues, and that makes all of my relationships complicated, too."

Sasha nodded sympathetically. "Well, you know my family issues. As in, I don't have family except my Bisa. It's made me weird about getting close to people." She gave Jay an apologetic look. He smiled his understanding.

"Well, for me, it's a long, ugly story and I won't bore you two with it tonight, but the short version is that my family is hardcore religious and doesn't exactly approve of the life I have now." Alex shifted uncomfortably. "Gabriel told me all the time that I should dump them, but I just can't."

"I get that." Sasha reached for his hand and clutched it tightly. "It hurts badly enough not to have much living family. I can't imagine what it must be like to know your family's still alive, but you're not able to be truly close with them."

He squeezed her hand. "Thank you. I'm a raw nerve where that's concerned. But—" He heaved a sigh and closed his eyes. "I really like you." His eyes flipped open, and he smiled shyly at Jay. "Both of you. I make no guarantees, but honestly, I'm not sure I could keep working with you two every day without being distracted by, well . . . my florid imagination."

Jay laughed. "Same here. That call we had last Wednesday, with the mini-hippo things? When you two were huddled together, trying to pinpoint the location of that rogue, I swear, I couldn't stop staring. It was rude, but I started mentally removing your equipment."

"Hey!" Alex protested. "I like my equipment where it is, thanks."

Jay flushed and squirmed. "That's not what I—oh, naughty-minded, aren't you?" He gave a gentle nudge.

Alex nudged back. "Of course. And if you wanted to inspect my equipment and make sure it's up to code, you're welcome to," he purred, cocking his head with a teasing smile.

"Well, you can consider me an official inspector, then." Jay grinned and put a hand on Alex's thigh, his fingers dangling close to his inseam. "Though my assistant Sasha will have to double-check my work." He raised an eyebrow at her.

Sasha giggled throatily. "Absolutely. Inspector Delescu reporting for duty, sir!" She dropped Alex's hand to trail her fingers up his other thigh.

Alex shivered and drew a sharp breath. His eyes fluttered closed, and he rested his head back on Jay's arm. In one swift motion, Jay slid his palm over Alex's crotch and leaned down to kiss him soundly.

Sasha could barely breathe. The kiss was so deep and so passionate that it was almost embarrassing to watch, but when Jay reached for her hand to help with his caresses, all sense of awkwardness vanished. She leaned over and began kissing Alex's neck, delighting in the soft noises he made as she did so. "I think," she murmured, her voice thick with need, "you're going to pass inspection."

To her frustration, only a couple of minutes later, they were interrupted by the arrival of the train. Reluctantly, they parted—Alex and Jay walking a little awkwardly—and boarded.

"I have a big bed at my apartment," Alex said as the train departed. "If you're interested."

Ignoring the bewildered look of the only other passenger in the car—an elderly gentleman with a stern face—Jay gave Alex a gentle goose and murmured, "I think that answer is a most definite yes."

* * *

As the fog of sleep left his mind, Alex couldn't stop smiling, despite the dark sky and the late-spring squall currently lashing against the bedroom window. Even when Remy slept there, his bed had felt empty, but now it was anything but. On the contrary, it was actually overfull. Sasha lay next to him, curled up tightly against his back, her hips nestled into Jay's. Alex found he was a little too warm and hoped Sasha, between them, wasn't roasting. She seemed to be snoozing contentedly, however, and Alex was loath to wake her, despite the suggestion by points south that he do so for a repeat of last night's mind-blowing activities.

"Awake?" A low-voiced whisper was barely audible.

Alex turned carefully, seeing just a bit of Jay's gold-flecked eyes through Sasha's sleep-mussed hair. "Getting there," he whispered back.

Jay chuckled softly. "I have been for about an hour. Brain's hard-coded for military time, I'm afraid. Got up to use the bathroom and have a quick shower, but I wanted to come back and cuddle while you two were still asleep."

"Nice idea." Warmth washed through Alex. He'd been concerned that last night might've been a one-off, followed by a quick parting this morning, but Jay, at least, seemed happy to stay. "I should go attend to biology, too. I can get you a cup of tea while I'm up."

"No worries." Jay smiled. "I can handle that myself, if you don't mind me poking around your kitchen. Can make breakfast, too, if you have supplies."

"That would be amazing. Pretty sure I have something that might serve."

"On it." Jay moved quietly, rolling out of bed and padding out of the room in just his boxers.

Alex watched him, marveling at the twitch of his ass, but then his body reminded him that there were other, more urgent uses demanded of his genitals. Grumbling under his breath, he finally peeled himself away from Sasha and went into the bathroom, which was still steamy from Jay's shower.

He had just finished up at the toilet and was turning on the shower when a soft knock echoed. "Alex? Mind if I come in?" Sasha asked, her voice thick with sleep.

"Yeah. I was basically done. Was going to wash up, but I can wait until you're out." He opened the door. She was still naked, and the sight reignited his arousal.

She glanced down, noticing. "Oh, feel free to use the shower," she said nonchalantly. "I'm not shy if you're not."

Alex blinked. That she was ready for that level of intimacy was a surprise, but he went with it. "Yeah, sure." He smiled and ducked into the shower, politely turning away while she sat on the toilet. "Jay's making us breakfast if you're interested."

"Ah! I thought I smelled something good. That's what woke me up." She finished and flushed. "If you don't mind some company in there, maybe we can clean up quickly and go get fed?"

"Be my guest!" Alex opened the shower door.

She smiled up at him, her face warm and relaxed.

"Hiya." She stroked a hand down his arm and leaned up for a soft kiss.

"Hi, yourself." His skin prickled at the touch, and he put a hand on her waist. He was fully aroused again, and he started wondering whether he should satisfy more than just food cravings. Excited as he was, however, it seemed off, somehow, not to have Jay in there with them. He almost laughed; a few months ago, having Jay present while he was with Sasha would only have made him feel angry and jealous. Now, the picture seemed incomplete without him.

Sasha seemed to have a similar feeling. "So. . . encore after breakfast? If you don't have other plans, that is."

"Unless we get a tessera alert, I'm all yours," he teased. "And his."

* * *

"So?" Josie nudged him with a foot under the table.

Jay tried to hide his smile behind his glass of beer. "'So' what?"

Her eyes narrowed, and she smirked. "I know that glow on your face all too well. You look exactly like you did after you spent that weekend at the coast with Tito. I take it your physics guy finally came through? Or did you hook back up with the cute biologist?"

He bit his lip and looked at the ceiling. The only person cannier than Josie about his expressions was his mom. "Well, yes, my physics guy came through," he admitted.

"Hooray!" she cheered. "About fucking time. I take it he got over his crush on her?"

He shook his head, grinning devilishly. "Not at all."

She raised an eyebrow. "OK. So . . . you distracted him from that, then?"

"Nope."

She sat back in her chair, cocking her head. "OK, now I'm confused. You finally got me, Lambert."

He laughed and took pity on her. "Sasha was . . . along for the ride."

Her mouth dropped open. "How did this happen?"

"Honestly? I dunno. We've been friends all this time—since the sub accident—and after that whole espionage mess finally settled out, it just sort of . . . came together."

She waggled her eyebrows. "I bet it did."

He kicked her playfully. "Filthy."

"Of course!"

"But, yeah," he continued. "She finally just asked both of us on a date, and we went back to Alex's place after. Stayed in the whole weekend."

She smiled. "Well, you look happy. Happier than I've seen you in a long time."

"I am happy. And calm, too. Not sure what it is about being with them, but even with how dangerous our missions are, I feel, I dunno, safe with them. I'm supposed to be the one keeping them safe and all that, but knowing they have my back—"

"—and your front, apparently."

He rolled his eyes, but couldn't help smiling. "And that, yes. I'm not jumpy anymore. Even the doc's commented on it. I ran low on my implant the other day and didn't even notice a difference. I feel normal. I feel . . . strong. This isn't just a fling, I know it. I think this is the real deal. I'm even surer than I was with Tito."

"That's awesome! And I expect to meet these two sometime soon, you know."

He nodded. "Yeah, definitely. I need more time as we're getting into the groove of being together, but once we're settled in, I'm sure we'll do the family introductions and all that."

"Family? Wow. You really are serious about them."

He smiled sheepishly. "I am. I really am. I'm in love, and it feels fucking amazing."

PARADISE

The cliché of rain at a funeral was lost on her. All Sasha knew was that it was cold and wet and her dress kept sticking to her legs. She wanted nothing more than to tear the thing off and go find her mother for warm, close cuddles. But her mother—or at least the body that had once contained her—was being lowered into the soggy ground in front of her. All around her in the cemetery were hundreds of other fresh graves, their dirt coverings only beginning to show signs of moss. Another grave nearby was still open, though. That one was for her Vovò, who was being laid to rest at the same time as his daughter. His graveside ceremony had just finished, and the casket already dropped into place. Her mother's ceremony was nearly done.

She knew she ought to be crying—everyone else around her was—but all she felt was damp and numb, like the time she'd spent too long outside in the season's first snow and her mother had had to put her in a hot bathtub to warm her back up.

Grandpa Joey squeezed her hand. "You can put the flowers over there now," he said quietly. Her Bisa, standing on her other side, gave her a gentle nudge.

Sasha glanced down. She had almost forgotten about the fistful of sagging daffodils. Their bright-yellow faces were out of place in this dim, dark corner of the world, but they reminded her of her mother's sunny smiles, which could light up even the dreariest January day.

Releasing Grandpa's hand, she shuffled to the graveside and tossed the flowers on top of the casket. As they started heading down with the box, however, she leaned over to pick them up again.

"Sasha?" Bisa called over. "What are you doing?"

"Mama can't see these now," she said matter-of-factly. "We need them more than she does."

Things seemed quiet so far, Sasha noted as she and the team disembarked from the hover. Paradise, as they'd called the tessera site near the small village at the bottom of Mt. Rainier, had been identified in Alex's first spectral scan, but it hadn't yet opened for any longer than a second or two. There was no telling what they might be in for: something dangerous, like the poison-spitting amphibians at Port Angeles, or something utterly benign, like the ambulatory but slow, small fungus that populated the planet on the other side of Kalama. Or it could be nothing at all. About a third of the tesserae that had opened so far connected only to lifeless moons, asteroids, or even outer space. The only danger they posed was in localized changes to gravity and atmosphere, and even that wasn't usually a problem except for the relatively few tesserae near populated areas. For those openings, the company, with assistance from the government, had constructed solid, airtight barriers. No one's Shih-Tzu was going to be trotting happily through a dog park only to get sucked onto a comet speeding somewhere near Orion's Belt.

As they kitted up and set out on the site scan, Sasha missed having Alex alongside her. After working together for more than a year and now dating for three months, it felt like missing a limb not to have him nearby for almost every waking moment. However, Angel was off this week celebrating her graduation by visiting family in Ireland, and Jason, who did mission control for the beta team, was on location, filling in for their usual tech specialist, who was home with a bout of food poisoning. That left Central Command to Alex, who actually seemed to like the idea of watching the whole thing remotely instead of traipsing about on the side of a mountain. Even so, he'd been chatty—and flirty—enough over the com that she missed him less than she might have otherwise.

"It's looking like a non-event from this end," Alex said confidently. "Satellite's not showing any incursion signs, and I'm not getting anything on the drones' IR. Amit, Jason, you're safe to send the probe through the tessera."

"On it, sir," Jason chirped.

"Please don't call me that!" Alex protested. "I'm only 23. Makes me feel like a grandparent."

Sasha laughed and glanced over at Jay, who gave her a knowing look. Alex might well be miles ahead of both of them in sheer intelligence, but sometimes, being younger—two years for Sasha, five for Jay—did come through in his personality. His youthful enthusiasm also showed up in other ways. For instance, when after a romp in the shower with Jay this morning, he was ready for another one with Sasha when she woke up 20 minutes later. Definitely something to be said for younger men, she had decided.

"Well, it looks quiet from our end, too, Alex," Jay said. "Tito, Hotchkiss and I are going to go patrol the perimeter anyway."

"Sounds good," Sasha said as they began to head up the hill. "I think I'll head south and go have a look around."

Cordy hesitated. "Hey, Sasha, is it OK if I go with Jay's team instead? Hotchkiss said he'd show me how to use the G-27. I'd feel a lot safer if I knew how to wield that thing."

"Of course." Sasha patted her back. She wasn't keen on the weapon—a higher-powered version of the stun guns they usually used—but it did make her feel better that more of the rest of the team might be using them soon.

Jay turned around, frowning. "Sure you'll be OK on your own, Sash?"

She shrugged. "I'm fine. Got my sidearm charged up if I run into anything."

"Or you could just beat it up," he said with a wink.

"Nah." She grinned. "Rather save that for you." They'd been spending some afternoons sparring lately, and Jay's combat training was oddly seeming to be no match for her capoeira expertise. She felt badly every time she knocked him on his ass so easily, but he seemed not to have a problem with it. On the contrary, the biggest reason he kept losing was that he was being distracted by arousal, and he was, she recalled with a happy shiver, pleased whenever she had him pinned.

They finally parted, and Sasha made her way down the hill, following Amit and Jason to the tessera.

Halfway there, a strange noise distracted her. After flipping down her visor and switching on its sensory-enhancement display, she crept quietly through the underbrush. From a few meters away, she saw the source of the sound. In a small clearing, dappled by the sunlight streaming through the cedars, was an enormous bull elk, its antlers dripping with the last bits of spring's velvet. It stopped grazing to look up at her. She changed her posture, not wanting to spook it or make it think she was a potential threat. Its nostrils flared, and it snorted, seemingly annoyed but not angered at having its lunch interrupted by the strangely adorned biped. For some time, she and the majestic creature merely studied each other— she figured it was probably used to seeing humans, due to the nearby hiking trail—but then it heard something it didn't like. Trumpeting in alarm, it quickly bounded away, off down the hill.

"What the hell?" Sasha muttered, looking back over her shoulder. Then her earpiece emitted a chorus of panicked shouts.

"We have xenos!" Jay bellowed. "Other side of the hill, by the river!"

"I have one at 10 o'clock!" Cordy cried, followed by several stunner bursts.

"What?" Alex's voice cracked in sudden panic. "I don't

see them. They're not on any . . . wait, I see movement. Radar. Satellite zooming now. But no thermal?"

Sasha was the first to figure it out. "They're extremely cold-blooded, guys! They haven't warmed up to local temp, so they're not giving off enough heat to trip the sensors."

She switched her visor's video feed to one of Alex's camera drones. The sight it displayed made her queasy. There were two of the creatures, both easily three times the size of the elk that had just dashed away. They looked like enormous arachnids: eight-legged and covered in a hard exoskeleton of a color that blended in with the surrounding evergreens, making them hard to pick out from a distance. Where an arachnid had compound eyes and mandibles, however, these creatures had oval heads and large, extensible jaws filled with backward-facing, jagged teeth. They looked, she thought with a horrified shudder, like oversized green tarantulas with the head of a great white shark.

But worse than the xenos' appearance was what they were able to do. Panicked by being surprised by noisy aliens in an unfamiliar landscape, they did what any frightened creature with a lot of teeth but little intelligence would do, and attacked.

Sasha's heart tried to leap out of her chest. A burst of strength she never knew she had flooded her limbs, and she sprinted up the side of the hill, her weapon at the ready. But by the time she got to the crest, it was too late. One of the creatures was dead, having fallen down a steep embankment, but the other was alive. Two of the team— Hotchkiss and Cordy—lay mangled and torn, utterly still. A third, Tito, was trying his best to fight off the creature's attack from the ground, without much success; the charges from their nonlethal weapons were simply bouncing off the creature's exoskeleton and not contacting any soft parts that would conduct the charges through to its nervous system.

Sasha looked around in panic, afraid that Jay might have already been devoured. But then she heard a soft moaning from a thicket by the river's edge. Jay lay in a bed of ferns, bloodied and clearly in pain, but moving. Thinking quickly, she realized that for Tito, it was too late. Trying to save him by distracting the creature would only put her and Jay in more danger. She crept over to Jay and covered him with her body, trying to keep as silent and still as possible.

Tito got off one last weapon burst, enough to finally make the creature collapse. In a few more seconds, he lay still, too.

"Jay!" Sasha cried, tugging at his torn clothing to see the extent of his wounds. There was only one, but it was horrifying: a deep gash running across his collarbone, and terminating under his right arm. The wound looked relatively clean, but it gushed blood. She tore off her overshirt to soak up the flow and apply as much pressure as possible over the area.

A camera drone whizzed past her head.

"Sasha? Is he OK?" Alex croaked. "What's his status?"

"He's alive, for the moment," he panted. There wasn't enough air in the world, not after that race up the hill, and not while Jay. . . while Jay. . . "Tito and Cordy are down, and Hotchkiss, too, so we don't have a hover pilot. We need medevac, *now*."

"Already called," Alex said. "And the tessera is closing. Amit, Jason, get down there!"

"Seconds away," Amit's voice cut in. "What can we do?"

"See if there's anything left of Cordy's med kit," Sasha said. "And hurry!"

"Coming as fast as we can!" Jason cried.

"He's bleeding out!" Sasha yelled when they arrived. "I need a cautery wand!"

Jason poked around in the med kit and came up with the device and a wad of absorbent nanosilk. Sasha sopped up as much of the remaining blood as she could and then went to work, sealing up the gashes before Jason gave Jay a blood-volume-increasing dose of saline. After a few moments, the major flow stopped, though the wounds still seeped. Jay lay quiet and still, his tan skin a sickly pale and his chest barely rising with shallow breaths.

"Alex, what's the medevac ETA?" Sasha asked.

"They're screaming, but they're still ten minutes out."

"That's too long," she muttered desperately, rubbing a bloody arm across her damp forehead. Then hope swept through her with an idea. Pushing a bewildered Jason aside, she pawed through the med kit.

"What are you doing?" Amit stared at her.

"Field transfusion," she said flatly. Finally she spied what she needed: a pair of syringes and a couple of butterfly needles with long tubes attached.

"Do you even know his blood type?" Jason asked.

"Don't need to." She smiled grimly. "I'm O-neg."

Amit, the team's engineering specialist, helped her cobble together a crude but functional device. She swiped at her skin with a sanitizing wipe, wrapped a nylon strap around her upper arm, and slipped one needle in his vein and the other in hers.

It took a moment for the flow to start. She sat back against a tree, massaging her arm, trying to get the blood moving as quickly as possible, giving back life to the unconscious man beside her.

"Guide in the medevac," she told Amit and Jason, and they hurried away. Truly, the pilot wouldn't have needed the ground guidance, having been talked in by Alex, but since she was about to cry like an exhausted baby, she didn't want an audience.

* * *

Alex was drowsing in the chair near Sasha's hospital bed, but nearly jumped from his seat when he saw her stirring. "Sasha?" he whispered, stroking her cheek as her eyelids fluttered. "Hey, love."

She looked bewildered for a moment, but finally focused. "Alex! Where's Jay? Is he OK?"

"He's still in surgery, but the docs say he's going to be fine. They wouldn't let me wake you up to tell you. Said you needed your rest, too."

She sat up, wincing at the pain from the hole in her right arm. The area was bruised from the impromptu transfusion, but she otherwise looked like she was well. The half-gallon of fluids that had been pumped into her probably helped, too. "How long have I been out?" she asked, rubbing a trickle of drool from the corner of her mouth.

"About three hours, give or take. Water?" He reached for the self-chilling bottle on the table next to her.

"Yeah, thanks." She sucked down about half of it before speaking again. "Did we lose anyone else?"

"Hotchkiss and Cordy died on-site—you know about that. The medevac couldn't save Tito; he died on the way in."

She twitched, her eyes filling with tears. "I was afraid of that. I feel horrible about leaving him with the xeno, but I figured he was basically gone already. My only chance to save Jay was if the xeno was distracted long enough."

Alex nodded in understanding. "Well, he did at least kill the thing. The G-27 works nicely." He smiled grimly

"Did he? Excellent." She echoed the smile. "I never thought I'd celebrate the death of any creature, but in this case, I would've killed it myself if I'd had the chance."

A purple-haired nurse poked his head in. "Hey, Sasha. Glad to see you're awake. I just got news that your . . . friend?"

"Boyfriend," Sasha corrected.

"Well, he's out of surgery. I'm prepping his room right now. I can help you in there so you can be there when they bring him in from recovery."

"Absolutely." Moving gingerly, with Alex and the nurse on either side, Sasha shuffled three doors down to the room and settled in to the large easy chair near the foot of the bed. Alex plopped down on the floor next to her. She began gently stroking his hair, and he closed his eyes, murmuring at the comforting touch. The nurse raised an eyebrow, but said nothing and left them alone.

Just a few quiet minutes later, the room erupted in activity as the surgical staff wheeled in Jay, transferred him into his bed, and set him up with med infusion patches and monitor strips. When they finished, Sasha and Alex dragged her chair as close to the bed as they could, and she leaned over to rest her head on Jay's leg. On the other side, Alex pushed aside a rolling bedside cart, and clutched Jay's hand. They remained there without a word for several minutes, watching Jay's pale face slowly pinking up. He was still delirious—fading in and out of sleep—and didn't acknowledge them for some time, but eventually, he began to come around.

As soon as they saw signs that he was indeed conscious, both got to their feet and began stroking his arms and face, reassuring themselves as much as him that he was there, he was alive, everything would be all right.

Alex smoothed a lock of shiny hair from Jay's eyes, chuckling a little with the knowledge that Jay probably felt like a wooly mammoth with hair so much longer than his usual neat, close style—growing it out had been his suggestion. "Good morning, sunshine," he said tenderly.

Jay couldn't move his mouth much—the bandage around his neck and jaw were far too tight for that—but he murmured their names clearly enough. Tears trickled from his eyes, and he blinked, trying to see through them. "You're OK!" he exclaimed as soon as Sasha came into his view.

"Yes, I'm fine." She smiled down at him, brushing away his tears even as her own began to fall. "Not going to run up the side of a mountain again right away, but I'm fine."

"Did we lose anyone else?" His breath hitched.

"We did. I'm sorry." She looked away. "Cordy, Hotchkiss . . . and Tito. I—I couldn't get to him."

The tears began trickling faster down his face, and he sniffled. "His kids. How can I tell his kids?"

Sasha cried harder, too. "I'm sorry. I had to choose between him and you. He was injured so badly I didn't think I could save him. I wanted to, but I knew it was too late, and I thought I could help you."

"I understand. It's all right," Jay whispered roughly. "Thank you."

"I had to," she said brokenly. "I've lost too many people in my life. I can't lose you, too."

Alex felt his chest tighten as he realized exactly how much he knew that feeling. He'd been trying to keep it together—trying to stay strong in case the worst happened—but now that Sasha and Jay were on the mend, he began to crumble. "Same," he whispered as he glanced between them. "Both of you. I can't . . . I need you."

Sasha turned to him, an unspoken question on her lips. Even in his barely conscious state, Jay seemed to read it, too, and nodded at him to continue.

Alex hesitated for a moment. The dressing-down he'd probably get from his mother when she found out would surely be spectacular. But for once, what she thought mattered next to nothing to him, compared to how deeply he loved the two people looking expectantly at him. Gathering his courage, he heaved a sharp breath and blurted it out. "This is probably the worst time ever to do this, but. You two are spending so much time at my place, and it's not really big enough for three, so I was thinking we should, if you want to, we can . . . that is, I'm open to—"

"Yes, I'll move in with you." Sasha interrupted. "Jay?"

Jay reached for their hands and squeezed weakly. "I was planning on asking if you two wanted to go apartment hunting this weekend, actually," he murmured through a tight, sad smile. "Though I was going to try to make it a little more romantic."

Alex chuckled wryly. "With our jobs? I don't think it could get any more romantic than this."

* * *

The weather was beautiful, which made the funeral all the more uncomfortable for Sasha. Her third this week, this one was for Tito. Hotchkiss and Cordy's services had been relatively tame; both of their families were quiet, stoic sorts who cried silently and otherwise tried to pretend they weren't actually laying a beloved friend and family member to rest. Only Cordy's daughter, a wiry, active girl with tanned arms and a freckled nose like her mother, broke down, and when she did, her father and Cordy's parents shuffled her out of the room.

By comparison, Tito's service was chaotic. He had four siblings, all of whom had children of their own, and his three children alternated between running around the reception area of the funeral home with their cousins and sitting in a corner to sob loudly on their Baba Yusuf's shoulder. His parents, grandparents, and a host of other family milled around, crying and holding each other, sharing memories of Tito.

Sasha felt out of place. She mourned the loss of her teammate, as did Alex, but they didn't have the strong emotional bond with him that the rest of the attendees did. The person whose bond did come close hovered near them as some of Tito's family seemed annoyed to have his ex-boyfriend there. To Sasha's relief, Angel had been running interference for them, busily chatting with people when they started getting testy.

"You OK?" Sasha asked Jay, who leaned against a wall, nursing a cup of orange-scented herbal tea. His chest and shoulder were still bandaged, and he moved slowly, but he'd been healing well.

He shrugged. "Better than I thought I'd be. I mostly just feel bad for his family, and that I couldn't do anything more to save him. Not that I could have, in my condition, but still. I wish I could have helped."

"Same." Alex, on her other side, looked over at him with a sympathetic expression. "I always wondered how soldiers—or people who used to be soldiers—handled death. Before this, I've never had a job where I risked my life, and now I've been in several situations like that: the sub, the raptor, now this. Is it different when you've had combat training?"

Jay nodded. "It's supposed to be, but for me, it never was. I got into the military because, well, to be honest, because I saw a lot of military guys around Hawai'i when I was growing up and I had a thing for men in uniform. I didn't take it seriously until the hell in Pakistan started, and even then, I had trained for mission logistics, so I knew I wouldn't be on the front lines. It wasn't until my bunker got bombed that I really saw the reality of war." His jaw tightened. "We lost seven people that day. Josie, one of the tech staff, and I were the only survivors. I'd never seen death—much less that kind of death—before, and it messed me up for a long time. That was just losing squad mates, though." He looked down at Sasha and settled an arm around her shoulders. "I can't imagine how it would feel to lose someone close."

Sasha shivered and leaned into him. He dropped a kiss on her head.

"My PTSD counseling did a help a lot, though," he continued. "One of the things that stuck with me was remembering that life goes on even after someone leaves it." He nodded toward Tito's husband and children. The youngest, Nala, was only four, and though every once in a while she asked where Papa Tito was, and wailed when told he wasn't coming back, she bounced back each time. Having her siblings and Baba—not to mention a host of other loved ones—around soothed her.

All at once, realization washed over Sasha, and she felt her eyes well up.

Alex frowned at her. "Sasha?"

She shook her head and brushed at her face. "I'm OK. It's just . . ." She shrugged. "I spent most of my life more or less alone, and I thought I was safer that way. I thought if I didn't love anyone, I wouldn't be hurt when they died."

"And now?" Alex asked, moving closer.

She smiled and relaxed into the warm feeling of being sandwiched between them. "Now I know love is the only way to be alive."

EPILOGUE

The air inside the room was stifling, and everyone in it was emitting nervous odors. Sookit tried not to twitch at the powerful smell, but his antennae itched with the information overload. Finally, the captain strode in, assistants and a handful of equipment in tow. After rising and dipping his head in deference, Sookit rested on his second legs again and watched the room's vid screen as it lit up with the captain's presentation.

In bright gold characters scrolling up the screen, the three lines of formal script introduced the meeting's topic: "Doorway Project Alpha: Earth."

ABOUT THE AUTHOR

Shawna Walls is a little bit of everything: Trained as a journalist, classical singer, and actor, she additionally dabbles in photography, video editing, Web design, and print graphics. She is also, according to her friends, a pretty darn good cook and full of enough useless information to rival Wikipedia.

She's a proud geek and nerd (and knows the difference between the two) and enjoys being a fan of others' work as much as she enjoys creating her own. Other hobbies include travel, birding, and fierce tooth-gnashing about politics and social justice.

Shawna lives in the Pacific Northwest with her husband and their son, a dear friend/housemate, and two incorrigible cats.